Rafferty felt her tremble.

He leaned closer and tucked his cloak around Thomasina's shoulders more firmly. "A glass of brandy is my prescription for you, Miss Wentworth. It's no wonder you're badly shaken after last night's events."

Thomasina fixed him with a steely eye. "I am not shaken, Dr. Rafferty, merely cold. If you'd taken care to examine the perfect stitches that I put in over your eyebrow, you would appreciate how steady my hands were."

Rafferty stared at her. Prattling on about stitches after the night they'd both been through. Did she even have the faintest idea how close she'd come to disaster? His Irish dander rose. "If that is your chief concern," he said hotly, "I'm more alarmed about the steadiness of your brain than of your hands. I have no doubt of your intelligence, Miss Wentworth. The fault lies in your judgment!"

Dear Reader,

December is a busy time for most of you, and we at Harlequin Historicals would like to thank you for taking a moment to find out what we have to offer this month.

From author Marianne Willman, we bring you *Thomasina*, the continuing story of a character from *Vixen*, Ms. Willman's first book for Harlequin Historicals. Set in the Mexican countryside, the heroine lives out her dream of becoming a doctor and discovers love along the way.

In *A Corner of Heaven*, newcomer Theresa Michaels has written the touching story of a woman reunited with the father of her child amidst the danger and hardships of the Civil War.

Isabel Whitfield's *Silver Fury* takes place in a California silver town where a stubborn washerwoman and a rebellious blue blood manage to overcome their differences and find happiness. Caryn Cameron's *King's Man* takes the reader to Tudor England where a lady smuggler and a loyal soldier outwit their common enemies.

We hope that you will enjoy our December titles. From all of us at Harlequin Historicals, our best wishes for the holidays and the year ahead.

Sincerely,

The Editors

Thomasina

Marianne Willman

Harlequin Books

TORONTO • NEW YORK • LONDON
AMSTERDAM • PARIS • SYDNEY • HAMBURG
STOCKHOLM • ATHENS • TOKYO • MILAN

Harlequin Historicals first edition December 1991

ISBN 0-373-28703-8

THOMASINA

Books by Marianne Willman

Harlequin Historicals

Vixen #7
Rose Red, Rose White #29
Tilly and the Tiger #55
Thomasina #103

MARIANNE WILLMAN

is an established author in both the historical and contemporary romance genres. She was born and raised in Detroit, and she now lives close by with her family.

As a child, Marianne haunted the local libraries, and she still manages to read volumes of history, as well as fiction of all kinds. When her hobby of collecting antique inkwells finally forced her to acknowledge that she wanted to be a writer, she gave up her critical-care nursing career and turned to writing. She's been busy ever since.

For Ruth and Jan and Nora—adventuresses all;
and for Kay Garteiser,
who was the first to ask for Thomasina's story

Prologue

San Juan de Baptista, Mexico, 1846

The land was deserted beneath a molten sky, except for a lone horseman. Brendan Patrick Timothy Rafferty rode up to the small adobe structure that served him as both house and doctor's surgery. The building sat on a stony hill a half mile from the village, backed by the snowy triple peaks of Los Tres Hermanos. Although the setting was vastly different, the house reminded him of the small white-washed cottage in Ireland where he grew up. It was a lonely life here in some ways, far from friends and family. But that was exactly what he wanted. There was such a thing as too much family—especially when one was part of the brawling lot known as the Roaring Red Raffertys.

He pushed back his wide-brimmed hat and slowed his horse to a walk. The sun had browned the doctor's skin, and he wore the loose cotton pants and wide-sleeved shirt of the villagers. It was his great height, dark blue eyes and his almost-black hair, polished with deep red highlights, that gave him away as a gringo.

Wearing the local clothes made it easier for the villagers to accept him; and as Rafferty had warned his new assistant, Dr. Pease, it beat the hell out of those damned starched shirts with stiff collars and the high-crowned hats that the man was addicted to. His well-meant advice had gotten him a pained look from Homer Pease, and stony silence. Rafferty had shrugged, exasperated. He'd only been trying to help.

He reined in before a red-painted door and patted Lugh's golden neck. "Home at last, old boy. Oats for you, and tortillas for me." Swinging down from the saddle, he walked his mount beneath the dusty trees.

Dr. Pease didn't come out to greet him, but that wasn't unusual. He was probably with a patient. A doctor would never get rich down here, but by the great Brian Boru, he'd never be bored. The stream of patients was constant, the challenges endless. The wind blew strongly, whispering into Rafferty's ear. He looked around for Domingo, who usually came out to see to Lugh. Rafferty shook his head.

"Where has that old rascal gotten himself to, eh, Lugh? Probably kissed the bottle a bit too thoroughly and is snoring in the hay again."

Rafferty's relationship with the gnarled Mexican was an unusual one. One fine morning, after a hard night with a difficult birth, Rafferty had awakened to the heavenly aroma of brewed coffee drifting through his unshuttered window. Outside a thin brown man with a red-and-purple serape was sweeping the stony ground and had made a proper walkway to the door by lining it with rocks on either side. He was going to be the servant of El Doctore, he announced. It was unfitting that a man of education and *medicina* had no servant, and he, Domingo, had nothing better to do than doze away his old age in the sun. All things considered, he would rather be useful. From that day on, Domingo had become a permanent fixture at the surgery.

Once, Domingo had gotten into the whiskey and tequila that Rafferty kept—primarily—for medicinal purposes. After finishing them off, he'd sampled a few of the decoctions from the pharmacopia, as well. That had led to a week-long hangover. Exasperated, Rafferty had ordered him to pack his things and go. Domingo had simply stayed. Short of tying the old man up and physically removing him to the other side of the mountains, there was no way to get rid of him.

Since then, firmly installed, Domingo had assumed the roles of groom, cook, honorary uncle and domestic tyrant. The surgery was El Doctore's domain, but in the house and stables, Domingo ruled supreme. Nothing short of the Grim Reaper's scythe would remove him from the premises. In the more frenetic moments of their five-year relationship, the thought of murder *had* crossed Rafferty's mind, but he always dismissed it wistfully. In the end, he had let his unsolicited servant remain and paid him what wages he could. He knew that Domingo had no family, and he suspected that the man had no place else to go. He and Domingo were two of a kind, it seemed.

Rafferty attended to Lugh, and took himself off to the surgery. A bath, a dish of beans and a tot of that medicinal whiskey seemed in order. The door was open a few inches. He glimpsed the neat interior. No patient, no Dr. Pease. Everything else was just as it should be. Except for the folded square of paper tented on the examining table.

"*Not again!*" Rafferty roared.

The bottles rattled in their locked cabinet, demonstrating that he'd inherited the voice as well as the looks of his ancient ancestors. He punched the door back against the wall with the same hand that could repair a nasty gash or soothe a crying baby. Striding in, he swooped down upon the paper, but before even scanning the crabbed lines, Rafferty knew what it meant: Dr. Pease had hightailed back to Los Alamos to catch the first ship bound for the States. The spineless, gormless, lily-livered weakling!

And it meant that Brendan Patrick Timothy Rafferty was going to have to put on one of those damned uncomfortable shirts with a stiff, starched collar and all the paraphernalia that went with it, book passage on a crowded and unsanitary ship and face once more the great sprawl of civilization that he so despised. Because this time, when he picked out a new assistant, he was going to do it the right way, instead of relying solely on an advertisement. Face-to-face.

And, by God, this time, he would get someone who could study hard and work harder, a man who would stick it out in San Juan year after year and count himself lucky.

A *real* man.

Chapter One

~~~~~~~~~~~~~

San Francisco, 1846

"Oh, Lordy, child, you do look fine!"

Only two people were present in Madame Lucine's exclusive establishment, one admiring the other.

"Fine feathers make fine birds," Thomasina answered, trying to smile back at the brown face reflected beside hers in the mirror. Her own image, of an auburn-haired young lady in floating white tulle, glimmered and blurred against the rose silk wallpaper. Quickly, she turned and posed, pretending to admire the elegant lines of her gown in the triple mirror, wanting to hide her distress from the modiste's keen, black eyes; but that was something Thomasina had never been able to do. Lucy, known to San Francisco society as Madame Lucine, saw through the ruse.

"What, are those tears I see?"

"I'm sorry, Lucy. It's...it's just—that I dread it so!"

The dressmaker adopted a brisk tone. "Dry your

eyes, missy, before you spot your dress. I won't have you spoiling my finest gown.''

The mock-stern tone provoked a tremulous grin and dim echoes of a happy childhood in distant New Orleans. How many times, Thomasina wondered, had Lucy's brown-sugar voice scolded her over the years? *Hold still, missy, you're wiggling like bait on a line! If you don't stop jiggling about, child, you're like to get a pin jabbed into your ribs. I declare, missy, you can smudge a clean dress just by walking on by it—and Lordy, child, how did you rip your petticoats like that! Sneaking into the garden at that fancy girl's school again? Why you need to be a-stealing oranges, when you've got all you want at home, is more than a body can figure....*

Thomasina had known Madame Lucine all her life, and their histories were inextricably woven. Born plain Lucy Selwell to a free family that could scarcely afford to feed and clothe all eight surviving children, the young black woman had been apprenticed to a seamstress in the city. Somehow, somewhere outside New Orleans—Thomasina suddenly realized she was very vague on the details—her mother and Lucy had met. The lives of the two women had been entwined ever since. Four years ago, Lucy had opened up this rose and gold establishment and become an instant success. The thin woman in a simple silk dress and yellow turban had transformed herself, by wit and talent, into an elegant modiste.

Now, the same clever hands that had embroidered Thomasina's Christening gown nineteen years before created a wonderful dress for her debut: a cloud of gossamer trimmed with seed pearls, crystals and knots of thin, silver ribbon. It was a masterpiece. But Thomasina knew it was all for naught. She would never achieve her mother's ambitious dreams. Her fingers trembling, Thomasina removed the gown with Lucy's deft assistance.

The money Maman had spent on outfitting her like a princess, the countless lessons in deportment, elocution and etiquette, the years of singing and dancing lessons at a fine boarding school in Connecticut, the two years of being "finished" at a select New York seminary, were all wasted. Not because Thomasina hadn't applied herself to absorbing her education and learning well the boring "accomplishments" that society deemed essential in a lady of quality. Not because she was still at heart the little tomboy who used to shuck her ruffled dresses for a stablelad's rough clothes and steal oranges from the gardens of the nearby convent school. Not because she was gangly or plain, for she had inherited at least some of her mother's beauty. Not even because of the masses of unfashionable strawberry-blond hair, whose color and rioting curls she deplored.

No, it was something deeper and unknown, a premonition of impending disaster that eluded her every time she tried to grasp its cause. She even dreamed of it—tangled nightmares that evaporated upon waking, leaving her filled with an uneasy dread. Her part in the annual debutante ball was going to be a complete disaster. The knowledge was cool and certain, like the chill of a bone-deep ague. Thomasina blinked and the crystal bobs on the gilt wall sconces shimmered through her tears.

Without commenting, Lucy handed her an embroidered handkerchief. The scrap of linen carried an elusive scent, like cinnamon and nutmeg with an undernote of the rose geranium Lucy used in her potpourri, familiar and dear. Thomasina dabbed her dark-fringed emerald eyes and blew her nose, chagrined at her embarrassing lack of control—she, who had spent ten years of exile at the Clovedale Academy for Young Ladies with only a rare visit from her mother, who had braved the cold, miserable winters, the terrible isolation and devastating homesickness without showing one tear or letting anyone even suspect her feelings!

Thomasina schooled her face. This ball and her debut in society were of great importance to her mother and were the culmination of all the years of mutual sacrifice and loneliness. It was small payment to ask, Thomasina was sure, and she loved her mother dearly. Their long separations had only served to deepen their bonds. She would walk barefoot over hot coals if it would make her mother happy.

"I—I don't know what came over me. I suppose it's quite normal to be a bit anxious about my first ball."

Madame Lucine pursed her mouth. "I've known you too long, child. You don't have to pretend. Not to me."

Thomasina slipped on her walking dress of apple green twill and fumbled with the cuff buttons. "Oh, Lucy, I don't know if I can go through with it!"

"I don't mean to be disloyal to your Mama, Lordy, no! Not after all she's done for me. But, child, have you told her how you feel? I don't believe she would ever force it on you."

"Everything my mother has done, she has done for me." Thomasina's face reddened as she remembered the scene she'd made when she'd first been packed off to school. She'd even run away, twice, in the early days. She flinched now, recollecting her heated accusations, the hurtful things she had said, so sure in her youthful righteousness that she had all the answers. It would take years for the memory to grow less painful.

"This is the only thing I can give Maman," she explained huskily. "And that's why I *must* do it. All these years she has had so many dreams and plans for me, and worked so hard to make them come true." Her voice faltered. "But it won't turn out the way she thinks it will. Oh, Lucy! I can't bear to see her hurt!"

"That's a lot of nonsense, and you know it. You've just got cold feet, that's what we called it in my day," Lucy replied briskly as she swathed the ball gown in its wrapper.

Thomasina's response was interrupted by the sound of a vehicle pulling up in the street below, and a moment later, the tinkle of the bell sounded. Lucy looked out the grilled window. "There's your carriage, child. Now, you go along home, and don't worry. Your mama knows what she's doing. I daresay, she's got a plan or two up her sleeve." Lucy smiled. "She always does. And once she sets her mind to something, there's nothing a body can do to turn her away from it!"

Thomasina tied the strings of her bonnet in a fashionable bow beneath one ear. "I suppose you're right. You've always warned me that my imagination is far too lively. I've been getting myself in a state of agitation for nothing."

Lucy picked a bit of invisible lint from her dress, then twitched a fold of Thomasina's light cloak into place, never once meeting her eyes. She personally escorted Thomasina down the stairway, a mark of attention she bestowed on few; but moments later, as she watched the carriage roll away from her establishment, her dark face looked suddenly old and tired. Thomasina was very dear to her heart; Lucy had played midwife at her birth.

Lucy sighed distractedly as she closed the door. Never had she known a mother and daughter to be so unlike one another. Patrice Wentworth was blinded by ambition for her only child, and that ambition might carry the seeds of destruction with it. It was wrong for her to hide the past from her daughter, worse to try to foist Thomasina upon the society that had rejected Patrice herself, so many years ago.

"Poor Miss Tommy," Lucy murmured. "Poor, poor, child."

Thomasina's carriage left the block of graceful buildings that housed Miss Lucine's establishment, and skirted the edge of the fashionable homes on Nob Hill. Far below, the waves of the harbor glimmered like strings of diamonds so bright she was almost blinded by them. Thomasina loved San Francisco with its steep streets and colorful houses, its interesting mix of people from the four corners of the earth and its babble of tongues. It was frequently said that one might easily find anything and everything in San Francisco—for a price.

As the carriage approached an intersection, she leaned forward and tapped Reed, the groom. "I promised to drop off a book at the house of an acquaintance," she said rather breathlessly.

She gave him an address in a distinctly unfashionable part of town and only his long training kept him from raising his eyebrows in surprise. "Are you certain you have that address correctly, Miss Wentworth?"

"Oh! Yes. Quite certain!"

Reed's misgivings grew but, as he had no instructions to the contrary, he obeyed his young mistress. Thomasina sat stiffly against the cushions. Two right turns brought them to a street of modest homes and shops with living quarters above. Their windows were streaked and dirty, their wood in dire need of fresh paint. At her direction, the vehicle stopped near the corner.

"I don't know how long I'll be. You may wish to walk the horses or—or perhaps have a glass of ale at one of the saloons in the area."

Reed wasn't about to leave Miss Wentworth for a glass of anything, despite his thirst. "I'll walk the horses, miss."

She got down without waiting for him to assist her and started up the narrow walk toward a narrow house that was marginally better than its neighbors. Once the groom was out of sight, however, Thomasina doubled back to the end of the block and turned the corner to a street of private homes that had once known better days. She stared up a moment at the boarding-house sign, then gathered her courage and knocked.

The door was opened by a large-boned woman with watery eyes and stringy blond hair pinned back at her nape. She looked the visitor up and down, curiosity warring with envy as she took in everything from Thomasina's smart bonnet to the tips of her stylish kid boots.

"And what would the likes of you be doing here?" she asked in a breathy cloud of alcohol fumes.

"I am Miss Wentworth. I have an appointment to see Dr. Rafferty." The words were scarcely out of her mouth when the door began to close in her face.

"Off with you, you bold-faced hussy! This is a decent house!"

Thomasina stuck the toe of her boot inside. "Please! I *must* see Dr. Rafferty."

"Not under my roof, you won't. There'll be no such goings on in *my* place."

Thomasina's dainty kid boot was now painfully wedged between the door and the jamb. At first she was as determined to gain admittance as the woman was to shut her out, but she was outweighed. The heavy oak slab was slowly crushing her foot. She tried to withdraw it and was shocked to realize she was unable to do so. "Please, you're hurting me!"

"Aye, so I am. That'll teach you to come around to an honest boarding house with your evil ways, it will!"

The impasse was resolved by a masculine bellow from the direction of the parlor. "Really, Mrs. Henson, there's no need for you to provide more patients for me by slamming doors upon hapless young ladies! I assure you, I do quite well enough on my own account."

Through the crack of the narrow opening, Thomasina saw a dark-haired giant stride toward the hall. His face was blurred by the involuntary tears of pain that stung her eyes, but she could see he had the air of authority and confidence of a man in his middle years. When he easily wrested the door from the irate landlady, Thomasina stumbled across the threshold and almost fell. Her foot seemed numb and paralyzed until she stepped on it; then the throbbing brought a sharp exclamation to her lips.

All the humor vanished from the man's face. He glared at the landlady. "Here now, see what you've done! The young lady is injured!"

Before Thomasina could recover, she was swept up and carried toward the front parlor. Having the weight off eased the pain considerably, but her foot felt twice its normal size. The giant propped her in an armchair and began to unlace her boot while the landlady watched, aghast. She placed her arms akimbo.

"None of that, now! There's only one reason a girl of her class would seek out a surgeon in this part of town, and I'll not condone her loose morals!"

Dr. Rafferty deftly slipped Thomasina's boot from her foot. "Madam," he said without facing the landlady, "You have an evil mind, and a temper to match. You've caused considerable bruising to the young lady, and if you don't want an unpleasant situation to develop, I suggest you bring me a bowl of cold water and some strapping tape. At once!''

After a second's hesitation, Mrs. Henson stalked out to do as he'd ordered, muttering beneath her gin-soaked breath. Dr. Rafferty probed Thomasina's foot gingerly. ''Nothing broken. A nasty sprain is all.''

He smiled a reassuring, professional smile, but it was still enough to make his bright, blue eyes twinkle. Thomasina realized he was much younger than she'd originally thought. It was his air of authority and the sober lines of his face in repose that had misled her. He was good-looking in a rugged way that she found quite attractive. His hand radiated heat, and Thomasina was suddenly conscious of the fact that he held her bare foot poised upon his firm palm.

In the moment that followed, Rafferty became aware of the awkwardness. Her foot was dainty—soft and finely arched—and no larger than his extended hand. He noticed the slimness of her well-turned ankle. Fleetingly, the thought intruded: Was the rest of her as delicate and exquisitely feminine? Startled, he felt himself blushing. How long had it been since he'd blushed like a schoolboy?

How long had it been since he'd touched a woman who wasn't a patient?

The landlady returned with the basin and tape and stood glowering until the doctor noticed. He nodded in dismissal. ''Thank you. Your assistance is no longer required, Mrs. Henson. I'll ring if I need anything further.''

''I'll *not* leave an unmarried man and woman alone in such a manner.''

His flush darkened with anger. "I'm not the kind of man to stoop to rape," he roared. "And if it were seduction I intended, my good woman, you may be certain I'd select a more romantic setting than the parlor of a third-rate boarding house smelling of cabbage and gin!"

The woman was too taken aback by his bluntness to argue. Still gaping, she turned and went out. When she was gone, Rafferty got up and pulled the pocket doors shut. "Meddlesome, quarrelsome creature!" he said, more to himself than to Thomasina. "It's the gin, you know. It's raddled her liver and pickled what few brains God gave her. And I must say, the Good Lord was less than generous with her in the first place."

Barely avoiding sloshing its contents, he arranged the basin and guided his patient's foot into the water with great gentleness. His face was still set with irritation, but it smoothed into a soothing, professional facade when Thomasina flinched at the frigid temperature.

"I'm sorry. It's not too pleasant, I imagine, but the cold soak will keep the swelling down. In a quarter hour or so, I'll bind it up properly for you, but there'll be no dancing till dawn for several days, Miss... er...?"

"Wentworth," Thomasina supplied.

Rafferty lifted his head and looked at her narrowly. "Miss Wentworth. Then you are the young lady who wrote requesting an appointment."

The glance that accompanied his words was comprehensive and clinical, as he noted the healthy color and texture of her skin, the brightness of her eye, the general level of vitality. "Your health, I would say, is quite robust. Nor do you look like the type of female inclined to disorders of the nervous system."

Thomasina blushed. "Oh, yes! I mean, no! I am never ill or out of sorts. And I have, so my mother claims, enough energy for a dozen people. That is one of the reasons I wanted to speak with you."

He raised his eyebrows. "You have too much energy? I admit that's a complaint I've never heard before, and I have no pat remedy to offer—other than fresh air and sufficient exercise. Perhaps you need to find something more than fashions and parties to occupy your time."

Thomasina leaned forward eagerly. Her eyes were level with his and radiant. "You understand my nature exactly, sir. I have not only a great need but an equal desire to occupy myself with some meaningful employment." Her face pinked with fervor. "You see, I have come in response to your plea of two nights ago."

He looked at her blankly.

"Surely you remember!" she exclaimed.

Rafferty sat back on his heels. Of course, he remembered. He'd spent half the night wrestling a sudden rush of loneliness and wishing he had a beautiful woman in his arms, but how in the devil this young lady knew of it, was more than he could tell.

She laughed at his stunned expression. "Perhaps you think it was improper for me to attend your evening lecture. There were very few women in the audience, but I didn't come unchaperoned."

"Oh!" he said as light dawned. "My *lecture.*"

"Yes. And I have come to apply for the position of your medical assistant and apprentice."

"To apply..." His words trailed off as the situation straightened itself out in his mind. He was dealing either with a madwoman or one of the hysterical types who attached themselves romantically to near strangers. Rafferty had suffered a hair-raising experience in Boston with an aristocratic spinster at her last prayers. Miss Kennedy had suddenly risen from the settee and thrown herself at him, babbling of past lives together in ancient Egypt and announcing passionately that she wanted to bear his children. Rafferty shuddered. And there had been the very lovely and very mad Lady Soppington....

He rolled his eyes. Why me, oh Lord? Out of thousands of physicians in the world, why do they always find me? And why, in Heaven's name, had he banished the landlady? If Mrs. Henson had returned at that moment, he would have greeted her with warm enthusiasm. But the doors remained closed.

Miss Wentworth was watching him, her entire body tensed.

"I'm afraid you have mistaken my intentions," he announced quietly. One thought was at the forefront of his mind: Keep her calm, administer a sedative, if possible, and get her out of here quickly, before she does God knows what!

Doubt crept into the young woman's eyes, turning them a deep sea green. She licked the corner of her mouth, an action that did strange things to Rafferty's peace of mind. Then she clasped her hands together tightly.

"Surely I didn't mishear, Dr. Rafferty. You *did* say you were quite desperate to acquire an assistant and... Oh! You haven't already taken someone on?"

Now Rafferty was certain she was mad. "I am desperate, Miss Wentworth, but surely you see that I can't possibly consider you for the position."

"No?" Her green gaze burned through him indignantly. "I do not."

"I'm afraid you're laboring under a mistaken notion. My practice is not here in San Francisco, but in Mexico. So you see, it is quite out of the question."

"But I don't see at all."

"Er... I would think the explanation is quite obvious."

"Well, I do not!"

Her chin was charmingly stubborn, and with her bowed mouth set firmly, she looked like a sulky girl in need of thorough kissing. Rafferty felt sweat break out upon his brow. What in God's name had come over him?

Thomasina hadn't noticed anything amiss. She nibbled thoughtfully at one gloved knuckle. "I can understand your hesitation. You would, of course, need to protect your reputation."

He tipped back his head and laughed at that. His blue eyes sparkled, but his tone was serious. "It isn't my reputation, Miss Wentworth, but yours that concerns me."

Thomasina mustered as much dignity as was possible to a young woman with one bare foot soaking in a basin of water.

"Your concern is misapplied. And in any case, if I'm to become a physician, I must necessarily travel alone and unchaperoned in the course of my duties, so it is better to start sooner than later."

Rafferty was in no mood to pursue the subject. "I'm afraid it is out of the question."

He lifted Thomasina's foot from the water and looked around. He'd neglected to ask for a towel. Without thinking, making do the way he had so many times before, Rafferty carefully blotted her foot dry with the corner of his frock coat.

Thomasina paid scant attention to the doctor's unorthodox methods. She had more important matters on her mind. Perhaps she hadn't made herself clear. "I don't see that it's out of the question at all. Let me first state my qualifications. Since the age of twelve, I have had only one desire—to be a physician. To further my plans, I have studied Brown's *Materia Medica* and Mrs. Junot's *Healing Uses of Herbs and Flowers* extensively. I—I have even obtained a copy of Dr. Mortimer's new anatomy text and am quite familiar with its contents."

Rafferty was surprised, but too much of an old hand to let it show. He imagined that some of the very realistic illustrations had made Miss Wentworth's green eyes positively goggle.

When the doctor didn't exclaim at her shameless disclosure, Thomasina took heart, speaking quickly and fervidly. "I am acquainted with the suturing of simple lacerations and have lanced a good many boils. In addition, I have worked extensively with the stablemaster and cowherds during the summer months while I was away, watching..." The doctor was staring at her with a curious expression on his face. She crossed her fingers hastily. "...watching and *assisting* with foaling and the applying of fomentations and plasters. I imagine it cannot be *too* different with human beings."

This time Dr. Rafferty threw back his head and positively roared with laughter. "I think, my dear Miss Wentworth, that you have been reading too many adventurous novels. One sight of the operating room would send you swooning."

She played her trump card. "Last September I watched... uh, assisted at the amputation of a gangrenous toe, and the subsequent cautery. I found it unpleasant, but I neither fainted nor screamed."

Thomasina didn't think it necessary to note that she'd been violently sick to her stomach later; after all, she'd fulfilled her duties before succumbing to human frailty.

Rafferty frowned. For the first time, he began to suspect the depth of this woman's desire to practice the art and science of medicine. His estimation of his extraordinary visitor went up in another great leap, but he wasn't about to let his admiration lead him afoul of good judgment.

"Miss Wentworth, I am not so abandoned that I would take an untrained, unchaperoned young woman with me on a long journey over land and sea, even sharing a ship's cabin."

"Well," she replied, giving the matter serious consideration. "If appearances are the prime stumbling block, I suppose I would have no objection to my masquerading as a young man until we reached Mexico City."

"No," Rafferty said firmly. "But I would. And, I imagine, Miss Wentworth, that you would have a great deal of difficulty pursuing that plan. You are, if you'll excuse so personal an observation, much too feminine in sha—er, in appearance to pass yourself off as a member of the opposite sex."

He bound her foot with strips of linen strapping and sat back to inspect his handiwork. "There. That should do quite well."

When he glanced up, his face was serious once more. "Furthermore, Mexico has certain social conventions which must be respected. Attractive young women cannot travel unchaperoned with men who are not related to them by either blood or marriage. My patients would have nothing to do with you. Or with me, under those circumstances."

With a quick twist of his wrist, he deftly wrapped a clean monogrammed handkerchief around her foot. "The injury is slight." Rafferty stood. "In a few days, you'll be over it." And, he hoped, over her foolish dreams of accompanying him to Mexico.

He turned away while she rolled her stocking up over the makeshift bandage and slipped her injured foot back into her boot. It was a tight fit and she gave a small gasp of pain as she pushed in the last inch of it. Rafferty heard it.

"You might have some difficulty putting weight upon it. Let me help you up."

With his strong arms lifting her, Thomasina was sure she'd have no trouble at all, but once she tried to step on the affected leg, she winced and lost her footing. Rafferty instantly took charge, sliding his arm about her waist for support. "I'll arrange for a carriage to come and deliver you safely home."

"There's no need. My own carriage is waiting for me at the corner."

She tilted up her face to his and he was caught by the appeal in it. "Please, Dr. Rafferty, don't reject my application out of hand, merely because of my sex. I would do anything to convince you to change your mind and take me with you."

That was quite enough for the landlady, who'd been eavesdropping at the keyhole. She burst into the room in righteous indignation to find the doctor clasping Thomasina around the waist, her head resting against Rafferty's wide chest.

"*Well!* I'll not have such goings on under my roof!" Mrs. Henson advanced on them. "Passing yourself off as a respectable physician to carry on I don't know *what* sort of carnal iniquities! And you, miss, with your fine airs and fancy clothes—why, you're no better than you should be!"

"Enough!" Rafferty bellowed, in a manner his ancestors would have approved. "There is no reason to subject this young lady to your foul mouth and worse temper. Or myself, for that matter. I won't spend another minute under this roof. Someone from the Bonaventure Inn will come for my trunks."

Ignoring the landlady's ire, the doctor swooped Thomasina into his arms and carried her to the door. She was mortified beyond belief. "I am so sorry, Dr.

Rafferty. If I hadn't come here, you wouldn't now be out on the streets."

The doctor's eyes flashed blue lightning. "I'll be happy to be shut of this...this *harpy*'s abode." He lowered his voice. "Furthermore, I can't abide the smell of boiled cabbage. That's the real reason that I left Boston in my youth," he said with a twinkle.

Thomasina chuckled at that, but was still upset that he'd left his lodgings because of her.

Rafferty found himself wanting to make her laugh again. He grinned down at her. "Be of good cheer, Miss Wentworth. Although I leave here of my own accord, I will tell you one thing—in their long and glorious history, Raffertys have been thrown out of far better places than this!" He threw the door open and marched out with her still in his arms.

Thomasina glanced nervously over her shoulder as he kicked the door shut with his heel. It wouldn't do to have Reed see them. It would spoil everything. "If you'll please to put me down now, I can manage as far as the carriage."

The doctor set Thomasina gently on her feet and saw her wince. "You've had a very disappointing visit here, Miss Wentworth. Perhaps I had better see you safely home."

"No," Thomasina replied, more sharply than she'd intended. "I can manage. That's my carriage approaching." She stepped gingerly away and hobbled a few yards down the street. She didn't want Reed to see her with the doctor, and she was even more anxious to be gone before she lost her precarious control

and burst into tears. She had so *hoped* that he would
consider her for the position.

Rafferty whistled softly when the carriage pulled up.
It was an elegant and expensive vehicle, very much in
the latest mode. He'd guessed from her clothing and
manner that his visitor came from a monied background, but he had apparently underestimated it.

As the carriage rolled away, all he could see of his
erstwhile visitor was the poke of her elegant bonnet.
He watched until the equipage turned the corner. Miss
Wentworth was certainly a paradox. Why would an
appealing and pretty young woman of good family
want to abandon her wealth and comforts to become
a surgeon? It didn't make any sense to him, and Rafferty was a sensible man. Ah, well. He liked tidy answers and neat endings, but he'd learned long ago that
life provided few. He tried to dismiss the incident as
the eccentric whim of a spoiled debutante. By tomorrow, she'd have forgotten all thoughts of medical
pursuits and be engrossed in her natural milieu—the
drawing room, the ballroom, the boudoir and the
nursery—and *not* the surgery.

In any case, her future would remain a mystery to
him, for the *Pride of Panama* would set sail in eight
days, carrying him back to his home in San Juan with
or without a proper assistant. Humming a plaintive
Irish aire, he turned and proceeded toward the docks
and the rough companionship of the Bonaventure Inn.

Thomasina was having a much harder time dis-
missing their encounter. Her disappointment was so
keen, she could hardly bear it. She had nurtured a secret hope that if she'd been successful in convincing

Dr. Rafferty to take her on, her mother would come to realize her earnestness. Then the dreaded ball—and all that would come with it—could be forsaken while Thomasina dedicated herself to her medical calling.

She was lost in reflection as her carriage wound higher over the cobbled streets toward the wealthy residential district. She was still deep in her private musings some time later, when the carriage pulled up before one of the oldest homes on the block. This was the residence of Agatha Fowlerville, a distant cousin of Thomasina's late father. Thomasina had not even been aware of Cousin Agatha's existence until six months ago, when her mother had sent her to San Francisco straight from finishing school. Although Thomasina's older relative had been a bit stand-offish initially, it had not taken long for a mutual affection to spring up between them.

Agatha was a widow of indeterminate years and vague mannerisms, with decided bluestocking tendencies. Until Thomasina entered her life, Agatha had lived happily among her growing collection of books and stray animals, fading gently into the decay that was the lot of impoverished widows. From snippets of information Thomasina had gained from Sarah, the friendly parlormaid, it seemed that Agatha had come into a recent windfall and was enjoying it immensely.

The Fowlerville house and grounds were mellow with age and showing their years, but there were definite signs of refurbishment in progress. The curved porch, tall window frames and the fancywork around the turrets and gables were freshly trimmed in contrasting shades of peach and green, and even the sleek tabby cat lounging before the side door had an air of newfound prosperity. It yawned and stretched gracefully, then, purring with bliss, rose to greet Thomasina as she descended from the carriage.

"Good afternoon, Ashurbanipal," Thomasina said with a laugh as she stopped to tickle behind the creature's ears. "Is it because I've returned that you're so pleased? Or because you know I'll wheedle another bit of fish for you from Cook?"

The cat refused to be insulted by such a cynical view of its behavior and rubbed against Thomasina's ankles in feline ecstasy. They went around to the side entrance together. The flagstone floor of the dim passage was freshly washed. Muffled snuffling and sniffling came from behind the closed door to the stillroom, interspersed with a gentle, reassuring voice. The name Mrs. Church was mentioned more than once. Clearly, the housekeeper had threatened to dismiss the young scullery maid again, and Cook was trying to soothe the girl's fears. Thomasina grimaced in sympathy. Mrs. Church ruled the household with a fist of iron and a heart to match. Even Cousin Agatha was cowed by her housekeeper's brisk and overbearing ways.

She set her small package down on a fine, old, pine hutch and removed her bonnet. A servant in a starched apron and frilled cap rounded the corner and threw her hands up in surprise.

"La, Miss Thomasina," said the head parlor maid, "I didn't expect to find you coming in through the service door. And carrying your own parcels! I'll give Reed a good piece of my mind over that, you can be sure. Why, if Mrs. Church had seen it, she'd have docked his wages!"

"Don't worry, Sarah, she'll never know. And don't blame Reed. I insisted." Thomasina lowered her voice to a conspiratorial whisper. "More books from Grinder's Apothecary Shoppe."

"Oh, Miss Thomasina, you haven't been there again?" Sarah shook her head. What the girl's mother would say if she heard of it, Sarah couldn't say. Not that Mrs. Wentworth didn't dote on the child, from all reports. The mistress, too. Why, the whole household was astir because Mrs. Fowlerville was planning to attend a ball for the first time in many years, to accompany her young charge. Perhaps there would even be a tea given at the house, or small reception. La, such goings on!

The maid picked up the discarded cloak and bonnet. There was a secret smile in the depths of her dark eyes. "I'll take these up to your chamber, miss. The mistress is in the Green Salon. She's been asking for you this past half hour."

"Thank you, Sarah. I'll freshen up and go to her at once."

Sarah took the twisting staircase at the end of the corridor, but Thomasina went through the pantry and up another set of stairs. She wanted desperately to go to her own chamber and leaf through her new medical books, but she couldn't keep dear Agatha waiting. A servant's door in an alcove led through to the dining room. The long table and carved chairs were highly polished. The grand silver-and-gilt epergne and matching candelabra gleamed upon it and Chinese vases held a bounty of roses.

Thomasina checked her reflection in the mirror above the ornate sideboard and smoothed her unruly hair into a semblance of neatness. It sprang back into wispy tendrils and defiant curls. At the doorway to the corridor, she paused, listening for the dragon of a housekeeper.

Mrs. Church was one of those dour, efficient creatures who seemed to care more for the gleam of the furnishings than for the comfort or convenience of the household. Her black-garbed figure roamed the halls and the servants tiptoed about in dread of her fierce temper. For some reason, Mrs. Church resented Thomasina's presence in the house and clearly wouldn't be happy until she saw her gone. Perhaps it was just that the housekeeper didn't like her routine upset but Thomasina suspected it had to do with the reasons her mother had left New Orleans. Someday, she meant to get to the bottom of that mystery.

Thomasina hoped to slip upstairs unnoticed. Mrs. Church's tattlings didn't bother her, but they did upset Cousin Agatha, and for that reason, Thomasina avoided crossing swords with the woman. Any infringement of decorum, real or fancied, would send the housekeeper straight to her mistress with a list of complaints. Agatha's rheumatism caused her great pain, and Thomasina knew that domestic scenes caused it to flare up. She didn't want to add any burden to her cousin's life—especially since Agatha's condition had quieted down in the past few weeks.

Thomasina peered around the corner. The hall was empty, and so was the curving staircase. She dashed over the inlaid marble floor. Home free! Taking the steps two at a time, Thomasina swept lightly up to the second floor, the gray-and-black tabby at her heels—and ran straight into the gorgon.

"So," Mrs. Church said with satisfaction. "Sneaking up the stairs like a servant. You have no more notion of how to conduct yourself in a proper establishment than...than..." she glanced down at the cat "...than that horrible *beast*."

Ashurbanipal, affronted by the housekeeper's lack of taste, arched his back and hissed sharply. Before Thomasina could reply, a door opened farther down the hallway. A tiny figure swathed in plum-colored silk was framed in the open door. "Ah, Thomasina," a soft voice said. "I have been waiting for you."

Thomasina brushed past the belligerent housekeeper and hurried to her cousin's side, planting a kiss on her rouged and withered cheek. It always shocked her to feel the frailty of the reed-thin body; it was as fragile as a bird's.

"The fitting took longer than I had anticipated," Thomasina said guiltily. "I'm sorry to have kept you waiting, Cousin Agatha."

"Not at all, my dear." The dowager stepped aside. "The refreshments have just been brought in. You see, I have a surprise for you."

Mrs. Church watched sourly until the door closed, sniffed and then started down the long staircase. In her preoccupation she neglected to note the cat stretched out in style on the fifth step from the top. For several long, loud seconds, the staircase and hallway reverberated with an outraged feline yowl, a high-pitched shriek and several heavy thumps. A blur of gray-and-black fur streaked past the heaving heap of black bombazine and zipped across the floor.

As curious servants opened the various doors along the ground floor, Ashurbanipal slipped into his favorite refuge beneath the tall case clock. Settled comfortably, with an excellent view of the pandemonium, the cat polished a delicate paw with his long, pink tongue, and smiled.

Upstairs in the Green Salon, the commotion went unnoticed. The room was daintily elegant, filled with light from the tall windows. Thomasina chattered brightly as she crossed the L-shaped room until she passed the high-backed chair that blocked the view. A sophisticated woman perched elegantly on the green brocade divan.

"Maman!"

Thomasina flew over the carpet and enveloped her parent in a joyful hug, crushing a great quantity of white ruffled silk in the process. Her mother's embrace, if somewhat more restrained, was no less sincere. The remembered scents of face powder and French *eau de toilette* enveloped Thomasina in a fragrant cloud.

"Darling!" Her mother offered an unlined cheek to kiss. Although she'd passed her thirty-fifth birthday, Patrice Wentworth looked far younger. There were few who would debate the fact that she was still one of the most beautiful women in the world. There were

none who would argue that she was not also the most
fashionable.

Exclamations tumbled from Thomasina. "Oh!
How I've missed you. What an exquisite frock! Is it
from Paris? And that bonnet—quite daring! When did
you get in? Why didn't you let us know you would be
coming home sooner? Oh, it is so wonderful to see you
again!"

"And you, my darling." Patrice disengaged herself, casting a rueful look at her newly crumpled bodice and the fresh creases in Thomasina's dress. "But
really, we will neither of us be at all stylish if you ruin
our garments like this. You mustn't be such a hoy-
den, my dear, now that you are about to take your
proper place in society."

Thomasina's face fell. For a moment, she had forgotten the coming ordeal. She sat beside her mother
more decorously. "We did not expect you for weeks
and weeks."

For just a moment, Patrice's dark lashes shaded her
eyes. "I was able to complete my business more
quickly than I'd anticipated, and I found myself bored
and lonely. And I wanted to give you this..." She took
a blue velvet box from her reticule. "A gift for your
debut."

Thomasina took the box and opened it slowly.
"Oh!..."

On a bed of pale blue satin lay a choker of glowing
pearls centered with a brilliant, pear-shaped sapphire.
"The Valnoy Bride's sapphire has been handed down
from mother to daughter in your father's family for

many generations." Patrice's voice was bright and brittle. "It was my wedding gift from him."

Thomasina touched a finger to the jewel. The sapphire felt like a piece of ice and glittered with a cold inner light. "It must be very old."

"Only the sapphire and its setting. Your father commissioned the pearl necklace to show off the jewel more suitably. It is," Patrice said with curious satisfaction, "quite well-known. You will, of course, wear it to the presentation ball."

It was worth a king's ransom and not at all the sort of jewelry suitable for a debutante, but Thomasina only nodded. She knew how important the coming ball was to her mother. "Of course," she answered.

She touched the sapphire again, and a cold little chill ran up her arm.

Chapter Two

The dolls and porcelain animals had been removed from Thomasina's dressing table to make room for crystal bottles of scent and covered dishes of powder. It was symbolic of the many changes to come in the days ahead. But the top shelf of her tall wardrobe was crammed with two dozen books on medicine and healing.

"How I wish your father could see you now." There was a wistful look in her eyes as Patrice clasped her own gold-and-pearl bracelet over Thomasina's gloved wrist. "Just one final touch to gild the lily, and then you'll be ready to leave for your first ball."

She took the heirloom necklace from its velvet box on the dressing table and placed it around Thomasina's neck. "This necklace is yours now, Thomasina. May it bring you good fortune." Stepping back, Patrice admired the effect with deep satisfaction. The Valnoy sapphire blazed dark blue against Thomasina's white throat. "My wonderful, beautiful daughter—you will outshine them all."

Even Thomasina had to admit that the combined efforts of her mother, Cousin Agatha and Madame

Lucine were not in vain. The gown floated about her like a shimmer of moonlight. The crystals and seed pearls winked and glimmered in the candle glow. She stared at her reflection in the pier glass. Her eyes seemed to take on some of the sapphire color. In the candlelight they looked more blue than green. Thomasina scarcely knew herself.

In contrast to the gossamer white, her peach-tinted skin and light auburn hair were startling. She was more used to herself in the simple day dresses suitable to a girl fresh from finishing school and not yet out in society. But in this elegant gown, with her hair dressed high, how very different she looked!

"No one will recognize me," she said, speaking her thought aloud.

The lines of her mother's face tightened. "Oh, you will be recognized, my dear. Have no fear of that."

"I wish, Maman, that you were coming with me."

"Nothing would give me greater pleasure than to witness your triumph. But when your father died, I chose to retire from society and have never regretted my decision. And, naturally, here in San Francisco, my acquaintanceship is limited. Fortunately Cousin Agatha has entrée to the most fashionable circles. She is the perfect sponsor for your presentation at the ball tonight."

Agatha wafted in on the last of these words. She was all adither both with anticipation of the evening's events and the satin gown that Patrice had brought her from Paris. "*So* kind of you, my dear. And my favorite shade of Pomoma green."

Thomasina turned. Agatha had taken her great-grandmother's necklet of diamonds and the matching drop earrings from the vault. Even though she had been in dire financial straits until her recent windfall, she would not have sold them except to keep from starving.

"How splendid you look, Cousin Agatha. Like a duchess." And indeed, with her snowy hair pinned up beneath a shimmering cap and her withered apple cheeks aglow, the older woman looked quite distinguished. Agatha pivoted slowly to show the cut of her gown.

"I feel like the cinder girl who went to the ball. It has been many years since I wore a garment so lovely. Or so fashionable, for that matter." A wicked sparkle lit her eyes, transforming her gentle features. "Regine Valnoy will be positively speechless with amazement. I can hardly wait."

Thomasina's curiosity was caught. "Valnoy?" She put her hand up to the sapphire.

Agatha gave a little gasp and fluttered her fingers.

Patrice reached out to clasp her daughter's hands. "There is something I have to tell you . . . perhaps you will think that I should have revealed it to you earlier."

Patrice took a deep breath. "Regine Valnoy is your grandmother. Your father's mother. That is why it is so important that you make a good impression upon her, Thomasina. I didn't want to tell you earlier and make you even more nervous."

A strained smile lifted the corners of Patrice's full mouth. "You see, we made a run-away match. I was an orphan and only sixteen. She forbade the marriage. He...he died. When I learned I was going to have a child I went to his mother. I had no ring—I had pawned it to pay the doctor and buy food—and no proof of our marriage. She didn't believe me, or so she said. But everything will be all right once she sees you. You are the very image of your father...and when Regine looks at you, she will see her beloved Thomas standing before her. She will open her arms to welcome you.''

The talk had made Agatha agitated. She glanced at the pink china clock on the mantel. "There is no time for chatter now, my dears. Thomasina, we really must hurry. The carriage is here and it won't do to keep the horses waiting in this wind.''

Patrice took the shawl of spangled silk from the back of a chair and draped it artfully over her daughter's shoulders. "Agatha is right. You must be on your way. But try not to worry. Everything will be all right.''

The shawl was light, but the invisible burden Thomasina carried upon her shoulders was much heavier. What a moment for such a revelation! She would have liked more time to assimilate what she'd just been told. Although she still didn't fully understand the reason for the estrangement between her mother and the grandmother she had never known, she was suddenly well aware of Patrice's ambitions: every lesson in deportment and elocution, all the schools and governesses and gowns were in preparation for this event. And no matter what had happened in the past between her parents and Regine Valnoy, she was determined to do her mother proud.

Thomasina cast one wistful look at her room, then she hurried down the stairs in a soft rustle of skirts. The clock was just striking the half hour and the cat shot out of his favorite hiding place like a furry cannonball. Ashurbanipal snarled as he flew past the parlor door and Thomasina turned her head.

The housekeeper was hovering in the shadows. Thomasina read her expression as clearly as if Mrs. Church had spoken aloud: *Trying to make a silk purse out of a sow's ear.* Thomasina lifted her head higher. She was determined that the ball would be a success, not for her own sake, but for her mother's. And not even Mrs. Church's sour scowls could spoil it.

Patrice tucked a ruffle on her daughter's shawl and embraced her lightly. "Have a wonderful evening, darling. And remember everything that you see and hear and do, for I expect you to go over it all for me when you return."

A concerned look flitted over Thomasina's features. "Please, Maman, don't get your hopes up too high," she said softly. "I was never born to play the role of social butterfly. I don't want to disappoint you."

"Nothing you could ever do would disappoint me. I know you too well, Thomasina."

Agatha was anxious to be off. "Come child, the horses are growing restive."

They descended the steps together and were handed up into the new town carriage Patrice had just purchased. It was glossy black with yellow trim, the interior lined with gold plush. The coach lanterns, of polished brass with beveled glass inserts, shone like miniature suns. The cream-colored horses between the shafts were fit to carry royalty, and Thomasina felt like a crown princess.

For the first time, her sense of anticipation took on a lighthearted tone. She was beginning to look forward to the evening. Perhaps it wouldn't be so bad, after all. When the groom mounted to his seat and snapped the reins, Thomasina heard Agatha give a tiny sigh of pure pleasure.

Patrice watched from the open door as the fairy-tale carriage disappeared into the darkness. There was more at stake than Thomasina knew. Much more. On the long-ago day when Patrice had left the house of Regine Valnoy, she had sworn she would have nothing more to do with her husband's family—not until the haughty matron issued her an apology and accepted Thomasina as her heir. The Valnoys were proud and stubborn, and no apology had been forthcoming. In fact, they had done everything possible to bring Patrice to her knees—but Patrice Wentworth had been more than their match. And tonight would prove it.

She only wished she could be a moth on the wall when Agatha presented her young houseguest to old Madame Valnoy. One look at Thomasina's eyes and rioting auburn hair, one glance at the great sapphire in her necklace, and Regine Valnoy would know that she'd been told the truth so long ago. It would be a bittersweet moment.

When her grandmother saw Thomasina for the first time, the old woman would melt. Regine had doted on

Thomas to an extraordinary degree. Seeing her only son's child would bring back a thousand memories. The past, with all it wounds, would be forgotten, and Thomasina would be welcomed into the family—as was her right. Patrice smiled. Victory at last. Suddenly she felt a need to celebrate the occasion.

She went up to the sitting room adjoining her boudoir and sat beside the miniature of her late husband. Splashing brandy from the decanter she kept hidden in her desk, she lifted the glass until it caught the light of the candles, and proposed a toast to the empty room.

"To you, Thomas—wherever you may be."

The room was small and the window wide-open in hopes that the night breeze might carry away some of the rum fumes. From the tap room below voices were raised in song and bawdy conversation. Brendan Rafferty's surgical kit was open on the scarred table by the light of the kerosene lamp. The doctor finished suturing the gash in the sailor's muscled shoulder and tore off strips of soft linen.

"That should do nicely."

The man grunted. A fresh bandage adorned his left calf, and his weathered face was pale despite thirty years of tropical sun. Rafferty taped the sailor's shoulder with a brisk economy of movement that spoke of long practice. This task finished, he eyed the man's plenitude of scars, old and new.

"Just keep out of brawls for a few days until it heals."

"Thankee, Doc." The seaman rose and pulled on his shirt with the physician's assistance. "Now then, what'd I be owing ye for yer patchwork?"

Rafferty gave the man a measuring look. "I'll not take your money, my friend."

The sailor frowned. "Tod Gumm always pays his debts. I'll not be taking yer charity."

"I didn't say I wouldn't exact payment," Rafferty said firmly. "This is the third time I've sewn you back together in as many days. I won't have your money. Instead, I'll exact a promise. You won't seek revenge of that young jack-o'-worts, Miles Stoker, and his gang. Too many bodies have littered the wharf. This foolish feud must end here and now."

"What? And have him stick a blade between me ribs while I'm catching forty winks?"

The doctor washed his instruments and put them to soak in carbolic. His face was flushed with sudden anger. "I've spoken to Stoker. He'll abide by the agreement or I'll cut his liver and lights out myself. Yours, too, by God. I'll see an end to this fighting and killing, one way or the other."

Tod Gumm shifted his bulk from one foot to the other. He was a big man, but so was Rafferty, and from the scuttlebut around the waterfront, the doctor was right handy with his fives. But it was a certain and indefinable air the physician had that swayed the sailor.

"Aye, I believe ye would at that. Ye've the look of the devil in yer eye when ye glare like that. Well, Tod Gumm's afeared of no man, but yer in the right of it.

It's time to end the feud." He stuck out a grimy paw. "Here's me hand on it, Doc."

Rafferty shook hands with him. "Now be off with you. And if you end up on my doorstep again, I'll sew you back together so crooked that you'll list to port with one step and to starboard with the other."

The sailor laughed heartily and went out, still chuckling to himself.

Rafferty washed up and put his instruments away. If he hurried, he could make the first presentation at the Scientific Society's annual symposium. And, if his luck would only change, he might find someone willing to join him in his Mexican surgery. The response to his advertisement had not been good: one tubercular young man, and an old sot addicted to drink or opium—or both.

Rafferty frowned and his thoughts turned briefly to Miss Thomasina Wentworth, his erstwhile visitor and would-be assistant. Gad, wouldn't she be shocked to see the primitive conditions he lived under—and the even more primitive surgery he'd set up. And, Great Grania, wouldn't the villagers be shocked even more if a confirmed bachelor like himself brought home a pretty young girl—fresh from finishing school, by the looks of her—without benefit of clergy, ring or wedding license.

Desperate as he was to find someone to share the burden and joys of his medical practice with him, the presence of the lovely Miss Wentworth, regardless of her enthusiasm, would create far more complications than it would solve. Rafferty blew out a gusty breath and pulled off his jacket. Whether he was successful or not, he must soon start on his homeward journey. Banishing all thoughts of failure, he put on a fresh shirt, slid his suit coat over his wide shoulders and ran a boar's-bristle brush through his unruly dark hair.

Before leaving he clipped the narrow leather case of his surgical kit inside his coat pocket. He wasn't about the leave his most prized possession behind in this den of roughnecks. Not with all those wickedly sharp scalpels inside. Rafferty left his rented room and went down the stairs and out into the dark street.

A block away on the waterfront, tall masts and spars were outlined against a starry sky. He took in a deep breath of fresh air, inhaling the mingled scents of salt sea and fish and tar. There was also a dankness on the breeze, promising fog and, perhaps, rain. Rafferty was quite at ease as he strode along, a stout walking stick tucked beneath his arm.

The cut of his clothes and the wink of lamp light off the brass head of the walking stick drew the attention of a cutpurse lurking between buildings. The man pulled down his cap and waited until the doctor was almost abreast. One practiced move, and the thief's long knife was out. The ruffian gauged his distance and tensed to spring.

A yard away, Rafferty passed beneath an inn's sign, his agile mind already jumping ahead to the Scientific Society meeting. An interesting paper on an experimental surgical technique was to be discussed tonight, and he was eager to hear it. Also, he was scheduled to participate in a debate on the current recommendations for women who had just given birth. Childbirth and the prevention of complications was one of his areas of research. He was sure that the dangerous milk leg could be avoided by getting women up and out of bed soon after birth. It was sure to be controversial. He hoped the evening would prove to be a lively one.

The would-be thief gathered himself for the attack. Just then two men came out of the inn behind him, guffawing over a bawdy remark, but turned into a brothel two doors down. The street was all but deserted, although the taverns were full as they could hold from the sounds of it. The robber made a swift change of plan, thinking it better to come up behind the man than to face a blow from that sturdy walking stick.

Rafferty's heels echoed hollowly in a rhythm as steady as his own heartbeat. The thug glided forward like a shadow as his victim passed the hiding place. Suddenly, he stopped, recognizing the wild Irish doctor who'd sewn up a few of his mates in the past week. If he stuck a knife in the man, there'd be a dozen more to cut up his own hide. He sheathed his blade resignedly and grinned to himself. Doc Rafferty would never know how close to death he'd come for a moment. The man melted back into the shadows.

Rafferty walked on without apparent notice; but as the ruffian vanished into the darkness, the doctor's strong fingers loosened their hold on the deadly pistol hidden in his coat pocket. With the small but accurate weapon, his stout walking stick and his pounding fists, Brendan Rafferty was always ready for action. But he was glad the confrontation had been avoided. It would be a great shame for a man dedicated to healing to inflict physical harm on a stranger, thief or not.

And the Scientific Society's meeting began in ten minutes. It would have been an even greater shame if he'd been forced to miss that first discussion.

Thomasina held on to the velvet strap as the carriage wound its way higher and higher. Her insides were knotted although she knew she looked her best in the gown Lucy had sewn with skill and love, and with her hair arranged so artfully. She meant to represent her parents proudly, and didn't know that the smooth center part and neat curls were already trying to spring back into their usual tumble.

"That is the Van Faulken house," Agatha said as the carriage rolled up the street between rows of turreted houses, their leaded windows glowing with light. "He's a prosy old dear, and she's as mean as a hungry dog. But their house is considered the finest in all of San Francisco."

When Thomasina peeked out, she was disappointed. The Van Faulkens' place was costly and beautiful, but could not compare with the picture of a tall brick house, fronted with white pillars and an ornamental garden, that lurked in her memory. It was only at odd times that she saw it in her mind's eye, and whenever she tried to picture it, the image dissolved into meaningless bits. She felt happy when she remembered that house.

There was another house that she saw only in her nightmares, a great sprawl of cold stone with a hundred blank-eyed windows, its corridors vast and never ending. Uncomfortable chairs of pale brocade with stiff gilt legs, mantlepieces carved with monstrous figures that were half human, half animal. And then running, running through a huge, empty ballroom with a great chandelier swathed in cloth, looking like the mummy of a gigantic spider...

Thomasina shook the memory away. This was not the time to dwell on childish nightmares. Not on the verge of her first—and hopefully last—ball. Although she'd protested the plan originally, she now looked forward to attending, but not for the reasons her mother imagined. To Thomasina, this was the last hurdle standing between herself and her true vocation. Once the night was over and she held firm to her purpose, her mother would see that the idle life of a society debutante held no charms for her daughter. And then Thomasina could turn her attention to the problem of finding a doctor who would take her on as an apprentice.

There had to be someone, somewhere, who would give her the opportunity.

She frowned, thinking of Dr. Rafferty. If he saw her now, all sparkles and ruffles and white tulle, he would certainly feel vindicated. The white-gloved hands did not look like a pair that could wield a scalpel or lancet—but Thomasina knew that one day, they would. And she would never give up until she succeeded.

Abruptly, the carriage pulled up in the half-circle drive behind a dozen others waiting to disgorge their occupants. "What a sad crush," Agatha said in an excited tone that put the lie to her words. "Why, I declare that half of San Francisco has turned out for Regine's birthday."

She sent Thomasina a smile that, in someone less kind, might have looked malicious. "A command performance, of course. No one would dare offend her. To do so would be to court social ostracism."

Some of Thomasina's confidence ebbed. She wished her mother had given her more time to get used to the fact that Regine Valnoy was her own grandmother. And what would the dowager think of her when they met? "She sounds a very unpleasant woman."

"Ah, no. I would describe her, instead, as a very powerful woman. But Regine—despite the fact that she's my elder by a good ten years—could still charm the clouds from the sky if she were so inclined."

Thomasina had known that Regine Valnoy's birthday was a special event for the families of French descent in San Francisco. It had become the custom to combine the select ball in honor of the matriarch's birthday with the presentation of the Creole debutantes to the cream of polite society. Any girl of fine family was eligible, as long as she had an approved sponsor from among the established families. Because of this, Thomasina had imagined Regine Valnoy was a kind and gracious aristocrat. In the past half hour, her mental picture had altered dramatically.

The carriage finally reached the entrance, and Agatha and her young cousin descended from it. Thomasina felt her pulse speed up as they entered the wide doors of the house and stepped into a spacious hall. Flowers were massed everywhere, stiff arrangements in pink and white. By the time they'd disposed of their cloaks and she had ruthlessly forced her curls back into place, the reception rooms were thronged. Thomasina was both surprised and relieved to find no formal reception line, as the guests streamed toward the back of the house. The walls of the public rooms were covered in maroon silk, the draperies encrusted with gold tassels and braid.

There was plenty of time to note the toilettes of the others as Thomasina and Agatha went through the first reception area and toward the ballroom beyond: fluttering tulle in pastel tints, gleaming silks and satins in all the colors of the rainbow, shades of shimmering taffetas that had no equal in nature. Silver floss, thread of gold, Brussels lace and French embroidery trimmed sleeves and shawls and graceful skirts. The place was aswirl with color and sound and already cloying with the scents of fine perfumes.

Thomasina realized that the other women were looking at her, too, whispering behind fans or gloved hands bedecked with jeweled rings and bracelets. At least she had the satisfaction of knowing she was one of the best-dressed young women there. "I wish they wouldn't scrutinize me so," she murmured to her cousin. "I feel as if I must have a smut on my nose."

"Pay no mind, my dear," Agatha said as she acknowledged one of the many polite nods and bows she was receiving. "A new and pretty face in such a closed society is bound to stir interest." She wondered if anyone had noticed Thomasina's resemblance to Regine Valnoy's son. "Before the night is out, you will have made several new friends." Agatha's eyes brightened. "And, I am sure, several conquests, as well." She nodded regally at two young men, who sent Thomasina looks of admiration. "I can safely prophesy that your dance card will be filled before the first dance."

Thomasina glanced at the young men and then away, blushing furiously. Their faces were pleasant, if rather inconsequential. Then she realized she was comparing them, to their detriment, with the craggy features of Dr. Brendan Rafferty. Strange, that she could picture discussing this ball with Dr. Rafferty, while by no stretch of the imagination could she imagine discussing the therapeutic effects of lime dust in treating scabrous disease with them.

This was nothing like the Musical Evenings at her finishing school or one of the informal parties her mother had given in New York. Thomasina felt like an overgrown schoolgirl, gauche and unsure of herself. Unsure of the reception she'd receive from the formidable Regine Valnoy. Her mouth went dry.

What on earth am I doing here? Thomasina knew she didn't belong among these shining people with their impeccable backgrounds and long-standing relationships. Despite her mother's hopes, the fine clothes and Cousin Agatha's sponsorship, she felt like an impostor. A nobody playing a role. Thomasina tried to quell the butterflies in her stomach and the growing wish that she was back in her bedroom at Cousin Agatha's, curled up safely with her copy of Mandell's *New Methods in Orthopaedic Surgery*.

Because of the nature of the ball, there was no receiving line set up outside of the ballroom either. The guests were to line up around the walls until Madame

Valnoy made her grand entrance. Once inside, she would take her place upon the dais with the other grande dames, and the procession of debutantes would begin. With a curtsy to the dais as her name was called out, and a curtsy to the crowd, the debutante would be officially launched upon her first season.

The thought of being "launched" struck Thomasina's funny bone: it sounded rather threatening, as if the debutantes were newly christened ships about to have bottles of champagne broken over their bows. Nevertheless she edged her way forward with Agatha, hoping her skirts wouldn't be crushed. The tall doors were thrown open, offering a tantalizing vision of the ballroom beyond.

The press of people briefly held them in place. Suddenly, the crowd surged toward the open doors like a tidal wave. The forward thrust ceased, and they were locked in place again. Thomasina looked up to admire the pink-and-gold chandelier fashioned of Venetian glass. The blaze of candles and the glitter of crystal dazzled her eyes.

She never knew how it happened. One moment, she and Agatha were side by side in the mirrored outer chamber. When she looked back, her cousin had been swept into the ballroom by the throng. Agatha frantically signaled that they would meet again inside, and Thomasina nodded. There was no way to get to her. It would have taken a Moses to part the sea of people. She felt very alone and vulnerable without her cousin's comforting presence. Thank God that Agatha had explained the procedure ahead of time. Thomasina settled into an empty space just inside the door of the ballroom, content to wait until the commotion should subside a bit.

Without Agatha for protection, Thomasina became the focus of several stares. Two young men hovered beyond the potted palms, obviously hoping for an introduction to the mysterious new girl at the earliest opportunity. A haughty but still-youthful dowager, meaning to launch her plain-duckling daughters at the affair, was ill-pleased to find a red-haired young swan only a few yards away. Her frosty looks and firmed mouth told Thomasina she would find no offer of friendship from that quarter.

Turning away, Thomasina was relieved to see a pair of warm blue eyes regarding her with patent admiration. They belonged to a handsome fellow with golden hair, a fine moustache and chiseled features. He edged closer through the crowd and made her a polished bow.

"May I procure you a glass of fruit punch, mademoiselle? Or will you send me packing on the niggling grounds that I've not a drop of French blood in my veins, and that we haven't yet been properly introduced?"

Thomasina blushed, unsure of how to handle the situation. While she debated, he stopped a pale youth just hurrying to his inamorata's side with a crystal cup of punch. "Monsieur LeGuin, how kind of you to fetch some punch for the lovely young lady. I'll be sure to introduce you afterward."

So saying, he plucked the full cup of punch from the other man without spilling a drop, turned his back and presented it to Thomasina with a flourish. "Ah, fortunate punch, to bedew such rose-petal lips..."

He looked perfectly serious, but Thomasina was sure no man would use such flowery speech in these enlightened times unless he meant it in jest. In any case, it was a great breach of etiquette to speak to a person to whom one had not been introduced. He was certainly bold, although she responded to the friendly twinkle in his eyes. Her blush deepened, but she'd gotten hold of herself. "Are you a poet, sir, or merely a hardened flirt?"

"Touché, mademoiselle. I am neither—only Douglass Wilks of Philadelphia, prostrate at your dainty feet." The glint of admiration was more pronounced. "And now, if you aren't already bespoken, may I be so bold as to solicit your hand for the first dance? It's to be a waltz."

Thomasina found him entertaining, and she would have liked very much to dance with him. "But first," she explained with a smile, "I must ask my Cousin Agatha if you are a respectable person or a gazetted fortune hunter more attracted to my expectations than my charms."

Douglass Wilks was still smiling, but his features altered subtly. His face seemed more thoughtful, his expression just the tiniest bit calculating. Then the look was gone, and Thomasina decided it was just a trick of the light. She hoped so, for she thought she might like to further her acquaintance with him. He was quite entertaining.

He acknowledged her hit with another bow. "Very prudent, mademoiselle. But you should know that even a gazetted fortune hunter might fall head over heels in love.''

He took her hand and bent low over it, brushing her skin with his soft moustache. It was a gesture far too familiar for either the place or the circumstances. She drew her hand back quickly, about to utter a quick censure; however, his attention was already focused elsewhere. A thin young woman with mouse-colored hair and enormous dark eyes watched them through a break in the company. Mr. Wilks made a gesture of apology.

"Please excuse me. I see my good friend, Miss Parise, is looking for me."

He vanished into the crowd, and Thomasina's view of Miss Parise was blocked by a stout matron in rust-colored satin trimmed with far too much ruching and lace. Thomasina was sorry to lose her audacious companion. Still, it was quite reassuring to know at least one person in this vast, glittering assembly.

The scents of flowers, perfumes and pomades became overwhelming as the company grew and filled the ballroom. Thomasina saw Agatha on the far side of the room, near the open garden doors. With everyone gathering along the walls now, it was difficult to squeeze across to her cousin's side. She rose and worked her way through the press, smiling, until she spied Agatha fanning her heated face only a dozen feet away. A portly man with a neat, white beard barred Thomasina's progress, but stepped aside when she murmured politely to him. He looked away, then back again. His pale eyes grew round with amazement.

Thomasina felt herself blushing. Perhaps this gentleman saw her resemblance to Thomas Valnoy.

Suddenly, a hush fell over the room. The crowd parted, and an elderly woman was framed between the open double doors that let out to the garden. She looked terribly fragile, too delicate for the blaze of diamonds that ringed her thin throat and crowned her gray hair. Despite the ivory cane in her hand, the woman entered with the measured tread of an empress, surrounded by her court of self-important dowagers. A respectful murmur greeted her appearance. "Madame Valnoy," some said from just behind Thomasina's shoulder, and she realized her mistake. She had expected Regine Valnoy to enter the ballroom from the reception area rather than the terrace; but there was no mistaking the air of consequence that surrounded the gem-bedecked woman or the effect of her arrival. The orchestra began a stately processional, and the white-bearded man came forward to escort the aged Madame Valnoy to the dais.

To her horror, Thomasina found herself directly in their path. As she was about to shift to the sidelines, Regine Valnoy stopped dead with an audible gasp. She fixed Thomasina with a basilisk stare. "You!"

Her voice was high and querulous. The crowd fell silent again, every eye fixed upon the unfolding drama. The orchestra faltered to a halt. Regine stared at Thomasina, then advanced, her aristocratic face suffused with emotion.

Thomasina felt as if she were trapped in a nightmare. If only she'd had more time to prepare for this meeting. If only it could have taken place privately and not in full view of four hundred witnesses. She held out her hands. "I beg your pardon, madame. I did not mean to offend you."

Regine Valnoy drew herself up. "The fact that you were born is offense enough!"

Thomasina was stunned to immobility. "Please, calm yourself, madame."

Regine stamped her ivory cane threateningly.

"Calm myself? *Mon Dieu.* You come here flaunting the Valnoy Sapphire, stolen from me, for all the world to see! Did you think to brazen it out, to force my hand before my friends and family? Well, let me tell you the same thing I told that woman. A Valnoy does not give in to blackmail." She was shaking with rage. "Well, if that... that *salope* who calls herself Patrice Wentworth thinks you will ever get your clutches on a penny of the Valnoy fortune, she is wrong."

The cane stamped again, sounding like gunshots in the artificial stillness. "Oh, yes, I know who you are. The misbegotten child of an *entremeteuse.* The daughter of the terrible woman who seduced my son and stole him away from me. The same woman, who, after his death, opened the most notorious bordello in New Orleans."

Thomasina felt the blood drain from her face, and there was a roaring in her ears. In the background, she saw Cousin Agatha rise unsteadily, and then sit down heavily again. Her dear old face was white with shock.

Not so Madame Valnoy. Her face was almost purple, her neck veins engorged. "Do you think I would make you, the illegitimate daughter of a whore, my heir? I renounce you as I renounced my weak son. You may have the Valnoy sapphire, but you will never have anything else, I tell you. I would rather throw it to the beggars in the streets than let you touch a penny of it."

The nightmare had taken on the terrible sense of reality for Thomasina. Bits and pieces of her life, little things from early childhood that she had never examined as an adult, fell into place. The stricken look on Cousin Agatha's face was like a blow to Thomasina's stomach. "The illegitimate daughter of a whore!" How much had her mother paid Agatha to try and pass off this tragic farce? For a horrible moment Thomasina felt as if she might faint. She fought for control.

The sick feeling was replaced by burning anger. Thomasina squared her shoulders proudly. The words poured out of her, hot and dangerous, like molten metal.

"Your heir? I would starve in the streets before I took a penny from you. If you think I came here to lay claim as your granddaughter you could not be more mistaken. I would rather be the daughter of Patrice Wentworth than a Valnoy any day. I renounce you and your name as you renounced my father."

Suddenly, Regine Valnoy struck out, not with her cane, but with a handful of sparkling rings. Thomasina drew back, but not in time. The prong of a gold setting grazed her face, and a line of fire burned along her cheekbone. The crowd gasped, but she didn't hear them. The colorful silks and satins of the guests blurred with the mist of angry tears that filled her eyes.

She touched a hand to her face and it came away streaked with blood.

"You are a cruel and hateful old woman. I see why my father had to leave. You need not worry that you will ever see my face again!" Reaching up, Thomasina unclasped the necklace with shaking fingers and dashed it down at Regine Valnoy's feet. The sapphire shone like a great, unblinking eye.

Thomasina gathered her skirts and whirled around. She fled the ballroom with what dignity she could muster, which, under the circumstances, was precious little. Blinded and bleeding, she rushed through the aghast company and out into the reception room. Without knowing how she got there, she found herself outside the house in the darkness. She had no idea of how to summon the carriage, but the thought of staying one more moment on Valnoy property was too onerous to stand. Thomasina stumbled down the drive, unaware that she was sobbing aloud with reaction.

A man stepped out into her pathway. She saw that it was Douglass Wilks, but she tried to push past. He caught her by the shoulders. "Miss...er Miss Wentworth, stop a moment."

Thomasina was unable to shake him off. His hands dug into her. "Listen, you can't very well set off on foot at this hour of night in a ballgown. You wouldn't get very far."

His voice was low and soothing. She knew he was right. "Please...will you help me? I don't know where our carriage is or how to get home from here."

The door opened behind them. In the lamplight, his face took on the quick, calculating expression it had worn before. He took off his jacket and put it over her shoulders. "Come with me, Miss Wentworth. I'll see to you."

She put her hand in his gratefully. "You'll take me home?" she asked as he led her to a waiting carriage.

As he helped her up into the vehicle, Thomasina was so awash in misery that she didn't realize that he hadn't answered her. Scenes of her recent humiliation flashed through her mind... And that hateful woman was her grandmother!

It wasn't until they left the mansion far behind and had reached the shadowy sections of a seedy residential area that she became aware of her surroundings. "This isn't the way," she exclaimed.

Wilks leaned closer and patted her clasped hands. "My driver is new. Perhaps he's lost." He rapped on the glass for the carriage to halt, and stuck his head out for a quick word with the groom. A moment later he settled back with a wry smile.

"It's just as I feared. Mason became confused in the maze of streets and has been trying to find his way back, hoping I wouldn't notice." The carriage rolled to a stop. "I've told Mason to pull up at this inn. It doesn't look too bad, really. We can have a light supper while he seeks directions in the tap room."

"Please, it is very kind of you, but I don't want to have supper with you in an unknown inn. I just want to go home."

"That you shall."

But even as he spoke, his groom opened the door and put down the steps. Wilks hustled Thomasina out none too gently. "Come, my dear. You have nothing to fear from me."

She was filled with foreboding. The inn looked squalid, and the company was sure to be rough. Her companion grew impatient. "Miss Wentworth, it won't look well for you to be seen out here in the street. I'll see that we're given a private parlor for our little supper. I am quite hungry."

It was true that the groom had to discover the route back to Cousin Agatha's house, and Thomasina was grateful to her rescuer. He had come to her aid and because of it, would miss the supper after the dancing at Regine Valnoy's mansion. She capitulated. "Very well."

The inside of the inn was dark and every bit as shabby as the outside. Everything needed a thorough cleaning as much as it needed paint. The drab green walls were cracked and peeling. Her stomach was already upset and rebelled further at the thought of food. Thomasina decided she would only take a cup of tea while Mr. Wilks dined.

Her companion pounded his knuckles on the worn hotel desk. "Landlord."

There was a muffled curse from somewhere in the back and the sound of a bottle being knocked over. Footsteps shuffled toward him.

Thomasina shrunk back when a paunchy man came out and assessed the newcomers with surprise. He took one look at Thomasina and a crafty leer came over his face. Wilks stepped forward. "The lady and I require a private parlor for the evening."

"'Zat so? Well we've none a'tall. There is a big chamber upstairs. Got a table and chairs. You'd be snug as bugs up there.''

"Lead the way.''

They followed him up the narrow stairs. The treads squeaked and groaned.

With every step, Thomasina's dread grew. The door opened, a lamp was lit, and she found herself alone in an unknown part of town with a man she had just met. How had she ever let herself get into such an untenable situation? She prayed her fears were groundless as the door clicked shut behind them.

A glance about the room was not reassuring. A section of grimy window was visible between the threadbare olive curtains, the table and chairs were rickety and covered with names and rude comments scratched into their flat painted surfaces, and there was a mouse hole along the wall. Worst of all was the tarnished bed, its mattress sagging, that filled most of the room. The counterpane was grey with age and infrequent washing. The whole place stank of mildew.

There was no way she could remain in such a place and under such circumstance. If Mr. Wilks was too hungry to take her home, she would brave the dangers of waiting in the carriage alone. As she was about to speak, she was startled by the sound of a bolt shot home. Thomasina turned on her heel to find Douglass Wilks bearing down upon her. The change in his manner was frightening and the look in his eyes even more so. She tried to sound calm.

"Unbolt the door, sir. I will not stay here another minute.''

"My dear Miss Wentworth—or should I say Mademoiselle Valnoy? I have no intentions of leaving the room."

She tried to push past him. "Then I shall leave without your escort!"

"Do you think so?" Wilks grabbed her arm bruisingly. "Get used to your surroundings, my dear. We shall be spending the night here together." He leered down at Thomasina. "I'm sure your esteemed mother has taught you many tricks of her trade."

Thomasina's anger changed to cold panic. It coiled up out of the pit of her stomach and snaked through her until she was paralyzed with fright.

"And," he added suavely, "you will have all night to practice them with me...."

Chapter Three

"Spend the night with you?" Thomasina was proud that her voice didn't quiver. "I wouldn't spend five minutes in paradise with an unscrupulous villain such as yourself!"

"So you really think you have any choice?" Brutally, he yanked her closer. Her left arm felt bruised to the bone, and her shoulder burned like fury. Pain and outrage overwhelmed her fear. Acting on sheer instinct, she swung her other arm back and slapped him as hard as she could. It was the wrong move and only angered him. His face flamed so red, the color blotted out the handprint she'd left on his cheek.

Wilks glared at her. "You'll pay for that." Grasping both Thomasina's shoulders, he shook her until she was dizzy.

Though she struggled as best she could, he bore her backward inexorably toward the waiting bed. When the high mattress hit the back of her legs, Thomasina knew she had only one chance left. She brought her knee up sharply and caught Wilks between the legs with all her might.

He released her and crunched up, moaning and cursing. He was still on his feet, but too agonized to stop her as she ran past him to the door. Her shaking fingers fumbled with the heavy bolt, and she lost several precious seconds. At last, she was able to loosen it from the slot and slide it open. Not a moment too soon. Wilks lunged for her with murder in his eyes.

The open door was between them. Thomasina waited a split second until he was almost upon her and then flung the door inward with all her might. It caught him in the nose. She didn't stay to observe the results, but raced into the hall and down the steps, accompanied by his cries and foul curses.

She managed to make it through the tiny space that served as a lobby and out into the street before she heard him clattering after her down the wooden stairs. A light fog had sprung up, sheer enough to see several yards, yet thick enough to obliterate any landmarks. Panicking when she heard Wilks somewhere behind her, Thomasina plunged blindly into the fog.

Dr. Rafferty strode angrily from the hall where the meeting of the Scientific Society had just ended. Abruptly.

From within, there was such a din that a passerby stopped to stare. As Rafferty came down the stone steps a man in a frock coat shouted after him. The words were unintelligible. Their tone was not.

Rafferty raised his fist at the man in the open doorway and the others crowding round him. "And the same to you, Harrison, you blithering son of idiot parents!" His volume increased with his intensity.

"How on earth you can expect a woman to recover from childbirth by spending a month in bed without activity, is beyond intelligent contemplation!"

His blood boiled with the wrath handed down through the ancient line of Rafferty, and he stomped away muttering of milk leg and lung fever and hidebound, bull-headed fools. Dr. Harrison's assertion that the lower incident of such occurrences in Mexico was due to the sturdiness among Mexican "peasant women," rather than the prolonged bed rest ordered for middle-class American mothers was utterly ridiculous! And the rest of those ignoramuses had agreed with their colleague. Rafferty stomped away, the long tails of his coat flying behind him. He had wasted his last evening in the States trying to argue with a pack of fools. Well, the more fool he.

Raising his collar against the growing chill, Rafferty turned the corner. There was a fine mist in the air that would soon coalesce into a clammy fog. If he was a judge of weather, it would clear by morning. A fresh rain would sweep in from the west, scrubbing the streets and buildings clean. The atmosphere and the soft sounds of the sea reminded him of home, but he shoved his hands into his pockets and didn't linger. He was in no mood for reminiscing.

What he *was* in the mood for was a damned good fight.

Thomasina didn't get far. The fog was disorienting, and once she'd gone a dozen steps, she'd lost her bearings completely. Was the inn behind her still or just ahead? Her heart gave a frightened leap when she heard low laughter near at hand. She bolted in the opposite direction. Her smooth-soled dancing shoes were no match for the slippery cobbles: She fell, painfully.

The fog curled like smoke around her, but as she struggled to her feet, she saw a tall figure coming her way, much distorted. It was dangerous to throw herself upon the mercy of a total stranger, but perhaps the man would help her. If not . . .

Her feet flew out from under her again and she went sprawling. The gray mist parted like a stage curtain. Douglass Wilks strode centerstage and bowed to his only audience. "Back in the gutter where your kind belong, I see."

She reached out for a stick, a stone, anything she might use as a weapon and gain a little more time. Her fingers scrabbled against the bumpy surface but found nothing. Wilks caught the back of her gown and began to haul her up. The sleeve ripped. Thomasina's faint cry was swallowed up by the damp air. She knew she must attract attention to her plight, but on the waterfront, cries of "Help!" or "Murder!" would more likely send passers-by fleeing. But there was one cry, in this area of close-packed wooden buildings, that might work.

"Help! Fire! *Fire!*"

"Stop it, damn you!" Wilks attempted to silence her, but she threw his hand off. Her flailing arms hit a post of sorts and she hung on to it for life and honor, screaming like a banshee. "Fire! Fire!"

In response she heard the welcome sound of running footsteps. A second later, Rafferty burst out of the fog and saw a woman in trouble. His Irish temper erupted. He grabbed the attacker by the coat collar and flung him away.

Wilks got up, cursing and blustering. Then he saw the fierce giant looming over him. He had time for one sharp protest before Rafferty hit him just beneath the angle of his jaw.

Thomasina, standing on the sidelines, had the best seat in the house. She saw the great rippling muscles beneath her saviour's coat and gasped at the speed and power of his hammering fists.

The round didn't last long. Rafferty struck again with the punishing one-two punch that had once made him a contender for the Boxing Championship of Ireland. His fists connected with powerful grace and Wilks folded up into rigid sections and fell. He didn't get up this time.

Thomasina ran to her protector's side, forgetting the way her slippers slid on the cobbles. She skidded toward him, out of control. For a precarious second, she almost lost her balance, but a strong arm caught her about the waist and lifted her right off her feet. Pressed tight against Rafferty's wide chest, her face half-buried against his shoulder, a great feeling of security poured through Thomasina.

She was safe.

But while she was sheltered by his brawn and took solace from the clean soap smell of him, a smothering sense of panic welled up from some hidden spring. She pushed at him blindly, struggling to be free.

Rafferty got a good look at her face, and was astounded to find his arms full of the same young woman who had come to him a week earlier, hoping to be his apprentice. He set her down with a bump. Thank God he'd sent her packing then. Any woman down on the waterfront at this time of night was looking for trouble.

"Calm yourself, Miss Wentworth. I mean you no harm."

Her face was sickly pale as she gasped for air, her eyes wide and unseeing. With visible effort, she forced the panic back. Her palms were damp and her throat constricted, but she was in command of herself once more. "Forgive me. I—I was frightened out of my wits."

His eyebrows snapped together in a dark line. "As well you should be. What in the name of hel...of grace are you doing down along the docks?"

His questioning was interrupted by footfalls and shouts heading toward them as men poured out of the taverns and brothels to investigate the cries. Thomasina was frozen to the spot.

Rafferty didn't hesitate. He bustled Thomasina into a space between the buildings and through the fog until they were far from the commotion. She was too stunned to think much beyond where to put her feet for several minutes. When she slipped on something slimy, Rafferty's strong arm was instantly there to save her from a nasty fall. Her muttered thanks were stifled by a quick word.

Refuse littered the ground, and furry things scuttled across their path, squeaking in alarm. As Rafferty and Thomasina turned a corner, her nose recorded odors of rot, mildew and spoiled food, and also detected a faint whiff of something vaguely sweet and medicinal. Her guardian led her through narrow dark places, through sodden pools and things that squelched unpleasantly underfoot. Thomasina went willingly, trusting that her companion had the situation well in hand.

Rafferty wasn't so sure about that. What he had on his hands was a young woman with disheveled hair and a torn gown, obviously in a state of near shock. If they were seen and recognized, it would ruin her reputation—and his, too. He weighed the odds of anyone of her acquaintance being out along the waterfront. It wasn't uncommon for the young sprigs of society to rub elbows with the rougher element in search for adventure. The soiled doves who plied their wares in the shabby stews were as likely to entertain the scions of wealthy families as they were sailors bound round the Horn.

And judging by the young woman's clothes, she moved in those same circles. The sooner he got her home, the better. He stopped and looked at Thomasina. Her face floated like a flower in the dim light. Her vulnerable beauty caught him off guard, and his voice came out sharp around the edges, "Where do you live?"

His curtness startled her. She stammered out her address. "It—it is my Cousin Agatha's house. The one with the peach-and-green trim, on the corner. My mother and I are staying with her."

Thomasina couldn't seem to stop babbling. Rafferty started her walking again. "It's too far for you to walk, especially in this damnable... er, this dense fog. I'll have to make arrangements.''

The Bonaventure Inn was only a short distance away. Rafferty made his decision. A few minutes later, he was smuggling Thomasina up a rickety back stairs to his room. If anyone spotted them going in, the worst that could happen would be for the landlord to mistake her for a damsel of the night and demand his share of her take. Rafferty shepherded her in, turned the key in the lock and plunked her down in the straight-backed chair.

Thomasina noted that the room smelled of soap and antiseptic, while the hallway had been rank with far-less-pleasant scents. Rafferty lit the lamp and faced her, arms akimbo. ''And now, Miss Wentworth—if that really is your name—I'll have the whole story from you.''

She fixed her eye on his coat button. ''It is not my story to tell, sir. I wish to go home.''

''You'll not go an inch until I learn what game you're up to and—''

He broke off in midsentence, suddenly a trifle woozy. Thomasina jumped up with a tiny cry and pointed to his breast pocket. A dark stain was slowly spreading over his chest. She frowned. ''You've been injured in the fracas, Dr. Rafferty. Sit down and let me have a look at it.''

Thomasina's voice was brisk as she took charge of the situation. ''Don't worry. It can't be too serious or you couldn't have walked all this way without effort.''

For the first time in his life, Rafferty was speechless. Thomasina slipped her hand inside his coat. "Don't squirm," she chided firmly. Quite doctor-to-patient, he thought.

Having the tables turned upon him was a novel experience. Having a warm, feminine hand on his chest was something else again. It made him feel dizzier. Rafferty yanked away and patted his chest gingerly. His hand came away wet. Wet but not bloody.

The room reeled. "Open the window," he commanded, ripping off his shirt. His voice seemed hollow and very faraway to his own ears. It was difficult to stand upright.

Thomasina stared at Rafferty wide-eyed. His chest was broad and tanned with a vee of crisp, dark hair across it, but there was no wound to be seen at all. A sweet miasma filled the room. She hastened to the window and threw it open. As she turned back, Rafferty staggered against the table, clutching his coat, and pulled out his portable surgical kit. He shook his head from side to side, like a great, shambling bear.

"Ah, the miserable cur, God curse him for a drunken sot! He broke my vial of..."

"Chloroform," she supplied.

"Chloroform," he slurred in agreement. The room spun like a top. And that was the last thing Rafferty remembered.

Faint light and chill air seeped through the narrow window gap. The wood was old and warped, and Thomasina had only been able to open it six inches. Dr. Rafferty's best coat was draped across the sill, airing out. On the other side of the streaked panes, the world was still wrapped in damp cotton wool. She couldn't see a thing for the thick fog, so she sat on the edge of the sagging bed and watched the sleeping giant at her feet. He looked younger and almost vulnerable, his dark lashes so long they cast shadows on his cheeks. It was his great size and intense expressions that made him so formidable in his waking state.

He was far too heavy for her to lift. She had placed a pillow beneath his head and had covered him with the dingy blanket. Now she needed some way to keep warm herself. The bare-shouldered ball gown, with its diaphanous layers and silky undergarments, was totally inadequate.

After a while she retrieved Rafferty's coat from the windowsill and sniffed at it gingerly. The chloroform had evaporated. She slipped her arms inside the sleeves, which were much too wide, and buttoned the garment up the front. Despite its battered condition it was, she discovered, quite comforting.

She only wished that her knowledge of medicine went a little further. Rafferty had been unconscious for some time now, and that worried her. She had read about the miraculous powers of chloroform for childbirth and surgery, but there her knowledge ended. She was unfamiliar with the duration of the effects and their potential consequences.

She was tired, hungry and increasingly worried. A shiver ran up the backs of her arms. The terrible thought, which she'd been trying to hold at bay, burst through her defenses. What if his sleep deepens into coma? What if he never wakes up at all?

"No!" she exclaimed into the silence. Dr. Brendan Rafferty was far too vital and strong to succumb. Why, look at his firm muscles and his—magnificent, really—chest. It would take more than a potent dose of anesthetic to keep a man like Dr. Rafferty down. She knelt beside him, the gauzy skirts of her ball gown incongruous against the stained boards of the inn's floor. Her fingers sought his wrist, but they trembled so, that she couldn't distinguish his pulse.

Without hesitation, Thomasina stooped down to put her ear to his bare chest. The maneuver took considerable agility and her gown was a hindrance. Once situated, she was forced to lean over him with her hand on the opposite side of his supine form. Her arm brushed his skin. The inadvertent familiarity embarrassed Thomasina, although she knew that Rafferty would never know. And, of course, with her goal of becoming a physician and surgeon, she would have to become used to touching the human body. The naked human body. She complimented herself on being detached enough to note that his skin was warm and dry.

Thomasina lowered her ear to his rib cage. The hairs on his chest tickled her cheek, and his breath was still tinged with the odor of chloroform. As he breathed out, she breathed in and became lightheaded from the chemical residue. As it affected her brain, she nestled against him involuntarily, until his body was the only thing keeping hers off the floor. His heartbeat was deep and steady as a drum. That reassured her greatly.

"You have the constitution of a bull," she murmured aloud. "Nothing will happen to you. I will not allow it."

Her soft voice and the warmth of her body reached down through Rafferty's drugged visions. He stirred and tried to lift his hand. It tangled in Thomasina's long hair, the bright locks streaming through his fingers like satin ribbons. The supple curve of her figure against his hard frame was very pleasant. He smiled and gave himself up to his dreams.

Rafferty mumbled something in his stupor, but Thomasina couldn't make out the words. It took too much effort. A fuzzy, warm vapour filled every corner of her mind, blotting out the power to think rationally. Her eyelids drifted closed. It was so nice to snuggle up and . . . and . . .

Thomasina sat bolt upright, fighting the siren lure of sleep. "The chloroform!" she mumbled, and shook her head to clear her brain. It didn't work.

With more determination than coordination, she crawled away from Rafferty and toward the window. Using the sill for leverage, she dragged herself up to her knees and put her face to the opening. Thomasina drank in breath after breath of cool, fresh air and felt the wooliness begin to recede. Anxious for faster results, she forced her head farther into the space between the sill and the window.

And found herself stuck fast.

Her position was extremely uncomfortable, not to mention mortifying. As she wiggled about, the sash dropped lower. The harder she struggled, the worse the situation became. Behind her, Rafferty was snoring softly. Her shoulder was in agony and the streak of pearly sky in the east announced that dawn was not too far away. Thomasina's birds-eye view was of a misty, deserted street where the cobbles gleamed wetly in the dull light.

A burly sailor sauntered out of a two-story building across the way and surveyed the street. He looked rough and dangerous. Possibly the kind of fellow who would rob an unconscious man... or worse. Thomasina was still weighing the wisdom of calling to him for help when a wall of fog scudded through, obliterating the scene. When it thinned out again, the man was gone. She ground her small white teeth in vexation.

Banging on the window in hopes of budging it, she scraped her knuckles and bruised her wrist. Thomasina bit back a vulgar expression learned from a stableboy in her youth. Interesting, she suddenly thought, how scraps of one's childhood intruded in moments of basic emotion. She wondered if Dr. Rafferty had ever noted this, and if he had a theory explaining it. Then she bumped her head again, and all cool, clinical evaluations were lost in a howl of pain. Her cry brought results.

A fist pounded on the door. "Wot's amiss in there? Open up, Doc. 'Tis Tod Gumm here to lend ye a hand."

Rafferty stirred and moaned behind her, but Thomasina couldn't free herself to look at him. A moment later, she heard the thud of a massive shoulder against the door. It burst open in a splintering of flimsy wood. Heavy footsteps sounded behind her.

"Well, I'll be blowed!" a gruff voice exclaimed. "Conked him on the noggin, have ye? And his purse tucked inside your bodice, no doubt."

A hamlike hand clamped down on Thomasina's shoulder. "Think ye'll slip out the window? Well, ye've got another think coming, ye louse-ridden, squint-eyed doxy."

The window jerked open wide with a squeal of protest and Thomasina was abruptly freed. She would have fallen headfirst to the street if not restrained. As she spun around, her surprise was no greater than Tod Gumm's. She'd never seen so fearsome a creature outside of storybooks. If he'd shouted out: "Fee fi fo fum," it would have seemed right in character.

For his part, Tod Gumm had been expecting a thieving waterfront whore. He'd certainly never been so close to a real lady in his entire life—and a lady was what this woman was, despite the doctor's coat over her crushed gown and the way her fiery curls had tumbled loose over her shoulders.

While the sailor gaped at her, Thomasina picked up the water pitcher and threatened him with it. "Not one step closer," she commanded coolly. "Lay a hand on him and you'll answer to me."

"Bless me, I don't mean the Doc no harm. I just heard him moan and come to see if he needed help. What in he—er, what's happened to him, er, yer ladyship?"

Thomasina decided he was sincere. "Dr. Rafferty was overcome with fumes from one of his vials when it broke. I was feeling it a bit myself." Her cheeks grew flushed. "Which is why you discovered me in such an unladylike position with my head out the window. And now that we've some fresh air, if you could put

Dr. Rafferty upon the bed, I'll see to that cut above his eye.''

Tod Gumm knew the voice of authority when he heard it. He picked Rafferty up as he were a child and whisked him to the bed, but when Thomasina set out the doctor's surgical kit and began threading a needle, he looked a bit anxious. ''Here now, ye oughtn't to be fooling with such things. . . .''

''Nonsense. I'm studying to be a doctor.'' She nodded toward Rafferty. ''If he begins to fuss, you might have to hold his hands for me.''

Gumm stood aside. The lady seemed to know what she was about.

Thomasina snipped off what she deemed to be the proper length of suture and turned her attention to her unwitting patient once again. There was a gash over the doctor's eyebrow, sustained when he'd fought her attacker. It was small but deep, and required her to place three small stitches.

''As neat a job as I've seen,'' the sailor told her when she'd finished.

He was obviously impressed and, although she tried to appear perfectly collected, Thomasina was ecstatic that her hours of practice had paid off. Of course, stitching together bits of chamois cloth had not been quite the same as suturing the gash on Dr. Rafferty's forehead, but the end result was quite satisfactory. Much more so, in fact, than her despairing attempts at embroidering pillow covers in her younger days. Once her patient awakened, he would surely see that she had the cool head and steady hands that were essential to a physician and surgeon—why, she'd hardly trembled at all.

And Dr. Rafferty would see with blinding clarity that she was not only perfectly suited to her chosen profession, but would be an ideal assistant for him.

If only he would wake up.

Thomasina's reading of Rafferty's character was wrong. An hour later, she sat beside him in a closed carriage on her way back to Cousin Agatha's house. Instead of gratitude, all she got from him was a stern lecture. "If you were my sister, I'd lock you in your room until you learned a little more common sense. The waterfront is no place for a young lady, whether by day or by night. And you haven't explained how you came to be there in the first place."

"I was not there by choice. And since you don't choose to believe me, I feel under no obligation to indulge your vulgar curiosity."

Her snappish answer had the effect she'd intended. Rafferty straightened his shoulders and sat back. From the stubborn set of his jaw, Thomasina knew that he'd rather eat ground glass than pursue the topic further.

Not that it would have done him any good. There was no way Thomasina could explain how she'd come to be on the waterfront at such an unseemly hour, not without bringing her mother's name and Regine Valnoy's horrid accusations into it. And during the time that Dr. Rafferty had been overcome by the chloroform he'd inhaled, Thomasina had had plenty of time to think.

So much fit into place. Things she had taken for granted as a child looked very different, when viewed through adult eyes. Thomasina had little recollection of her life before arriving at the boarding school, and the memories she did have were confused. She frowned as images assaulted her.

Beautiful ladies dressed in rainbow colors. Ladies living in her home, who slept by day and descended the curving staircase when the sun went down. Herself in a nightgown, peeping over the railing of an upper landing as guests arrived for dinner parties. Male guests. Laughter by moonlight. Weeping from shuttered rooms at midday. Those visions were misty and blurred, like half-remembered dreams.

Before that, Thomasina recalled moving from place to place, city to city. A dozen houses in all. There had been a succession of older gentleman who had come to visit her mother, bringing little gifts for the young Thomasina, as well. Then, after months—or perhaps years—another house and another man. And then the packing would begin again without explanation. There were dimly remembered visits to a vast country house where she and her mother had been the only guests and Thomasina had been free to roam the house and grounds undisturbed, unnoticed.

And just before she'd been sent away to boarding school, the coldly elegant chateau with the pale carpets, stiff gilt furniture and long, chill corridors of white marble that haunted her nightmares still. Awake now, beside Rafferty in the clear morning light,

Thomasina felt a shiver run through her body in remembrance.

Rafferty felt her tremble. He leaned closer and tucked his cloak around her shoulders more firmly. "A glass of brandy is my prescription for you, Miss Wentworth, followed by a long sleep. It's no wonder you're shaken badly after the night's events."

Thomasina fixed him with a steely eye. "I am not shaken, Dr. Rafferty, merely cold. If you'd taken a moment to examine the perfect stitches that I put in over your eyebrow, you would appreciate how steady my hands were at the time."

Rafferty stared at her. Prattling on about stitches after the night they'd both been through. Did she have even the faintest idea how close she'd come to disaster? His Irish dander rose. "If that is your chief concern," he said hotly, "I'm more alarmed about the steadiness of your brain than of your hands."

"My mind is perfectly sound!"

"I have no doubt of your intelligence, Miss Wentworth. The fault lies in your judgment."

Thomasina drew in a breath, prepared to tell him off in fine fashion, but never got the chance.

Rafferty skewered her with a shrewd look. "You've got beauty and brains and, if I'm not mistaken, the backing of wealth. Everything you want is within your reach."

"I want to be a doctor," she said firmly. "And the only thing preventing me is the fact that I'm female. If I were a man, you'd have taken me on as your assistant immediately."

"If you were a man, my dear Miss Wentworth, this entire situation would not have come about." The words came glibly, but Rafferty felt a prick of conscience. He pushed it away. "I can't help you, but there are means and opportunities if you know where to look. You can accomplish much if you put your mind to it in the right way."

Thomasina turned her head away. Nobody understood how serious she was. Not even Dr. Rafferty.

"If you please," Patrice murmured, ushering them into the hall, "this is not a suitable place to hear all that I am sure that you have to tell me. I'll take you up to your bedchamber, Thomasina, and when you're settled, I'll join Dr. Rafferty for some light refreshments."

Rafferty bowed. "Thank you, madam, but I'm afraid I won't be able to avail myself of your kind invitation. I'm setting out on my return journey to Mexico in three hours' time."

Patrice made all the proper responses, but Thomasina was speechless with disappointment. Mexico! For a few short hours, she had dared to dream. Now it was time to wake up. She stood in the hall and watched Rafferty's departure. He went down the steps into the morning sunlight, taking her last ray of hope with him.

Rafferty understood more of her feelings than Thomasina knew. He thought he'd glimpsed in Miss Thomasina Wentworth something of that same fire that had driven him to become a physician. If she had the necessary grit and steel, and if fortune favored her, perhaps one day she'd attain her goal—but the odds were strongly against it. He certainly wished her well.

As he reached the walkway, Rafferty paused and glanced over his shoulder. Thomasina stood framed in the open doorway, her face flushed with emotion. She didn't speak aloud, but he read her thoughts clearly: *You haven't heard the last of me, Dr. Rafferty. I won't give up. I'll never give up.*

If fierceness and heart had anything to do with it, he decided, the odds might not be so insurmountable, after all. And she did have a steady hand with the needle. "I wish you good fortune in all your endeavors, Miss Wentworth."

Rafferty tipped his hat to her and went away.

Thomasina slammed the door with all her strength. The brass knocker banged against its plaque, and the lead glass sidelights rattled in their frames.

She turned to face the triumvirate of her mother, pale and strained beside her, Cousin Agatha, pink and flustered on a needlepoint chair, and Mrs. Church, malevolent in triumph on the upper landing. Thomasina squared her shoulders.

"There is no sense stewing about it. 'Least said, soonest mended.' This has been a most unpleasant incident but it is over."

The housekeeper was too spiteful to be discreet. She came down the staircase like a squat black shadow in her black bombazine dress. "You're wrong about that, indeed you are. By morning, this whole sorry affair will be all over town."

Agatha stiffened. "That is quite enough, Mrs. Church."

"Not half enough, it isn't. I said from the start that taking in the likes of those two guttersnipes would make nothing but trouble."

Patrice's face went completely white, and the breath hissed in between her teeth. Thomasina put a restraining hand upon her mother's arm, but before she could act, Cousin Agatha had risen to her feet. The elderly widow was trembling with indignation. "How *dare* you speak in such a manner to a member of my family—especially one who is a guest beneath my own roof!"

"It's nothing but God's own truth I've spoken." Mrs. Church's face was as red as the wattles on a turkey. "I'll be that glad to see the back of them both, I will. Trash is what they are. Nothing but common trollops, is what I said when—"

Agatha folded her hands and drew herself up to her full five foot height. "Enough! The only one who will be leaving is you, Mrs. Church. You are hereby given your notice, effective immediately."

"But...but..." Mrs. Church sputtered, looking from Agatha to the others and back again. "I... they...surely..." She gasped in a breath, shaking with suppressed fury. "You can't do this to me!"

"Oh, can't I? Because of my age and ill health, I have let you bully me with your overbearing ways for far too long. You have run this household as if you were the mistress and I a mere pensioner. The fault was mine for letting you usurp my authority. But *I* am the mistress in this house."

"You can't dismiss me out of hand."

"I can—and I have. I will give you six months' wages, providing you are out of here by tea time. There is nothing further to discuss," Agatha said crisply. "I will not allow anyone—servant or aristocrat—to speak or act so rudely to any guest beneath my roof. And especially to dear Patrice and her daughter."

It was the longest and most forceful speech Thomasina had ever heard her elderly cousin make. Until this very moment, Thomasina had never guessed at the depth of frustration and humiliation Agatha had suffered once the dragon of a housekeeper had taken control.

Thomasina was so fascinated by the change in her cousin that she stared in surprise. She had never dreamed there was so much iron in her. In fact, if Agatha's dignified cat had suddenly turned into a seven-hundred-pound lion, complete with fang and claw, the effect would have been about the same.

Mrs. Church was stunned into silence. The housekeeper had never expected the worm to turn, especially not with such disastrous results for herself. Agatha tugged the bellpull and Sarah, the head parlormaid, appeared with such alacrity that she must have been eavesdropping at one of the doors.

"Yes, madame?"

Agatha put her gnarled hand to the hair brooch at her throat. "Mrs. Church will be leaving the premises permanently this afternoon. Please see that the carriage is ordered, and ask Reed to bring her trunk down beforehand."

"It shall be done, madame!" Sarah's radiant face told its own story: the servants would be as delighted as their mistress to see the overbearing housekeeper gone. Thomasina was glad—there would be no more frightened faces, and no more weeping in the scullery.

Mrs. Church sent off a parting salvo as she clumped off to pack her possessions. "I only hope you will live to rue this day's work."

Thomasina didn't think that Agatha would rue it at all. Already, the atmosphere in the house had changed. She heard muted laughter and then Sarah's humming as the maid dusted the dining room.

Even the cat sensed the difference. Ashurbanipal was stretched out in a pool of sunlight in the center of the hall, languidly licking a paw. The sound of his contented purring filled the room.

Agatha turned to Patrice and Thomasina. Some of the lines of care had lifted from her face. "My dears, pray do not let this upset you. I should have sent Mrs. Church packing years ago." A gentle smile curved her wrinkled mouth. "And I believe that Sarah has the sense and experience to be a wonderful housekeeper." She sent a speculative look in Patrice's direction. "But first, I would like to have a few moments with Thomasina. Alone."

Patrice was surprised. "Very well. I've some letters to write."

Patrice went up the stairs, while Agatha led Thomasina into the cheerful morning room and shut the door. The draperies were open onto the sunny back garden. A cardinal perched on a branch, preening its scarlet feathers. Its color was matched by the painting of bright poppies that hung over the mantel. Agatha went to the fireplace and gazed up at the picture.

"I painted that when I was eighteen," she announced. "It's unsigned, of course, but that little design in the lower righthand corner was my special mark."

"*You* painted it?" Thomasina was startled and impressed. "It's a wonderful painting! So full of life that I can almost touch the petals and see the flowers wave. But—I never knew that you painted."

Agatha's tired face was transformed. Beneath the ravages of age, a young and vital woman looked out. "It was my dream," she said. "I had a drawing master, who was himself a gifted artist. But he told me the pupil would far surpass the teacher. I was fired with the passion to paint. I wanted to travel, to see all there was to see, to capture the light and colors of wonderful foreign places. And to put it down on canvas so that others might share my visions with me."

Her face suddenly crumpled, and the light that had shone within it went out like a snuffed candle. Thomasina wanted to run to Agatha and enfold her in her arms. She wanted to comfort her—and to ask her why, if she had had the passion and the talent, it had come to naught. Something stopped her. Perhaps it was the way that Agatha squared her thin shoulders. She seemed to have divined Thomasina's thoughts exactly.

"You have courage and determination, my dear. I had neither. Because of that, I let my dreams wither and die. Instead of standing up to my father and going off to Italy to study, I stayed at home and married the man my father chose for me."

The old woman's face grew pensive. "Everett was a good man and very kind to me. But by the time I was twenty I'd lost heart. At twenty-five, I put away my paints and brushes forever with my lost dreams. And I have always regretted it."

Agatha crossed to the door. "Don't let it happen to you," she whispered fiercely. "Don't let anyone take away your dream."

She went out, and Thomasina had the wisdom not to follow. Agatha had dug up old, painful memories and needed to be alone to bury them once more. Walking to the mantel, Thomasina stared up at the brilliant poppies until they sparkled and blurred through her tears.

When she heard the door open, and close behind her, she blinked and turned slowly. Her mother had entered. Patrice took a place on the settee and signaled for Thomasina to join her.

"I'm so sorry, my darling, that words fail me. Thank God for Dr. Rafferty! I shudder to think what might have happened if not for him . . . and I don't know how to ever make up to you for the horror of last night. Perhaps . . . perhaps a trip to Europe . . . Paris . . ."

Thomasina didn't sit down. She stood with her back to the mantel, feeling the heat and color of the poppies warming her determination. She could feel it through the thickness of Rafferty's cloak, which she'd forgotten to give back.

"There is only one way to make up for the horrors of this past night, Maman, and we both know what that is. You wanted to make me a respectable and fashionable debutante. It didn't work. It never will. I will never be the society belle you intended."

Rafferty's words echoed in her head. *You can do anything if you put your mind to it—in the right way.* Agatha's fierce voice joined in. *Don't ever give up your dream!*

Thomasina faced her mother squarely. She had grown up overnight, and the shy schoolgirl was gone forever. "From now on, my energies will be focused on a single goal. I will be a doctor, come hell or high-water."

Chapter Four

San Juan de Baptista, Mexico, 1848

Rafferty was spent, and so was his golden gelding, but the sight of home, as they crested the rise, gave man and beast a burst of energy. The valley lay nestled in the gap of the green hills, and high above them, floating like an insubstantial cloud, was the snow-covered cone of the extinct volcano with its two side vents from old eruptions. The inhabitants of the area called the three white peaks Los Tres Hermanos. Today, the three brothers looked heavenly and benign, giving no hint of their ancient cataclysms.

Lugh neighed, and Rafferty patted the gelding's neck. The horse was eager for the shade of the stable and a trough of fresh water, followed by a good rub-down from Domingo and a ration of feed. Rafferty's wants were almost the same. The cool interior of the adobe walls, a bath, some beer from the stone jar in the well and whatever food he could scavenge from his scanty stores. Then he planned to sleep the clock around. God willing.

What he *didn't* want was to find another disaster or emergency waiting for him. The last time he'd been gone so long, he'd returned to discover his assistant had bolted—the fourth to leave in the two years since he'd returned from his abortive visit to San Francisco. It was hard managing the practice alone, but it would be worse trying to break in another feeble-hearted, weak-kneed, limp-spined assistant. He ground his teeth. Not for the first time, he wished for a real man, one with the mettle to live and learn under harsh conditions. One who had heart, as well.

He tipped up his sombrero and wiped the sweat from his brow. After two weeks up in the hills with Alonzo de Vega's people, Rafferty was baked to a cinder. As his skin had burned bronze, his hair had lightened to deep auburn, providing quite a contrast with his strong, white teeth. Except for the medical kit in his saddlebag and his high leather boots, he might have passed for one of the minor landowners in the vicinity.

Riding up to the small building that was house, surgery and hospital, he was relieved to see no one about. That was always a good sign. Right now, with the old recurrent fever only beginning to subside, rest was his best chance of preventing a relapse.

Rafferty expected Domingo to come shuffling out as he rode up to the stable, but there was no sign of the old man. Shaking his head, the doctor dismounted wearily and led Lugh toward the stable. He had a distinct sensation of déjà vu. Like the time two years ago when Homer Pease had packed up and fled the place—only different, somehow.

Rafferty took Lugh into his stall, removed the saddle and tack, and rubbed the horse down thoroughly. He wished the horse could do the same for him in return. His every muscle ached, every cell in his brain protested five nights without sleep, his eyes felt like poached eggs.

Steel will and long practice had kept him in the saddle on his return journey. Now that he was safely home, tiredness hammered at him. His vision was suddenly bleary, and his fingers felt like swollen stubs. The fever he thought he'd conquered had come back with a vengeance. Rafferty lost all desire for a bath and food. Just a few steps away was his lumpy and familiar bed. He might just flop down upon it, boots and all, and sleep until he awakened.

Once Lugh was settled comfortably, Rafferty staggered out into the blinding sunlight, heading for bed like a homing pigeon going to roost. He was so exhausted, he thought the rumble he heard was the drumming of blood in his ears. Then someone called out to him and he wheeled about. Señora Valdez and her small daughter came out of the shade of a twisted olive tree, their faces all smiles. The woman carried a basket of fresh vegetables and fruit.

Rafferty was so glad to see the child walking again, that it gave his flagging fortitude a boost. Señora Valdez held out the basket. "It is not much, El Doctore, but when the lambs come in the spring, one shall be yours. Our debt to you is a great one."

He squatted down before the child and ruffled her gleaming dark hair. "To see Consuela up and about again is all the payment I require."

"May God bless you and keep you safe." Seeing how exhausted he was, Señora Valdez did not linger to chat. She knew that a village woman came in to clean and do his laundry, but what El Doctore really needed, she thought, was a good woman to look after him.

After mother and daughter started back toward the village, Rafferty staggered groggily across the sandy yard. He was even beginning to hallucinate: across the dry land beyond the surgery, the ground seemed to rise up and form a moving cloud, topped by Domingo's ancient sombrero. He blinked. It was no illusion. Domingo's image slowed down as it neared the surgery, and the outlines of a sturdy wagon and gnarled driver emerged.

Rafferty was startled. *Damn!* He'd felt in command of himself, but was evidently so abominably tired, he hadn't even noticed that the wagon was missing. They'd gotten supplies two weeks earlier, so what on God's green earth did Domingo have piled up in the wagon? And where the *hell* had all those trunks and valises in the back of the wagon come from?

A soft whicker from the stables surprised him. Rafferty squinted into the light. An elegant horse with intelligent eyes looked back at him. He shook his head. And where in creation had Domingo gotten that mare?

Domingo pulled up in a flourish of whip and reins. He was clearly delighted with himself. "*Buenas tardes.* I am glad you have returned on this day."

Grinning widely, which was most unusual, the old man clambered down from the high, wooden seat. "This mare, she is a fine surprise, no?"

"No!" Rafferty put his hands on his hips. "Whose horse is she, and what have you got in the wagon?"

"Why, the *señora*'s horse, of course. And the *señora*'s things."

Rafferty was so tired, he swayed. "*Señora?* Which *señora?*" He was beginning to feel like a damned parrot.

Domingo's grin grew sly. He cast a knowing glance at the doctor. "Señora Rafferty."

The doctor rubbed his eyes. He knew what this was. He was dreaming. As with most dreams, this one was rapidly becoming senseless and stupid. Any moment, if he was lucky, he'd wake up in his bed, refreshed and restored. The dawn light would be filtering through the half-closed shutters. The air would smell of earth and piñon, of tortillas and beans. Domingo would knock softly, steal into his room and ask him if he'd like a mug of coffee—

"Would you like a mug of coffee?" a soft voice said from somewhere behind him. "Or would you prefer some beer? Domingo said there's a jug kept cooling in the well."

Rafferty spun about so swiftly that he staggered. Now he was positive he was dreaming. A vision in embroidered white lawn and a straw hat with blue ribbons, hovered just on the edge of his vision. "Oh!" the vision exclaimed. "You're ready to drop in your tracks. Here, I'll take that basket of vegetables from you. Now, come inside at once."

Gentle hands hustled Rafferty into the surgery and through the room where he examined his patients. The same hands propelled him firmly to the small bedroom beyond. He had only a glimpse of a fine-featured, oval face and a wing of Titian red hair as they passed through. In his private chamber, the shutters were drawn. As he blinked his eyes, the furniture seemed to waver, like objects seen through rippling water. A cup was placed in his hand. He downed the water quickly.

"Lie down," the soft voice said firmly. "Don't bother to take off your boots."

It was exactly what he wanted to hear. If this was a dream, Rafferty decided, he didn't want to awaken, after all. He lowered himself onto the mattress, feeling every weary bone and bruise. Gad, it was good to lie down! Rafferty closed his eyes in bliss. A cool cloth was applied to his brow, and a light blanket thrown over him. Before the door closed, he heard Domingo's voice from the surgery. "Where should I put this trunk, *señora?*"

"Over on the wall beneath the window, if you please."

The soft voice murmured something else before the door shut. Rafferty was already out cold.

A donkey brayed nearby, bringing Rafferty out of his exhausted sleep. The sun was halfway to the western horizon. Four o'clock or a bit after, he judged as he stretched and yawned. The fever was quenched. He felt like a new man, filled with vim and vigor and ready to tackle anything. He thanked the saints that, along with the temperament of his ancestors, he had inherited their amazing physical stamina.

He swung his feet over the edge. Bring on *banditos* and breech deliveries. Bring on colic and quinsy and dropsy. Brendan Patrick Rafferty could handle them all, by Gad. And with one hand tied behind his back. He leapt up, stark naked, as the door swung open. A young woman in a crisp shirtwaist and navy skirt stood gaping at him. The light streaming over her shoulders struck bright fire from her red curls. Rafferty cursed and grabbed for the blanket. His litany of likely contingencies hadn't included this.

"Madam, I would advise you to knock before walking into a man's bedroom," he roared.

She bit her lip and lowered her eyes at once. "My profound apologies, Dr. Rafferty. However, there is a man with a great gash in his arm lying on the examining table."

"What? Then get out of here at once," Rafferty ordered, "and let me get my pants on."

"Don't worry about your modesty," she replied calmly.

He could see that she was biting her lip to keep from laughing. "I'm not in the habit of putting on my clothing before women."

Her eyes twinkled. "Well, you can scarcely blame me for not knowing that. But, after all, you have few secrets from me. I saw you yesterday when I undressed you."

With a hint of a smile and a faint waft of lemon verbena, she waltzed out of the room.

Rafferty gaped at the closing door. If the laws of nature had allowed for such a thing, boiling steam would have come out of his ears. He pulled his trousers and shirt on hastily. Two minutes later, he erupted into the surgery.

He stalked toward the examining table where the woman Domingo referred to as Señora Rafferty was leaning over a recumbent form. Yesterday her wide straw hat and his own exhaustion had confused Rafferty. Just now, her cool composure and air of youthful maturity had thrown him off. But that classic oval face and Titian hair had given her away. Oh, she'd changed since their two meetings in San Francisco, grown in character and purpose and determination. Grown even more startlingly lovely than he'd have imagined possible.

Rafferty frowned down at her. "Miss Thomasina Wentworth, I presume."

"Your deduction is correct."

"What the deuce... What are you doing in my surgery?"

She didn't even look up, but continued with her work. "We'll talk later, if you please. I'm occupied with suturing this gash." She spoke to the man on the table. "The worst is over. Just a few more minutes, and I'll be finished."

"He can't understand you," Rafferty growled. "This is Mexico, Miss Wentworth. The natives of San Juan de Baptista speak Spanish."

"I think you'd better return to bed, Dr. Rafferty. Your brain is befuddled. Domingo has been speaking to me in English since my arrival."

Puzzled, the doctor stepped around her and pulled up short. Domingo was indeed the patient on the examining table. The old man's skin was a bit moist, but his color was good considering the circumstances. As Rafferty watched, Domingo's eyes closed and his mouth went slack.

"Good Gad, what have you done to the poor fellow!"

"Given him enough of your whiskey to take the edge off his pain." She knotted the suture and snipped the ends. "While I normally look upon the imbibing of large quantities of alcoholic spirits as a character flaw, in this case, I'm rather glad that you're a drinking man. Your private stores came in handy."

"I'll have you know that liquor is purely for medicinal purposes."

"Oh?" Thomasina's tone was caustic. "Then why, may I inquire, was it locked up so securely that I had to take the key from your pocket and break the chain to get at it?"

"Broke the chain?" Rafferty's indignation rose. "You barge into my bedroom, take over my surgery and break into my medicinal spirits, talking like an encyclopedia the entire time and...and..." He was so angry he could only sputter. That made him furious.

Thomasina watched with interest, sure that Dr. Rafferty was going to tie his tongue into knots out of sheer spleen.

Rafferty fought to master his temper. It was difficult to do when he felt like a volcano inside, ready to explode. And the way she was examining him to see how he handled the situation made it worse. Saints and Angels, but he'd show her that a Rafferty had will power to spare.

The doctor heaved in a deep breath and started again, relieved that his voice flowed smoothly. "I've had about enough, Miss Wentworth. I don't know what you're doing here or why you have shown up in San Juan—but I advise you to take yourself off again immediately."

"Really, Dr. Rafferty, if this is the way you speak to your assistants, it's no wonder that every one of them has packed up and left." She applied a snug bandage over the gash on Domingo's arm. "I, however, am made of sterner stuff."

Rafferty's brow clouded. "You may be made of pure, brass-plated presumption, but you are not going to stay here. By Gad, the village would be scandalized."

Thomasina put a blanket over Domingo and tucked him up in it. As a final precaution, she buckled the safety strap over his skinny hips. "If it's scandal you're afraid of, then you should have thought of that before agreeing to accept me as your assistant."

"Agreeing to accept . . ."

Thomasina noted the way the doctor's veins stood out at the sides of his tanned throat. "You must strive to ease your choler, Dr. Rafferty, or I'm very much afraid you'll have a stroke of apoplexy."

After a major struggle with himself, Rafferty lowered his voice to a growl. "Miss Wentworth."

"Yes?"

"It is an amazement to me that no one has strangled you yet. I have never met such an overbearing female in all my days."

Thomasina turned her back to him. "There's the kettle on the boil now. Sit down. We'll have a cup of tea, and we'll discuss this like civilized people."

Rafferty sat. There was nothing else to do. It was becoming clearer with every minute that his first assessment of Miss Wentworth in San Francisco had been on the mark: the woman was mad. She had no sense of modesty—at least where *his* body had been concerned—no scruples and a devastating lack of logic. How and why she expected him to take her on as his assistant boggled the mind.

But, damn, she'd done a fine job putting Domingo to rights. And, after all, Rafferty had no hesitation about having a cup of tea with the woman, mad or not, before shipping her back to— That *was* Earl Grey, wasn't it? He was sure he smelled bergamot....

Thomasina glided forward gracefully, bearing a tray. A blue china pot, which Rafferty had never seen before, was capped with a knitted cozy and flanked by a matching cup and his heavy pottery mug. A plate of Domingo's tortillas in green-chili sauce was on one side, a blue china plate filled with fancy shortbread was on the other.

Rafferty's mouth watered, and his stomach growled encouragement. He realized he hadn't eaten a bite in twenty-four hours.

Thomasina poured his tea. "You haven't said a word yet about the quality of my work on Domingo."

"Don't look to me for flattery. It was competent aid for a superficial scratch."

"Scratch! That gash was a good inch deep. Why, I doubt he'll even have a noticeable scar."

Rafferty took a hearty swallow from his mug. Admirable tea. "My compliments to your sewing teacher. I imagine you're quite adept with the embroidery needle."

"A misdiagnosis, Doctor. My talents don't run in that direction."

Rafferty couldn't resist a quick barb. He took another piece of shortbread from the plate. "And you have misdiagnosed your calling. You'll make an excellent housewife."

Thomasina thunked down the plate of shortbread with more effort than she'd intended. "I have no intentions of confining my tasks to the domestic sphere. I am determined to devote myself to the practice of medicine. I shall never marry."

Rafferty was unconvinced. Her cheeks were rosy, her eyes clear and bright, and tiny ringlets had escaped her tight chignon to halo her piquant face. "A waste," he murmured, more to himself than to her. Then he turned his attention to the food.

They drank their tea in a silence broken only by Rafferty's sigh of satisfaction. The shortbread seemed to melt in his mouth. He accepted another cup of tea. It was fragrant and steeped exactly right for his palate. The doctor admitted to himself that there would be a few benefits to having a female about the place. What a shame that Domingo and the widow Estevez had quarreled just when it seemed that wedding bans were imminent. He quirked an eyebrow.

"You certainly have mastered the fine art of afternoon tea, Miss Wentworth. But, how are you, I wonder, at wringing chickens' necks and butchering a joint of beef?''

Thomasina set down the pot with an alarming thump. "I am not here in the capacity of a hired maid and cook, Dr. Rafferty. I am here at your express invitation." She pulled a letter from her reticule. "As you may see quite clearly for yourself."

Rafferty frowned at the envelope, addressed in black ink in his own scrawling script. "Really, Miss Wentworth, do you take me for a complete fool? This letter was written in response to an inquiry from Mr. Thomas Y. Valnoy."

She folded her hands precisely. "I'm afraid that you jumped to a conclusion, Doctor. Nowhere in my letter to you did I so much as mention my sex. And you have been under another misapprehension. Valnoy is my actual surname."

Rafferty leaped up and stormed into his bedchamber. After sounds of violent rummaging, he came out with a sheet of paper in his hand. He glared at Thomasina and then back at the letter. Only after reading it twice and holding it up to the light did he see the small dot after the signature: "Thom. Y. Volnoy."

"Thom." for Thomasina, not for "Thomas" as he'd thought. Rafferty scowled. "Why, the period after the abbreviation is so small it would take a magnifying glass to make it readily visible." He put his palms down on the table and leaned across it. "A devious and unethical ruse!"

Thomasina rose, put her hands on the table and leaned across toward him. "You are a fine one to talk of ethics. If this rude hovel is the 'hospital' you boasted of, then you are either the greatest liar or the worst scoundrel known to modern medicine!''

Rafferty tried to stare her down, but couldn't. She was in the right. His "hospital" existed mostly on paper and in his mind. But, by Boudicca's bones, he'd have it before the year was out. It was just a little awkward to explain at the moment.

He went on the offense. ''When did you get such a tart tongue, Miss Wentworth—or rather, Miss Valnoy? Perhaps your change of name has resulted in a change of personality, as well. You were much more subdued when I last saw you.''

To his surprise, she went quite pale and dropped her teaspoon. Then a tide of hot color swept over her face. She lifted her chin and faced him straight on.

''That was not very kind in you, Dr. Rafferty. I have spent the past two years trying to banish that evening from my memory.''

Rafferty felt like the gauchest schoolboy who'd ever had a prank backfire on him. He flushed to the roots of his hair. He thought of apologizing. He thought of explaining that he'd spoken in jest and without thinking. He thought of touching her fevered cheek with his fingers to soothe her—and to see if her skin was as rose-petal soft as it looked.

Instead, he banged down his mug. His craggy features molded into stern lines. ''I am staunch in my loyalties, steadfast in my duties and stubborn in my opinions. I am too busy to be hospitable, too impatient to be affable and too rushed to be patient. Furthermore, another thing I am not, is kind.''

Thomasina had recovered herself. She picked up her china cup. "You paint a formidable picture of yourself, sir. But on the way from Los Alamos, Domingo and I had a long talk. What he told me contradicts your words completely. He said that you are gentle, compassionate and deeply committed to your profession." She smiled at the doctor over the gilt-edged rim of her cup and sipped her tea. "A veritable paragon of virtue—if a bit hotheaded."

Rafferty's eyebrows snapped together in a straight, dark line. "If you are to stay on here, Miss Wentworth, you will learn that Domingo's vivid imagination is fueled by the potent liquor the villagers make."

The words were no sooner out of his mouth than Rafferty realized his blunder. Thomasina capitalized on it at once. "Well, then," she announced, "now that we're in agreement about my staying on, where shall I put my things?"

"We are not at all in agreement. You have come here on false pretenses. For all I know, your references are equally fictitious."

"I'll have you know that I have brought with me several letters of reference under my entire name of Thomasina Wentworth."

She began ticking them off on her fingers. "One from Sister Mary Louise, who ran the dispensary for the Sisters of St. Martin, where I worked as a volunteer in the Contagious-Diseases Ward. A second from the Foundling Hospital, where I assisted with birthings and the care of infants, and a third from Cordell McGillicudy..." As she said the last name, a flush began to rise from Thomasina's throat and continued upward to the roots of her hair. Rafferty watched, fascinated. "... Who let me assist with the setting of bones and stitching of flesh wounds... among other things."

Rafferty laughed harshly. "Those other things being the care of injured dogs and cats and birds. You see, my dear, I'm not totally ignorant of McGillicudy's charitable veterinary work. Not just because the newspapers occasionally run a story about the 'Quack Doctor,' as they so rudely refer to him, but because he is a remote relation on my mother's side of the family." Little devils danced in his eyes as he observed her discomfiture. "It's a very small world, as they say."

Thomasina refused to let the doctor mortify her further. "The newspapers may think what they will of Dr. McGillicudy, but I am convinced that the man is both a saint and a genius."

Rafferty grinned. "My mother's family will be gratified to hear of your opinion. However, Miss Wentworth—or Valnoy, or whatever you choose to call yourself—that is neither here nor there. You can't stay on as my assistant. Which poses a minor problem. It's too late to send you back tonight, but either Domingo or I will take you back to Los Alamos first thing tomorrow morning."

Thomasina clasped her hands together before her waist and held them so tightly, her knuckles blanched. "Then you are reneging on your signed contract with me? It clearly states that I am bound to you for one probationary year, to be extended another two years if I prove able in the art and science of medicine. I warn you, if you try to wriggle out of our contract, I shall seek legal representation.''

Rafferty glared at her. "A contract made under false representation is not worth the paper and ink in a court of law. I suggest that you get a good night's sleep, Miss Wentworth.''

She looked around the surgery. "And where am I supposed to sleep?''

"Perhaps you should have thought of that earlier. I suppose that the stable is as good a place as any,'' he said, more to provoke her than anything. "I'll be damned if I'll give up my own bed to you when you've come here unannounced and uninvited.''

Thomasina waved the doctor's acceptance letter beneath his nose. "Hardly 'uninvited.' And where do you think you're going?''

Rafferty rose and strolled toward the door. "It is my usual custom to take a walk to the village to visit my patients after returning from a journey.''

Thomasina reached for her hat. "Excellent. I will accompany you.''

"That you will not! If word leaked out that I had a woman staying here who was unrelated to me by blood or marriage, the elders would throw me out lock, stock and barrel. You will stay here, safely hidden away until morning. I won't let your impulsive and ill-thought-out behavior ruin everything I've worked for.''

Rafferty stalked out and escaped down the road to the village. He was still angry but felt the situation was well in hand. Let her stew awhile. A little time alone in a strange place with none of the amenities she was used to, and his "guest" would be more than ready to depart at first light. In the meantime, he'd promised to see young Manuel Valdez about a horse, and he wanted to check on the Oporto twins, as well.

There was not a house in San Juan de Baptista where El Doctore was not heartily welcome. Rafferty spent some time in the village square, hearing the news and passing the rest of the afternoon pleasantly. After making the rounds of his chronic patients—old Señora Ramirez, little Pedro Nunzio and the Hernandez sisters, he stopped to visit the padre. There was a definite pattern to Rafferty's routine. He managed to time his visit to a particular home with the arrival of dinner. The Valdez family members were warm and generous. The deal for the horse was struck with mutual good feelings and celebrated with one of the *señora*'s feasts. It was also washed down by the same fiery fluid that had been Domingo's downfall.

The evening was advanced when Rafferty wended his way back, grimly smiling. By this time, Miss Wentworth should be fit to be tied. Tired, too, after a long day's travel. He'd get a little peace and quiet. In the morning, barring any medical emergencies, he would pack Miss Wentworth and her traveling show into the back of the wagon and take her to Los Alamos himself. Domingo would be fully recovered, but Rafferty wanted to see the woman's departure with his own eyes. Her determination was formidable.

As a wisp of cloud came between him and the stars, Rafferty realized that he hadn't thought things out well. He should have asked one of the women of the village to come play duenna for the night. Should he turn back now? He came to a halt and pondered the matter. No, his first instincts were right. The fewer people who knew of Miss Wentworth's arrival, the less chance of stirring up any scandal. The people of San Juan might not understand what a young and refreshingly lovely woman was doing at his surgery. Rafferty decided that he and Miss Wentworth would be on the road to Los Alamos well before cockcrow.

He'd tell Miss Wentworth that she could have his bed for the night, and he would bunk out in the stable with Domingo. As he strolled down the road, feeling much more amiable, it occurred to Rafferty that having a woman in his bed was a rather interesting situation. One he would have to enjoy vicariously. Meanwhile, he was in the mood for a proper set-to with his unwanted guest. There were few things a Rafferty—any Rafferty—looked forward to with more vigor than the thrust and parry of sharp wits.

He stopped first to check on Domingo. The old man was snoring beneath his striped serape. Rafferty grunted. No reason to awaken the man to check beneath the dressing. Rafferty acknowledged that his unwelcome assistant had done a competent job of treating the wound. More than competent. She had a good eye and steady hands. If only she'd been born a man!

The stray dog that had adopted Rafferty—much as Domingo had done—woofed a soft welcome as the doctor crossed the yard. Then it tucked its nose beneath a paw and settled down for a quiet night.

Evidently, Rafferty's visitor had done the same. The surgery was dark and empty. It irked the Irishman to think that Miss Wentworth had climbed into his bed and gone to sleep without a by-your-leave. But the chamber door stood open. Perhaps she was still awake.

Disregarding the propriety of the situation, he crossed the surgery floor to his bedroom—and found it empty. The bed was neatly made up and turned down, the pillow plumped and inviting. But there was no sign of his unwanted guest. What now? Rafferty thought angrily. Then he laughed at himself. First, he was indignant that she had taken over his bed; then he was indignant because she had not. It was a good thing she'd be gone by morning. The woman was addling his brains.

He went back into the surgery and discovered that Miss Wentworth's trunks and valises had been removed. Where in the hell could she have gone?

He stepped outside and saw long scuff marks in the dirt that he hadn't noticed before. They led straight to the stable. With Domingo out of commission, it was clear that Miss Wentworth had done the dragging. Rafferty was torn between irritation at her stubbornness and grudging admiration of her strength and stamina. At least his would-be assistant was no dainty, die-away miss.

He followed the trail to the empty end stall, which had once housed Domingo's late mule. For the past year, it had been a storage room holding a jumble of odds and ends. The jumble had been put into order and stacked neatly against one wall. Trunks and bandboxes lined another. Along the third wall, a blanket had been thrown over a pile of straw. Rafferty stepped inside.

Miss Thomasina Wentworth, erstwhile San Francisco debutante, was curled up on it beneath an embroidered silk coverlet, fast asleep. She was still wearing her shirtwaist and skirt. Rafferty smiled. She seemed younger and more vulnerable. More like the soft, inexperienced girl he'd met two years before. What on God's green earth did she think she was doing down here in the wilds of Mexico?

From the little he knew of her, she obviously came from a family of wealth and some degree of status. Her head should be filled with visions of ballgowns and formal dinners, not compound fractures and gangrene. Why, when he was her age he...

Rafferty found himself pulled up short. At her age, he had been totally immersed in medicine. He had started young. First, following the veterinary on his rounds, then reading the books in the squire's library—for which young Rafferty had been soundly beaten, first by the squire's lackey, then by his own older brother, for having anything to do with the hated Englishman. Poor, angry, shortsighted Kieran, not seeing that his people were enslaved as much by the ignorance forced upon them by English politics as they were by guns and taxes. On that day, Rafferty had taken a vow to break away from the cycle of poverty and despair.

And, like the woman before him now, opposition had only made him more determined. To his dying day, Rafferty would never forget the look on his mother's face when he had asked for a student's dissecting kit for his birthday, instead of the pair of brogues he needed and that she'd saved to get him. A good stout pair of brogues distinguished the hopeful poor from the hopeless poor, and she had scrubbed her knuckles raw cleaning the squire's hall to get the money to have them made.

A smile of remembrance softened Rafferty's rugged features. When the important day had come, he'd unwrapped the bulky parcel expecting to find the shoes inside. To his utter joy, he'd found the kit rolled up inside an old shawl, instead. His mother, God rest her soul, had been a great one for little jokes like that.

Staring down at Miss Wentworth, he suddenly thought what very remarkable creatures women were. And he wondered, for the first time, where Aileen Mary O'Bannion Rafferty had ever found the kit and the wherewithal to purchase it.

He sat on one of the trunks and pondered the situation. The very fact of Miss Wentworth's presence in San Juan said a lot for her depth of character and determination. If the same desire for knowledge and its practical application burned within her heart as it did in his, he would be three times a villain to deny her the opportunity.

Rafferty rubbed his eyes. It was a quandary worthy of a Solomon's judgment, yet he hadn't that wisdom. An unchaperoned woman living at the surgery compound would scandalize the countryside. He might be able to arrange one of Ramon Mondragon's numerous old aunt's to serve as duenna. Or perhaps Señora Rivera would take Miss Wentworth in as a boarder.

A yawn interrupted his thinking. He should have straightened this all out earlier while they were awake and thinking clearly. Rafferty was too much of a gentleman to let a woman sleep in the straw while he was snug in a comfortable bed.

"Miss Wentworth?" No response. He shook her arm. "Miss Wentworth..."

Thomasina didn't budge. She'd been traveling for two weeks, and now that she'd reached her destination, she was enjoying a deep, refreshing sleep.

After a moment's hesitation, Rafferty turned back the cover and scooped her up in his arms. She sighed and snuggled against his chest.

It had been a long time since a woman had nestled so trustingly in his arms. A pang of loneliness shot through Rafferty, surprising the hell out of him. He almost dropped her. No, he decided abruptly. It wouldn't work. He'd have to send her packing at first light.

Pushing past the half-open surgery door, Rafferty carried her through to his own room. "It won't work, Miss Wentworth," he said softly to her sleeping form. "Nice as it would be to have a woman's touch about the place, and much as I should enjoy your company, the situation is impossible." He pulled the blanket up and covered her.

Thomasina was having the most wonderful dream. She sighed and slipped her hand beneath Rafferty's pillow. He tip-toed quietly out of the room.

A few minutes later, the doctor was himself asleep in the storage room, the shaggy curls at his collar ruffled by the edge of Thomasina's silk coverlet. A light scent clung to the fabric, and he dreamed of green, flower-filled meadows where the Shannon flowed down to the sea.

Only Domingo was wakeful, no worse for the wear and tear on his arm. He had at least a dozen scars on his body, all far more serious than the one the *señora* had repaired. By the morning, he'd be up and about, as usual. He rearranged himself on his straw pallet. Not an hour past he had seen El Doctore carry the woman into the house.

Unfortunately, he hadn't seen Rafferty return to the stable alone.

Earlier Domingo had realized that El Doctore and the *señora* had quarreled, which was why the *señora* had made herself a bed among the boxes and bales. *Ai-yi*, the freedom allowed to young women these days! Of course, it was true that after so long a separation, the *señora* had some right to be angry. Women were tenderhearted creatures. El Doctore should not have gone into the village, leaving her alone on their first night together.

It had worried Domingo. Disharmony in a home could disrupt everything. Ah, well, it had turned out right in the end. El Doctore was back from the village now.

As he drifted into a deep, dreamless sleep, Domingo was relieved to know that the *señora* was also back in the house, safe and snug where she belonged—in her husband's bed.

Chapter Five

An hour before dawn, Rafferty started out of a sound sleep. He was momentarily confused to find his bed a combination of straw and silk, his bedchamber the storage room. Then it all sorted out and he recognized the approaching thunder of galloping hooves. He'd heard that same, frantic pounding a hundred times before. Hopping up, he was into his trousers and boots, his shirt buttoned and jacket on before the rider reached his doorstep.

A man rode in on a lathered horse and reined to in the yard. At first, Rafferty didn't recognize Señor Zavala, a stolid local farmer who looked half-crazed with fear. His skin was gray, and his horse spent.

"El Doctore, you must come at once—my son..."

"I'm on my way. Domingo will see to you and your horse." He helped the man dismount.

Domingo had already saddled the doctor's horse and was attaching the special bags that held emergency medical items. Rafferty was relieved to see the old man acting as if his injuries of yesterday were no more than a flea bite. There was no need for explanations, and they fell into their practiced crisis routine.

Rafferty ducked inside the surgery to grab his satchel of equipment and his hat. Thomasina had heard the commotion. She threw on her robe and peeked around the doorway as the doctor strode in. "What is it?"

"An emergency. Go back to bed, Miss Wentworth. We'll discuss what to do with you when I return."

Exiting the surgery like a flying cannonball, Rafferty tucked his satchel into one of the special pouches and mounted his horse. To Domingo he said, "Tell the American *señora* why I've been called away." He started off without waiting for a reply.

Señor Zavala's *jacal* wasn't far beyond the village outskirts. Rafferty sped down the road on his faithful Lugh, wondering what he'd find at the end of it. During the long ride he had plenty of time to ponder the possibilities. The sun rose in a ball of orange flame. In the distance, the emerald flanks of Los Tres Hermanos rose into the blue dawn. To the east, where the ground was jumbled and rocky, the hot sun had dried out the wild vegetation. In contrast, the irrigated orchards and fields rose in green tiers on the southern and western slopes, rich in nutrients from ancient lava flows. The Zavala family had lived at the head of the valley for three hundred years.

The sun was considerably higher when he reached the Zavala home, almost hidden between the trees that lined the riverbanks and a screen of leafy vines. Dappled with sun and shade, its walls blended into the scenery like the spotted lizards basking on the nearby rocks. Away from the protection of the village, it was wise not to draw too much attention. Bandits often swooped down from the rugged hills to the east, preying on rich and poor alike.

Rafferty dismounted when he reached the stand of trees beside the house. The old wagon parked beneath it was streaked with drying blood, and an ominous dark trail led to the door of the house. The doctor removed his satchel and began to unstrap his saddlebags with quick, sure fingers. The tattoo of approaching hooves surprised him. The horse was coming too fast and fresh to belong to the father of the injured boy.

Rafferty glanced up, expecting trouble, and saw a horsewoman racing up the road toward the *jacal*, bright hair streaming from beneath her bonnet like flames. He swore beneath his breath. The horse trotted up at a smart pace as he removed the saddlebags and swung them over his wide shoulder. The entire operation had taken him less than twenty seconds.

Thomasina swung down from her saddle. Her dress was liberally coated with dust and her cheeks were as red as her hair. "It was stupid of you to leave me behind like that. Four hands are better than two."

Rafferty started across the yard to the house. "This is no place for amateurs. Look at the blood, Miss Wentworth." There was no way to avoid it. Great gouts of it marked a trail from the wagon to the house. Brown where it mixed with soil, glistening red in other spots.

"Arterial blood!" Thomasina exclaimed. A sudden queasiness formed into a tight, hard knot in her midsection, and her mouth went dry. This was not a passage in a textbook. Somewhere inside the house, a living, breathing person was in pain and mortal jeopardy. Frightened and fearing she was in over her head, Thomasina still followed the doctor in without hesitation.

Rafferty had seen the way Thomasina's face paled and the way she'd squared her shoulders. Miss Wentworth had resolution. Now, to see if her stomach was as strong as her courage.

The woman of the house rushed to meet the doctor with a spate of rapid Spanish. "Thanks be to the Virgin of Guadaloupe and her Most Holy Son!"

"He still lives?"

"*Sí*, El Doctore—" The woman broke off, somewhat taken aback to see a fashionable young lady with the doctor. "My son is here," she said, leading them to the single rough bed at the back of the house as she explained his injury.

The woman's son had been gored by a neighbor's bull. Rafferty didn't ask why the young man had been at the neighbor's place so early in the morning. He'd probably been playing toreador to improve his skills in order to impress some blossoming beauty. It didn't matter. Rafferty's first concern was to save the boy's life.

The patient was stretched out on his back beneath a woven blanket. Sweat broke out on Thomasina's forehead. The youth's skin should have been a golden caramel like his mother's. Instead, it was gray as clay.

Rafferty stripped off the worn sheet. The young man's cotton trousers were soaked with blood, as was the makeshift bandage wound over them. "Boil some water, *señora*." He nodded to Miss Wentworth. "Cut his pant leg off."

Thomasina took the scissors from her own medical kit and began cutting the wet fabric. Her hands became smeared with blood, but she was proud that they didn't shake. Rafferty slit the bandage holding the garment in place, and Thomasina pulled the cloth away. When she saw the hole in the boy's thigh, her ears buzzed with the sound of a million flies, and her vision dimmed.

She'd gone deaf, too. Rafferty was speaking, but whether to her or the boy, she didn't know. His lips moved, but nothing reached her ears. Thomasina took a deep breath. Her eyesight returned to normal. So did her hearing. The doctor was in midsentence.

"...swear to God and all the saints," he said urgently, "that I'll send you packing at once if you faint."

Thomasina bristled. "I have never fainted in my life."

"Good. Don't start now."

"And, if you will recall, Dr. Rafferty, it was you who ended up in a heap on the floor in San Francisco."

He didn't rise to the bait, although the provocation was keen. Only a cad would throw the circumstances of that night in her face. He snapped open his satchel, put a clean, white rectangle of linen on the table beside the bed and began laying out scalpels and an array of metal objects that had the young man's mother gaping in alarm.

Thomasina stared at them, too. The injured fellow before her was not a neat diagram on the page of a lifeless book, but a human being. Flesh and blood. She glanced at his face. His eyelashes lay thick and dark against his pale cheeks, and his mouth was soft and vulnerable as a child's. So full of life a few hours ago—and now lying on the blood-soaked bed. Pity filled her chest until it ached.

Rafferty's gruff voice shattered the spell. "Don't just stand there. Get out the large vial of powder, the jar of green unguent and the linen strips. They're in the upper compartment."

Thomasina jumped. She was angry with him for startling her, and angrier with herself for acting like a spectator when she had her own role to perform. She followed his orders efficiently, but couldn't resist one shot. "Perhaps you'd care for a little chloroform."

"No need. Our patient won't feel a thing until he awakens. And then I'll prescribe something stronger than the medicine you gave Domingo yesterday."

She quickly overcame her twinge of annoyance and in a minute, all personal thoughts were emptied from her head. There was much to learn and much to do.

When the boy's father arrived, he hurried in and stopped short. Señor Zavala seemed to be angry, and a torrent of words poured out. Rafferty cut them short with a few of his own. Thomasina didn't understand the exchange, but she knew the cause: the man didn't want a strange woman present. The word *gringa* was one she'd come to understand quite well. Rafferty held his ground and the farmer retreated. Thomasina wondered what he'd said.

The sun had already reached its highest point before they finished. Then the waiting began. Thomasina used the rest of the hot water to wash her hands. There was nothing she could do about her bloodstained dress.

Rafferty went outside to the well. He was in good shape, but bending over the bed for so long had stiffened his muscles. His head felt full of cobwebs. He hauled a bucket up and sluiced water over his head and shoulders. The cold should have cleared his head. It didn't. Rafferty prayed it was only weariness that made him feel feverish and clouded his thinking. Since his days in Africa, he'd been subject to recurring fevers complete with bouts of delirium. He took his wet shirt off, rubbed at the stains and set it aside.

Thomasina's seat beside the bed offered an unobstructed view of Rafferty at the well through the open window. She stared, first out of curiosity and then out of fascination. He drew up another bucket. His skin was sunned to a dark golden brown, and the muscles of his back rippled beneath the sheets of dripping water. Sleek and supple as an otter, she thought, and strong as a bull. And just as bullheaded. But Thomasina found it hard to dwell on Rafferty's iniquities when he stood, half-naked, just a few yards away.

A third bucketful of water sloshed over him, plastering his thick hair to his head. He turned his face up to it as if it were life giving, and she wondered what a man, born on the green island of Ireland was doing in a land so brown and sere. A place where water was scarce and he was hundreds of miles from the sea. There were intriguing mysteries surrounding Rafferty. In time, she decided, she would find out some of the answers to them.

Rafferty looked up and their gazes locked. For a moment, Thomasina felt breathless and slightly dizzy. A normal reaction to the morning's events, she assured herself. Then Rafferty strode into the house, frowning, and she found herself shrinking back into the rickety chair. *Not* a normal reaction at all.

He stood over her and put out his hand peremptorily. "You look like you've been butchering a hog. Come with me."

Thomasina settled more firmly into the wooden chair. "I won't."

"You will." He caught her hand and dragged her up. "The first rule of my practice is that cleanliness must always be maintained." His frown deepened. "The second is that my assistant—or anyone aspiring to be my assistant—obey my rules implicitly."

She didn't have the chance to argue the point. The doctor gave a quick look in his patient's direction, then, satisfied that all was as well as could be expected, he propelled Thomasina out the door.

The sun was hot. In the bright light, Thomasina saw what Rafferty had meant about her condition. In fact, he'd been rather kind. She looked as if she'd slaughtered an entire herd of hogs. Head high, but more cooperatively than he'd anticipated, she accompanied him to the well.

As Rafferty turned his back to haul up another bucket, Thomasina tried not to look at the doctor's

astoundingly developed musculature. Tried and failed.
Rafferty was magnificent. Beneath his bronzed skin,
she could see the outline of the tapering triangle of the
trapezius, and she noted the bulge of anterior del-
toids and triceps...why, seeing the human body in
action was *much* more instructional than outline
drawings in her medical texts. Thomasina applied
herself more fully to the lesson.

Rafferty straightened and turned back just as
Thomasina became deeply engrossed in the splendid
interplay of muscle, sinew and bone. A deep crimson
flush spread upward from his admirable chest to the
strong column of his throat and all the way up his face
to the hairline. Even the tips of his ears grew pink, she
noted with what she sincerely imagined was clinical
detachment. Her assessment was rudely interrupted
when the doctor moved suddenly. He dashed the icy
contents of the bucket over her.

While Thomasina yelped and sputtered, Rafferty
drew up another cold draught from the well and tossed
it over her as well. Her hair streamed with water,
coming loose from her chignon and covering her eyes
like a soggy veil. She gasped, pushed the hair out of
her face and sent the doctor a glare that would have
done justice to Medusa; in fact, he seemed to have
turned to stone.

Rafferty stood frozen in midmovement, the wooden
bucket still gripped in his hands. His face was white as
marble and chiseled with strain. Then the red flooded
over him again, deeper than before. Señora Zavala
came out of the house, took one look at Thomasina
and threw up her hands in horror. She ducked inside

and hurried out with a gaily striped rebozo, which she flung across Thomasina's chest. Chattering like a scolding hen, she shooed the *gringa* into the house. The woman opened a small, carved chest and removed an embroidered skirt and blouse, indicating that her scandalous guest should put them on. *"Por favor, señora."*

Thomasina peeled off the rebozo and looked down at her bodice. No wonder he'd stared at her. It was plastered to her like a second skin.

Her blush was as fiery as her hair. In her haste to catch up with Rafferty, she'd decided there was no time to lace into her light corset, which she'd removed before going to sleep in the stable storage room. She'd just treated Rafferty to a sterling demonstration of her own anatomy, from the waist up. She tried to temper her mortification with the fact that at least she wasn't lacking anything in that department. It didn't help at all.

Still blushing, she took off her shirtwaist and put on the garments left for her, then went to check on her patient.

He was floating in poppy dreams from the dose of thick, brown liquid she'd given him, but his color had greatly improved and there had been no further bleeding.

Thomasina set about cleaning the surgical instruments and putting them back neatly in their fitted case. When she'd left San Francisco, she'd been consumed by her passion to become a doctor, determined to let nothing stand in her way. In her single-minded pursuit of her goal, she'd deliberately forced away thoughts of anything else. Upon arrival in San Juan, she had been smacked in the face by reality and jolted out of her rose-colored fantasies.

She'd been expecting something more than a tiny country village. Rafferty's reply to her had clearly stated that San Juan, although small and remote, held all that any man of good sense could need or want. After such encouragement, she'd been devastated to discover that meant a surgery, a church and a cantina. Clearly, her needs and wants differed significantly from his.

Worst of all was the lack of an inn or regulation boarding house. Thomasina had come prepared to make do in cramped quarters and to take her meals at a communal board, but she'd never in her wildest flights imagined there would be no inn at all. And she couldn't stay alone at the surgery with the doctor.

There must be some family willing to take her on as a boarder, she thought. That would solve the problem of where she would sleep, but the days would still be long and filled with strain. If she could talk Dr. Rafferty into keeping his contract with her, they would be thrown together for long hours. They would be forced to spend the greater part of their days together. And she didn't know how she was going to look him in the eye after this incident.

As it happened, Thomasina didn't have to worry. It was a long time before Rafferty came back inside.

"He'll be feverish and in pain when he awakens," Rafferty told Señora Zavala. The day was far advanced, the sun looming closer to the horizon. "Give him the medicine as I've shown you and he'll sleep until morning. He's a lucky young devil and should do fine. But if there's any fresh bleeding or other problems, send for me at once."

"But you have not eaten." The woman waved her hand at the scrubbed wooden table. "You and the *señora* must refresh yourselves."

Thomasina didn't understand the words but got the message all the same. The aroma of garlic, tomatoes, beans and onions was heavenly. While they'd worked over their patient, she hadn't been aware of time passing or the pangs of her indignant stomach. Now she was famished. Rafferty was about to refuse. She could tell by the tilt of his chin. "A fire must have wood for fuel," she announced as she plopped herself down on a stool. "And the human body requires sustenance also. Go, if you like. I shall accept Señora Zavala's kind invitation." She eyed the unfamiliar food eagerly.

"Perhaps you're right, Miss Wentworth."

Rafferty's sudden smile should have given Thomasina pause. She accepted the frijoles, wrapped in a thin, soft corncake, and took a bite.

It was delicious, but far spicier than anything she'd tasted in her life. In seconds her mouth and tongue were on fire. The heat seemed to incinerate the lining of her mouth and go straight up to her brain. Her eyes watered, and her breath was trapped in her chest. She dared a glance at Rafferty and found him watching her with a knowing gleam in his eyes. Thomasina had only one course of action. She swallowed the hot coals that filled her mouth. They seared a track of pain down her throat and into her chest, where they seemed to burst into flames. A film of tears caught on her lower lashes, blurring her vision.

She dabbed at the corner of her mouth. "Quite tasty," she said, and then she took another bite. It was worse than the first. Her mouth felt blistered and swollen. Tears streamed down her face. Thomasina kept a smile frozen on it. She'd be damned to hell and back before she let Dr. Rafferty laugh at her.

But he wasn't laughing after all. There was a glint in his eye, but it held neither humor nor malice. He held out a small dish containing a thick cream and dabbed a piece of tortilla in it. "Here. This will quench the fire."

Thomasina was sure it would be a more incendiary dish. "Thank you," she managed to say. Her tongue felt like a wooden plank. To her surprise, the cream was cool and soothing. It put the flames out and she found that she could breathe normally again. Rafferty sat back. "It takes time to get used to the local food. You'll adapt. If you stay on, that is."

All the pain and humiliation was worth it. Thomasina wiped her eyes on her sleeve. The doctor hadn't so much as said so, but it appeared that he was becoming resigned to her staying on as his assistant. She watched as he dipped his rolled tortilla and frijoles into the cream, and she followed suit for good measure. This time, the food went down more easily. The lining of her mouth only smoldered instead of bursting into flame, and her eyes only watered half as much.

Rafferty polished off his tortilla, grinned and started on another. Miss Wentworth had guts...er, no, she had *fortitude*. If he could solve the logistics of where she would stay and who would chaperone, she might serve very well in the role of his assistant. Gu—er, fortitude, courage and determination were exactly the qualities his former assistants had lacked. But it would be damned ticklish business to get the villagers to accept her if the circumstances held even the slightest hint of irregularity. They certainly would be up in arms over a young—and, he had to admit—a desirable unmarried woman working and living beneath his roof.

The remembrance of her in the sunlight flashed before his eyes. Her hair touched with sun, her firm breasts and small waist outlined by the wet bodice...

Rafferty choked on the tortilla. Coughing and sputtering, he reassessed the situation.

In the past few years, he'd tried to make himself one hundred percent physician and to forget that he was a man with a man's potent needs. He had put his passions into his work and had planned to keep them there, safely buried. No, it would not be wise to have Miss Wentworth at his elbow day and night.

He would have to have Domingo drive her back to the nearest town where she could arrange return transportation to San Francisco. If she proved unwilling, he'd deliver her straight to the ship himself. A young and lovely woman traveling alone in a foreign country was trouble waiting to happen.

It really was only too bad that she couldn't stay on a few days. He enjoyed Miss Wentworth's company.

That last thought surprised him. Loneliness, Rafferty mused, is an insidious thing. He loved the people of San Juan de Baptista, found them interesting and intelligent and good of heart. But he longed for conversations with someone who'd read Yeats and Shakespeare. Someone with whom he could discuss the finer things in life, like... like the potential for successful abdominal surgery and his developing theories about the true causes of malaria and typhus.

Rafferty took a swallow of beer from the cup Señora Zavala had given him. A shame that there was no one of Miss Wentworth's acquaintance with whom she could stay in San Juan. He tried to convince himself that she lacked the skills or the temperament to become a physician. Even if there were some way she could stay on, she would soon tire of the endless work, the lack of amenities, the dirth of the social activity that had been hers in the States. No other outcome was possible.

By the time they thanked the Zavalas and were returning to his surgery, Rafferty had settled into a state of silent thoughtfulness. Nothing broke the silence except the steady sound of their horse's hooves and an occasional birdsong.

Thomasina wasn't eager for conversation, either. She was young and fit and hadn't expected the day to take such a toll upon her, but she ached all over. The back of her neck was knotted and kinked, and her eyes felt as if they'd sunk a few inches into her head. She was tired to the bone—and felt absolutely, incredibly, wonderful!

The doctor saw the glow on her cheek. Flushed with the success of the first case she was really involved with, he realized she was setting herself up for a painful fall. He brought his mount up beside hers. "Riding high, Miss Wentworth? Don't count your chickens prematurely. The boy may yet succumb to loss of blood or to infection."

She sent him a wry smile. "Don't spoil it. Let me enjoy the feeling of accomplishment for however long it lasts before you start puncturing my illusions."

"A doctor must have no illusions where his patients are concerned. If you can't learn to anticipate what might go wrong and what steps you'll take to counteract it, you should be back home sipping tea."

His words stung. Thomasina bridled. "You'll have to admit that my presence made your own task much easier. It's a good thing I was quick in following you."

Rafferty shrugged. "It took you long enough to catch up with me."

"I have a few more garments to put on than you have, *Doctor* Rafferty."

"Nonsense. *I* put *you* to bed fully clothed, Miss Wentworth—gentleman that I am."

Unfortunately, their exchange reminded them both of the cold shower he'd given her and its results. She gave him a withering look. "Your diploma says physician and surgeon, Dr. Rafferty. I saw no mention of 'gentleman' at all—nor have I seen any indication of one in your abominable manners."

It was clear that they were spoiling for a fight. Thomasina wanted to force him into admitting that he couldn't have succeeded so well without her help.

Rafferty wanted her to admit that the reality of it had been more unsettling than she'd expected.

He had noticed her pallor, and now there were blue shadows of fatigue beneath her eyes. For some reason, that infuriated him. He stabbed at the first thing that came to mind. "It would have been better if you'd removed the boy's pant leg with one or two major cuts instead of snipping them to ribbons. His mother will have a devil of a time patching them up. These people lead simple lives. They don't have the benefit of the vast wardrobe contained in the half dozen traveling trunks you brought with you."

Instead of responding to the provocation Thomasina nudged her horse from a trot into a canter. *If he thinks he can goad me into losing my temper and leaving, he is sadly mistaken!*

For the next hour they maintained a steady distance between them. Rafferty was growing increasingly tired and had the strange sensation of being physically removed from his body. Then the pounding began at his temples and the base of his skull. He couldn't pretend to himself any longer: his recurrent fever was, indeed, returning, this time with a vengeance. This stage would last an hour or three, followed by days of high fever. If left untreated, the fever could leave him prostrated and delirious again. If his luck held, a dose of Langanberg's Elixer, followed by Greene's Smartweed Compound mixed with a bit of pleurisy root, might prevent the full-blown symptoms.

He felt a cold prickling along his skin. If not for the emergency this morning he'd have had Miss Wentworth packed up and on her way home. Although she had proved useful today, he couldn't let her stay on. But, a small voice warned inside his head, if he succumbed to the fever, she would seize the chance to stay while he was helpless. He decided to hurry back to the surgery on the pretext of catching up with her. Sunset was fast approaching.

The western sky was blazed with orange light, and the hills to the east had faded to misty lines of purple and blue. It was a scene of peace, of utter serenity. The land, like the people, had remained unchanged through generations.

Thomasina felt the weariness and anger seep from her body as they drew nearer the surgery. And then, the tranquility was rent by bloodcurdling cries.

She reined in instinctively. Two dozen horsemen galloped over the western ridge and swooped down upon them. Thomasina's heart raced. *Bandits!* One rider came straight up to her and leered. His eyes were as dark as olives. She could almost count the individual hairs in his enormous moustachio. As he reached for her bridle Thomasina found that she could neither move nor breathe.

Her brain was numbed with fear. Her limbs had turned to stone. Even the blood in her veins seemed to have solidified. The man caught her bridle and pulled it from her leaden fingers. The mare offered no resistance, and Thomasina sat rigidly as the bandit led her off the road toward the others. She fought the blinding panic with all her strength and will. It took every ounce of energy she had. Movement came back, and she dragged in a deep, shuddering gulp of air. Mere seconds had elapsed.

Freed from the grip of fear, Thomasina's first thought was to escape across the fields. She wheeled her mare about, but it was too late. She was surrounded. The riders circled her, waving lariats and hats and shooting their sidearms in the air. She saw a group close in on Rafferty, who disappeared in a hail of blows.

"No!" Thomasina cried out. She jerked the bridle from her captor's hands.

Surprised, the man lost his balance and his horse reared back in alarm. He was too busy trying to control his mount to stop the woman.

Thomasina rode at the men surrounding Rafferty, screaming like a banshee as she whirled her riding crop overhead. She was no longer the young woman who had been petrified by panic. Now she was an avenging fury.

The bandits turned in amazement, and their horses sidled away from the charging madwoman. Thomasina burst into their midst, flailing left and right. In the noise and bustle, she didn't hear Rafferty cry out her name. His cries turned to an eardrum-bursting roar. *"Stop!"*

The doctor lunged toward her as she struck out at a man in a brown-striped serape, and caught her around the waist.

Thomasina found herself suspended between her saddle and Rafferty's strong right arm. Then she was up before him, clasping at his neck to keep from falling. Lugh pranced and plunged to keep his footing among the other milling horses. One of the men caught Thomasina's riderless mare and kept it from bolting.

Rafferty's arm tightened about Thomasina's ribs painfully. "By Gad, will you hold still, woman? You'll break both our necks if you're not careful!"

Thomasina was confused. The doctor looked more irritated than concerned. Pinned against his chest, she hung on for dear life. It was the work of mere moments before Rafferty brought the situation under control. It took slightly longer for Thomasina to grasp the truth: the men surrounding them weren't murderous attackers. They were an overly friendly welcoming committee.

"But who are they?" she exclaimed.

"These are the young men of San Juan and some of the *vacquerros* from a nearby hacienda. Their leader is Andres Zavala, uncle to the boy who was gored by the bull."

Thomasina eyed Zavala. He was a hawk-nosed man with a fierce gaze and a wonderful mustachio. He rode up to Thomasina and the doctor, laughing and shouting something that Thomasina didn't understand. The others picked up the refrain, repeating the same words over and over again in what sounded like a cheer.

Rafferty, for all their merriment, looked increasingly grim. He should have known that Domingo wouldn't hold his tongue—the old man was an incorrigible gossip. But never in his worst nightmares had the doctor anticipated anything like this.

Thomasina rubbed her wrists where the marks of Rafferty's fingers burned red on her skin. "Why are they shouting so? And what are they saying?"

Rafferty sent her a dark look. "They are celebrating your arrival."

Andres Zavala rode up to them, rose in the saddle and doffed his hat to Thomasina while executing a splendid bow. His knowledge of English was slight, but effective. "Welcome to San Juan, *señora*. It is a good thing that you have come to join *El Doctore* and work beside him." A great smile split the man's seamed face.

She smiled back and nodded, hoping to show her appreciation for his warm welcome.

With a rousing cheer, the whole cavalcade moved forward, escorting Thomasina and the doctor right past the surgery and on toward the village.

As they approached, the church bell rang and the villagers came out to meet them, dressed in their Sunday clothes. Even Domingo was fancied up in a colorful serape and a fine embroidered shirt that Rafferty had never seen him wear before.

Rafferty swore under his breath and clung to his saddle horn, a brief dizziness making him sway. There would be no quick dash to the dispensary just yet. He thought he could hold out another hour at the most.

Meanwhile, Thomasina was utterly charmed by their welcome. Girls with flowers in their hair sang out from the sidelines, and the young boys raced along on foot beside the cavalcade. When the crowd reached the village square, the mayor gave a speech, and the old priest gave everyone gathered his blessing.

Thomasina was delighted. She had expected resistance, perhaps hostility, toward a foreign woman studying medicine in their village. It was gratifying to see how wrong she had been. She nodded and smiled to everyone, enjoying the spectacle wholeheartedly. A glance at her companion said that Rafferty was not enjoying it half as much as she. Indeed, he looked rather grim.

Rafferty was still in his saddle by sheer willpower and little else. The dancers, the singers, the little village square all blurred together for him. The effects of the fever were coming upon him more strongly with every passing minute. He had to get back to the surgery at once. At the earliest possible moment, he tried to extricate them from the crowd.

"Come, Miss Wentworth. It's been a long day and we have much to discuss."

"Yes, but the villagers have gone to such trouble. We wouldn't want to offend them."

A young mother stepped forward and offered a posy of flowers for the *"señora"*, that Thomasina accepted graciously. "This reception is quite overwhelming. I really didn't expect the people of San Juan to accept me so readily. And the courtesy by which they call me *señora*."

Rafferty gritted his teeth. "They've welcomed you with open arms, all right. But for the wrong reason. *Señora* is not a courtesy title for a female doctor. It is the title for a married woman, Miss Wentworth."

"I don't understand."

"I do. Unfortunately, all too well. And what the devil can be done to straighten out this coil is beyond me at the moment." Rafferty's voice was strangled with chagrin. "You see, they believe that you are Señora Rafferty."

Thomasina's eyes widened. "Do you mean to say that...that..."

"Right you are, Miss Wentworth." Rafferty's voice was harsh. "Domingo—and all the people of San Juan de Baptista—are under the indelible impression that you and I are man and wife."

Chapter Six

"Man and wife!" Thomasina was appalled. "But that is ridiculous!"

Rafferty sent her a sharp, warning look. "For God's sake, hold your tongue. Do you want to create a public scandal?"

"But you must tell them . . . explain to them . . ."

"Explain what? That the woman who spent the night under my roof—in my very bed—is almost a total stranger to me?" His reply was angry, but low enough that only Thomasina could make out the words.

Her face flamed. "But we weren't . . . we didn't . . . You slept in the stable, and I slept alone inside."

"Look at their faces. Do you think anyone here would believe that? We must tread warily, Miss Wentworth. It took me years to earn the trust and goodwill of the people, but one hasty word from your lips will wipe it all away."

She lifted her chin. "Very well. We'll discuss that later."

There was no time for more. Thomasina and the doctor were separated by the cheering crowd. Friendly hands took the reins from Thomasina's hands and helped her alight from her horse. A garland of wild-flowers was placed on her fiery curls. Looking at the happy faces surrounding her, Thomasina knew that the doctor was right. They would have to think of an explanation acceptable to all before the night was over. If only she could steal ten minutes alone with him, surely they could concoct something suitable. But Rafferty was on the other side of the plaza, and that hope died aborning.

The women crowded around Thomasina, exclaiming at her red hair and fine kid boots. They seemed pleased that she was wearing the garments Señora Zavala had lent her, as if Thomasina had offered them all a fine compliment.

Soon they led Thomasina to a table set up in the square, where a feast had been prepared. Dishes of food were pressed upon her, one after the other. She learned to nibble delicately until she'd assessed whether or not her still-tender mouth could accommodate the spices.

As the festivities continued, the town leaders rose one by one, cups in hand, and made long, courtly speeches interspersed with many bows. "Toasts to the bride and groom," Domingo explained.

Thomasina didn't understand a word of what was said, but the spirit of the occasion more than made up for it. She reached for her cup and took a healthy swallow of the clear liquid. The effect was worse than Señora Zavala's frijoles. Her entire throat and chest burned. She gasped and sputtered and coughed. Her eyes swam with tears.

Rafferty had been watching from the corner of his eye. When Thomasina rose to her feet, clutching at her throat, he thought she was choking. Pushing unceremoniously through the crowd, he made his way to her side. He swung back his hand and clapped her between the shoulder blades so hard, her knees buckled. As she dropped, he caught her deftly and picked her up in his arms.

"Clear the way! She needs air!"

The villagers only saw an eager husband swooping his wife up in an embrace. When Thomasina grasped at Rafferty's collar the villagers cheered more loudly than before.

The sound buzzed in the doctor's head until his skull seemed to be filled with angry hornets. A light sweat broke out upon his brow. Oh, no! he thought. Not now! But the buzzing continued long after the shouts and laughter ceased, and there was a hollow throbbing at the back of his head that promised to turn vicious soon. He had to get back to the surgery and dose himself with Langanberg's Elixer before the attack came on.

Suddenly Thomasina was taken from him and he was lifted off his feet. Rafferty found himself carried around the square three times, riding high on the shoulders of the men. He looked around worriedly for his "bride" and saw that Thomasina was being carried along also, seated on a cushion someone had placed on a board. It was a relief to know that she had recovered from her choking fit and a greater one to see that she was being taken in the direction of the surgery.

Rafferty prayed he'd get there quickly. Every jounce and jostle aggravated the pounding pain in his head. The sweat stood out on his forehead now in huge drops. As the men set him down, he blotted his face with his handkerchief. The buzzing in his ears increased as the happy villagers poured down the road toward the surgery, sweeping him along with them.

Rafferty was increasingly dizzy. *Concentrate!* Right foot, left foot, right foot. Oops. He had bumped into the corner of the cantina, stubbing his toe. Hands were ready to support him amid the laughter. Dusk was settling rapidly.

When they reached the surgery, Rafferty's fever was coming on more strongly. Every beat of his heart was like the throb of a kettledrum inside his head, and he was alternately suffused with heat or shaken with cold. Just a few more seconds. He only had to hold on a few more seconds. By the time the procession reached the surgery yard, his grin had turned to a rictus of desperation. Dammit, if only he could keep from collapsing too soon!

Suddenly Rafferty found himself inside the surgery, weaving slightly. Thomasina came through next, propelled by laughing women, and the door was slammed shut behind them.

"Bolt the door," Rafferty ordered hoarsely. "Quickly."

She gaped at him. "Surely they mean us no harm."

He didn't want to waste time explaining. "Never mind, I'll do it."

He stumbled toward the door and slid the long piece of wood across its frame, then fumbled about, closing all the shutters. The crowd outside roared its approval. Thomasina watched him in amazement. Soon the place was dark as a cave.

Rafferty knew every inch of his surgery by heart. He made for the lamp, muttering beneath his breath when he barked his shins on a wooden crate where there should have been nothing but empty floor. Fortunately, the matches and striker were where they had always been kept. He scratched the match and the bright flare dimmed to a small flame at the end of the wooden stick. Although his fingers were beginning to shake, he got the wick lighted almost immediately. The darkness fled to the distant corners of the room.

Just in time. Where Rafferty had felt warm before, he now felt cold. The chill began stealing up from his toes and down from the crown of his head simultaneously. He began to shake so hard, his teeth rattled.

Thomasina hurried to his side. As her hand touched the sleeve of his shirt, she felt the heat pouring from his body. He was burning up with fever.

"You're ill! You should have told me at once. Come. Lie down on your bed and I'll attend to you."

Rafferty resisted. Despite the ague shaking through him, he was incredibly strong. "N-n-no...I n-need s-s-ome L-Lang-g-g-an-berg's..."

"Langanberg's Elixer. I'll get it at once." Thomasina hustled him into the bedroom. "And a little of Greene's Smartweed Compound, mixed with a bit of pleurisy root, is said to be most efficacious."

Rafferty's reply was a groan. He fell onto the bed. She pulled off his boots and piled the blankets on him. He was warm and his skin lacked the marble pallor and cool touch she'd read about in her books. Not fulminant malaria then. The sick feeling in her stomach lessened. "Have you ever had this before? When did it begin?"

"S-s-stop...p-playing...d-doctor..." He pushed the covers off again. "I'll...b-be...better...s-s-soon. I have t-to...g-get up...."

"No, you don't."

He tried anyway, and she pushed him back, firmly. She was frightened by his fever and the suddenness with which it had struck. Thomasina took refuge in putting his condition into medical terms. "My diagnosis, Dr. Rafferty, is that you have a touch of periodic fever aggravated by insufficient sleep. A little medicine and some bedrest will have you as good as new."

He opened his eyes and stared at her. "N-not b-bad. It's...m-monkey f-fever. G-Got it in Af-frica. N-not as s-s-serious..."

Thomasina remembered reading of monkey fever but couldn't recall enough to know if Rafferty was telling the truth. He certainly looked bad. Her heart turned to a lump of ice. Once he was settled, she mixed the medicine and urged a dose past his chattering teeth.

She also gave him an infusion of Peruvian bark and tortoiseshell plant, which was recommended for miasmal fevers in her favorite tome. Hecker's remedies were said to be the best. After thinking it over, she poured the medicine into a stiff shot of the Irish whiskey she had packed in her medicine trunk.

Within an hour, Rafferty's fever had lessened and he dropped into a restless slumber.

"It's all right," she told him softly. "I'm here." Rafferty shifted and smiled in his sleep. She took that as a good sign. Sleep was often the best medicine of all.

After her journey and the day's introduction to emergency surgery, Thomasina would have liked a little rest herself. Unfortunately, the people of San Juan were continuing to celebrate the nonexistent marriage. A guitar serenade had begun and was soon augmented by a chorus of mellow masculine voices. When they tired, other singers took up the slack. Soon, there were shouts of "Viva! Viva, El Doctore! Viva Señora Rafferty."

Thomasina realized they were having a sort of chivaree to honor the "newlyweds." The entire situation was so embarrassing she didn't know how she'd have been able to face Rafferty if the fever hadn't come on him so suddenly. While she regretted the brashness that had sent her pelting to San Juan without first discovering more of the physical situation, she still didn't regret her decision to come here.

A good thing, too, she thought, for it appears that I've burned my bridges behind me.

The chivaree went on and on, but Rafferty slept deeply for more than two hours. With his cheeks roughened with more than a day's beard growth and his hair in tousled curls, he reminded Thomasina of a big, rumpled stuffed bear. She had brought her own with her. The toy had been a gift from some unremembered soul amid her childhood wandering, a creature with jointed limbs and rootbeer eyes and half the fur loved off its fuzzy little face. As she watched the rise and fall of Rafferty's wide chest, she pushed a lock back from his wide forehead and began to appreciate the resemblance even more.

But the moment he awakened, Rafferty turned from teddy bear into the king of the veldt. He yawned like a lion, shook back his dark mane of hair and pawed the sheets away. "By Gad, the Langanberg's Elixer has worked like a charm. The cursed fever is almost licked," he announced as he attempted to sit up.

Thomasina was able to keep him down simply by placing her palm on his forehead. "Just slightly warm," she announced. "How do you feel otherwise?"

The doctor winced at a particularly loud shout from outside. "I'd feel like a king if I could just get a few hours of uninterrupted sleep."

"You've been snoring so hard for the past two hours that you almost drowned out their noise."

"Balderdash. I wasn't asleep for a second." He glared at her. "And I never snore."

"How do you know that, if you're asleep at the time?"

Her calm logic wasn't appreciated. Rafferty put the pillow over his head to shut out the din. It was no use. The good people of San Juan were making enough noise to wake the dead for the Last Judgment. Thomasina covered her ears, too.

The chivaree continued into the wee hours of the night: singing, shouting and shooting. The sounds of hoofbeats and *guitaros* were interspersed with the beating of small, hand-held drums.

Rafferty had insisted on getting up the moment he felt better. He paced the surgery floor from one end to the other and then back again, until Thomasina wanted to scream. "It isn't my fault they think I'm your wife," she said for the fifth time in a minute.

Rafferty answered for the first. "You should have told Domingo your correct name immediately. He's the one who has spread the 'happy news' about the countryside."

"Then the mistake is Domingo's, not mine."

Rafferty turned on her, his blue eyes glowing in the warm light of the lantern. "What else could he think, when you traveled here unchaperoned, carrying enough baggage to set up housekeeping in the wilds of Antarctica?"

Her cheeks reddened. "I brought nothing but essentials."

"Like shortbread, I presume."

It was a severe struggle to keep from retorting in kind. Thomasina lost. "You seemed to enjoy it. There wasn't a crumb left for a mouse when you'd finished. I'm only thankful it was shortbread and not the Kilimore Whiskey stores."

Her retort had the desired effect, but for the wrong reasons. Rafferty was not a drinking man, but the name of Kilimore Whiskey called up memories of peaty warmth that flowed down a man's throat like nectar, of his grandfather sitting by the fire with Gavin Sloane, the gnarled storyteller, their voices spinning the old heroic tales that had been passed orally from one generation to the next since the English conquerers had banned written Gaelic and forbidden speaking of the ancient language. So much lost and gone.

Thomasina watched Rafferty's face soften, then harden again into stern lines. She wondered what complexities lay beneath his brusque mannerisms. There had been tenderness in his face, and great sorrow. Both vanished in a blinking.

Rafferty waved a hand at the china dishes on the table and the boxes stacked along the walls. "Furthermore, you cannot blame Domingo for jumping to conclusions when you arrive with an excess of baggage amounting to a bride's trousseau. Why the dev—er, why on earth you thought you needed so much in the way of clothing and creature comforts is beyond me."

Thomasina gave the doctor a look that would have shriveled a lesser man. She began throwing up the lids of the trunks she'd unlocked earlier. They were filled with marked boxes and oilskin-wrapped packets. She rummaged through the layers and selected one. Inside, nested in cotton wool, was a curious contraption of metal ribs and wire mesh. Freeing it from the packing, she clamped it over her face. It covered her from the dimple in her chin to her eyebrows. She glared at the doctor through the mesh and metal, feeling like a monkey peering out through the bars of a zoo cage.

"Is this dainty item part of what you consider a fitting trousseau, Dr. Rafferty?"

"By Gad, is that a Schumhoffer-Braus chloroform mask?" Scorning fever and throbbing headache, he was across the room in a few great bounds. He took the wire mask from her and turned it over and over.

"Excellent! Yes, I see what a vast improvement this is over previous models. Look at that beautiful workmanship!" His face filled with eagerness. "What other wonders have you brought?"

Thomasina could have laughed aloud. The man who would have fallen asleep on his feet except for the noisy chivaree was suddenly wide awake. His enthusiasm transformed him, lighting his craggy features from within.

"Here. Perhaps these will interest you, as well."

She opened another box and was rewarded with his excited response. "By Jove, it's a veritable treasure trove you've brought."

Thomasina grinned in satisfaction. The way to most men's hearts might be through their stomachs, as the old adage had it, but the route to Rafferty's was quite different. From his enthusiastic reaction, the physician was more likely to respond to an Emery clamp or a bone saw, than to Veal Napoleon and poached pears in cream. A tiny smile of satisfaction played about the corners of Thomasina's mouth. Despite the passage of two years and their brief acquaintanceship, she had read Dr. Brendan Rafferty like the proverbial book.

Her self-congratulations didn't last long. The doctor set down the chloroform mask and rubbed his chin. Something didn't add up. "Tell me, Miss Wentworth, where does your mother come into all this?"

"My mother? She doesn't." Thomasina felt her face reddening. She suddenly felt like a guilty schoolgirl.

Rafferty leapt on her hesitation with the eagerness of a trout to a fly. "You can't convince me that your mother approved of you setting out alone for the remote fastness of a Mexican village."

"That is neither here nor there. I am of age and have independent means."

She thought gratefully of Cousin Agatha, whose legacy to her had financed the trip. Agatha, for all her twittery ways, had believed in her young cousin's dream. Her support and encouragement had helped Thomasina to come so close to achieving it.

Rafferty watched the emotions flicker over Thomasina's face. He knew she was hiding something. Before he could probe further, his train of thought was derailed by a volley of shots. The ruckus outside grew even more alarming.

Thomasina jumped a foot when the zing of a wildly-fired bullet clipped the corner of the house. Adobe chips spattered down the louvered shutters with the sound of falling hail. She clamped her hands over her ears. "I can't stand another minute of this caterwauling. When are they going to stop?"

"When they drop in their tracks! Or when I get out my shotgun and take a few potshots back at those sons of—" Rafferty bit off his words. The men raising the hullabaloo were his friends and neighbors. "You brought this on yourself, Miss Wentworth. They are only celebrating the happy—and fictitious—event of our marriage."

The din worsened. Thomasina winced. "I suppose this is some old Mexican tradition which must be honored at all costs."

Rafferty scowled. "I don't know. This is the first time I've taken a wife in San Juan and—"

The sound of breaking crockery stopped him. The cries of merriment took on an argumentative tone. Rafferty muttered an oath. "If they don't go home to their beds soon, there's liable to be trouble."

It sounded to Thomasina as if something—or someone—was trying to climb onto the roof. She was exhausted. Her eyes felt as if they were filled with hot sand, and she could no longer distinguish the beat of the drums from the incessant pounding in her head. She swayed in her chair, willing herself to remain erect, and wondered how close to dawn it was getting to be.

Her exhaustion wasn't missed by Rafferty. Although he was used to long hours and little sleep, he was feeling the effects of the long day's events and his energy-sapping fever. It sounded as though a herd of cattle were stamping on the roof. Dust rained down from above the vigas, and the bottles rattled wildly in the medicine cupboard. Noise was one thing; the potential for damage to his surgery was another. Rafferty brought his fist down on the desktop so hard, his heavy brass ink stand clattered.

"By Gad, that is enough!"

He shrugged out of his jacket. "There's only one way to stop them."

As she watched in astonishment, he stripped off his shirt and ran his long fingers through his shock of hair until it looked as though it had been combed with a rake.

She hurried toward him. "You're not going out there!"

Rafferty blocked her way. Suddenly Thomasina was incredibly aware of him: the heat from his body, the way the light glinted on the crisp hair that matted his chest and the strength and power in his tall frame. She couldn't help staring. "Stand aside, Miss Wentworth."

She did as he said, expecting him to go to the door. Instead, Rafferty unshuttered the window and leaned his upper torso out. His appearance was greeted by resounding cheers and catcalls. When they ended, Rafferty called out to the men in rapid Spanish. His voice sounded amiable, if a bit weary. The response was a burst of raucous laughter. Rafferty answered and waved. The next thing Thomasina heard was the sound of hoofbeats fading away toward the village proper. It was like magic.

Rafferty closed the shutters and latched them firmly. In the newfound silence, the tiny click of the latch was clear and final. There was a satisfied expression on his face when the doctor turned away from the window. "They won't be back."

He went into his private chamber, then returned with a couple of blankets. "I'll sleep out here for what's left of the night. You can take the bed."

Thomasina was still amazed at the way he'd dismissed the revelers. "What on earth did you say to them? And why didn't you say it sooner?"

"To spare your blushes, that is perhaps better left unexplained."

She glared. "I am not a child. If it concerns me in any way, I have a right to know."

Rafferty rubbed his eyes. The tiredness he'd been holding at bay came crashing down. It made him indiscreet. "Very well. I merely announced that if they expected a man to keep at peak performance all night long, they'd have to stop ruining his concentration."

It took a moment for his meaning to sink in. Thomasina was speechless. Rafferty barked out a hoarse laugh. "If you didn't want to know, you shouldn't have asked. And, as you pointed out, it was quite effective."

Thomasina was torn between embarrassment and fury. She turned on her heel and went into the other chamber, slamming the door behind her.

Rafferty threw a thick blanket down onto the floor and stretched out upon it, congratulating himself. He had managed to silence both the raucous villagers and Miss Wentworth at the same time. He felt rather proud of himself. They'd still be able to catch a few hours of sound sleep before dawn. And in the morning, he'd see about getting his unwanted guest on her way home.

Much as he sympathized with her desire to become a physician, the surgery of a bachelor in a village of devout Mexicans was not the place for her to learn the profession. And if Don Valverde learned that he'd spent the night, however innocently, with an unmarried young lady, Miss Wentworth might not be the only one sent packing. Don Carlos had influence in high places.

Rafferty sighed and rolled over. He knew that Thomasina would not take his decision well. Perhaps his old friend, Roscoe Sparrow of Boston, would be able to take her on at his school. Of course, Miss

Wentworth would be barred from the anatomy classes and some of the lectures, and she would have to find accommodations nearby instead of living on the school premises like the young men did but Rafferty was sure she could cope. She was quite a remarkable woman. Yes, he'd write her up a very fine letter of recommendation. It was the least he could do. Having made up his mind, he bundled up his shirt for a pillow, and fell almost immediately into a deep and untroubled sleep.

An hour later, he awakened from that sound slumber with the horrible knowledge that he'd been hoist with his own petard. By his own words, he had made it impossible to tell the truth now. The young woman who'd spent the past two nights under the roof of El Doctore was either his wife, in which case everything was fine, or a common doxy whom he had smuggled into the village—in which case, everything was most definitely *not* fine.

God knew if only she were a man, there would be no problem. Rafferty spent a good half hour examining the situation from all angles. It was unfortunate that his brain was still muddled by the fever, but after much consideration, he was inspired by a burst of genius. Miss Wentworth was determined to be a doctor. The road for females in medicine was uphill and rugged. Roscoe Sparrow might decline to take on so controversial a pupil. In that case, it might be years before she found someone willing to take her on and share the knowledge gleaned from books, lectures and years of hard-won experience. Rafferty, on the other hand, needed an assistant desperately in order to provide the appropriate level of care that the people of San Juan and its environs required.

The young Mendoza boy was going to need ongoing treatment and Consuela Chavez was due to deliver twins soon. In addition the outbreak of summer fever would begin to take its grim toll in the next month. Rafferty hoped to travel to the more isolated populations in the hills to begin a course of inoculations. All in all, there was enough work for a dozen trained hands and minds.

He rubbed his eyes. For some reason, his previous assistants had failed to see the charm of village life. They had pined, instead, for the evils of modern civilization, which he himself had gladly left behind.

Miss Wentworth, however—for all her soft exterior—appeared to be made of sterner stuff. She was blessed with a lively intelligence, a quick mind and a warm heart. She had steady hands, a willingness to learn and the dedication to succeed. It was a damned shame that she had been born female!

A nightbird called outside the shuttered window and a small creature scurried for the shelter of its burrow. Rafferty was too engrossed to notice. An idea was taking form in his mind. He rolled it around in his head, examining it from all sides. Domingo's mistake, compounded by his own actions earlier, might be a blessing in disguise. It would keep Miss Wentworth's reputation intact and help him, too.

Yes. It could work out well. Rafferty was very pleased with the solution he'd arrived at. All in all, it would be much easier on everyone if Miss Thomasina Wentworth *was* his wife.

With the matter settled in his own mind, Rafferty rolled over on his side and went back to sleep.

"Are you out of your mind?" Thomasina set down her coffee cup so hard, its contents sloshed into the saucer.

"You don't have to sound quite so revolted," Rafferty snapped. The fever wasn't entirely gone, but he felt ready to tackle the world—and more than a little testy. "I'm not proposing that we share a bed—or anything else but the medical work here. But I won't allow your impulsive and foolhardy arrival to spoil everything I've worked for over the last eight years. The entire village thinks you are Señora Rafferty. And, by Gad, if you intend to stay on and work in San Juan, you will answer to the name of Señora Rafferty from this moment forward!"

Thomasina's face settled in outraged lines. "It's no wonder your previous assistants packed their bags and fled! You're mad as a hatter."

Rafferty realized that harsh words would only get her back up. He softened his tone—as much as any Rafferty had ever been able to do. "Think it over, Miss Wentworth. It is the only true solution. I need help, and you want to become a physician. I'm only pointing out that a marriage in name only is the one workable way out of this impasse. And when you are qualified, if you choose, you can return to the States without hindrance."

Thomasina rose, almost knocking over her wooden chair. "A rather drastic solution, you must agree. I don't understand why *I* should have to suffer for Domingo's mistake.''

Rafferty's intense frown changed to a scowl. *Suffer?* "May I point out, Miss Wentworth, that I will find myself in an equally untenable position. I have no more desire for the wedded state, real or counterfeit, than you do.''

Without replying, Thomasina began pacing the floor as the doctor had done the night before. As she understood the matter, there were two choices open to her. She could admit defeat, slink back to San Francisco with her tail between her legs and begin crocheting antimacassars—or she could grit her teeth and make the best of an exceedingly awkward situation.

In accepting the position of Rafferty's assistant, she had signed an agreement to work as his probationer for one year. After that, if she were deemed suitable by Rafferty, he had contracted to train her rigorously for a period of two years, until she could be considered a physician in her own right. Back in San Francisco, it had seem marvelous: three years, doing what she loved best, three years of making her most cherished dream come true. At the moment, three years sounded like a lifetime.

She glanced warily over at Rafferty. His dark eyebrows were pulled together in a straight line, his jaw squared and his firm mouth set in intractable lines. He had a lion's roar and a fiend's own temper. But she had seen his hands at work, sure and gentle and greatly skilled. And in them, he held the key to her future. She could learn a great deal working at his side.

She continued pacing until the wall loomed an inch before her nose. Thomasina turned and went back the other way. The soft tap of her boots was the only sound in the room. Her pulse had quickened. Could she live here in San Juan with Dr. Rafferty for three years and keep up the pretense of wedded bliss? A shiver danced along her spine. Surely there was nothing to fear from him, yet she felt a definite edge of danger. Thomasina stopped abruptly.

"What arrangements would you make for slee—for privacy?"

"I'd planned to add on to the building next year when—" He stopped. "I suppose I'll have to change my plans to accommodate your arrival."

Thomasina knew that the trick she'd played on the doctor was going to cost him no end of inconvenience. Although she was the one in the wrong, his attitude still made her hackles rise.

"It seems that I'm going to cause you a good deal of trouble, Dr. Rafferty. Perhaps you'd find it simpler to just marry me and be done with it."

Her sarcasm fell flat. Rafferty glared. "You may get that idea out of your head at once, Miss Wentworth. I am the last man in the world that someone like you should ever marry—and even though you may be willing to enter such a loveless contract, I would not."

Thomasina felt a rush of heat to her face and knew she was more splotched with red than a pomegranate. "I spoke in jest. If you'll recall, I have already told you that I have no intention of *ever* marrying."

"Good. Then I won't have to go to the trouble of breaking in another assistant."

Rafferty felt a paradoxical sense of relief. If he had known the true identity of the Thom. Valnoy who had answered his advertisement, he would never have answered the letter. And in that case, he wouldn't be in the pickle he was in now. But her arrival had made him aware of his isolation and loneliness. It would be good to have someone to discuss his medical cases with, and it would be interesting to have a face—a very pretty face—across the table from him at breakfast and supper.

He leaned against the side of the instrument cupboard. "If you choose to stay on, Miss Wentworth, you may have my chamber. I'll make do with some blankets on the surgery floor until something better can be worked out."

Thomasina flushed. "I would feel guilty throwing you out of your bed, Dr. Rafferty."

He rose, unfolding his long body and moved toward her. "What are you suggesting, Miss Wentworth?" Rafferty's eyes held a strange, amber light. "That we share the bed?"

Thomasina's heart thudded in her chest, and she felt another wave of hot color rush up to her face. She fought the urge to step back, away from the doctor and his burning gaze. Away from the danger. It was difficult to think with him so close, watching so intently while her hopes and dreams hung in the balance. Thomasina knew she was being tested. He was trying to frighten her.

She wouldn't let him know that he had.

"Nothing so ridiculous," she replied levelly. "Remember, this is to be a partnership, not a real marriage. I'm sure Domingo can fashion some kind of platform to serve as sofa by day and a bed for you by night. I shall be more than glad to sew a mattress and pillows for it. In my spare time.''

Rafferty stared her down. She didn't blink. A long moment passed before he smiled. She had passed the test. ''Very good, Miss Wentworth. You'll do.''

Thomasina took a deep breath. Her palms were damp. ''Then I suggest you stop calling me Miss Wentworth.''

He laughed. A deep rumbling sound that seemed to start at his toes and roll upward. Before she could re-act, he took her hand in his warm clasp and raised it to his lips. ''Whatever you say, *my dearest wife.*''

She would have snatched her hand away except that Domingo entered at that exact moment. He stopped on the threshold, grinned like a jack-o'-lantern, and bobbed his grizzled head. ''Ah, Señora Rafferty, it is an excellent thing that you have come to San Juan to take care of El Doctore!''

Rafferty released her hand and asked Domingo a question. Thomasina didn't even hear it. She was stunned to immobility. If she looked at her hand, she was sure she'd see the warm imprint of Rafferty's mouth branded on her skin. It was very unnerving—but perhaps that was what the doctor had intended. She was almost sure that he had seen Domingo from the corner of his eye before he took her hand and kissed it.

Her mouth turned up wryly. It would be just like Rafferty to test her ability to keep up the pretense by practicing in front of Domingo. In her first forty-eight hours in San Juan, she had already had a few glimmers of the doctor's reckless sense of humor, and she was sure that this was just another example of it.

But she would feel a bit less ruffled if she could be absolutely certain.

Chapter Seven

Rafferty flung his saddlebags over Lugh's golden back. "Did you pack that chloroform mask and the Rickles blade?"

"I put them in my kit." Thomasina bit her lower lip, thinking of Geraldo Zavala. So young! "Do you really think you might have to—" she paused, unable to say the word or contemplate the thought "—to do something drastic?"

"Let us pray that it won't be necessary."

Thomasina had done so frequently during the restless hours of the night. Domingo led out her mare and Rafferty helped her up into the saddle. She was reminded again of the great strength in him, and the gentleness, as well. Then he mounted, and they rode out of the yard in the still morning air. Lugh was frisky, and Thomasina's mare picked up the gelding's high spirits as they trotted briskly down the dirt road. Even Rafferty looked fresh as a new starched shirt, but Thomasina felt rumpled around the edges. She supposed she'd get used to the irregular routine after a few days.

A bird with gay plumage rose in flight, greeting them with a cheerful melody. "And good day to you," Rafferty called out to it. He began to sing an old air in his rich baritone while Thomasina listened and fumed.

"When I was single I wore a fine shawl,
but now that I'm married I've nothing at all,
but still I love him, I can't deny him,
and I'll go with him, wherever he goes . . ."

Thomasina frowned at the doctor when the poignant chorus ended. "You are deliberately trying to annoy me."

Rafferty's expression was guileless. "Why, no. That song was always a particular favorite of my mother's."

Thomasina tucked a strand of hair back behind her ear. It was going to be a hot day. The sky already shimmered like molten silver overhead, except along the distant horizon, where it was bluer than a cornflower. Blue as the sapphire signet ring that Rafferty had taken from his own brown hand and slipped on her finger that morning.

"Until I can find something more suitable," he had told her.

The ring was so large, she was afraid of losing it. The waxed cord she'd wound around it felt odd when it touched her palm. It was a constant reminder of their agreement. *Mrs. Brendan Rafferty.* She said the name over and over in her mind, trying to become accustomed to the sound of it. One slip, and she'd ruin everything.

It all seemed unreal to Thomasina, as if she were caught up in a dream state as illusory as the peaks of Los Tres Hermanos, which seemed to float disembodied in the sky. The rest of the mountain was almost invisible, mere layers of translucent smoke lost in the dazzle of sunshine.

Rafferty noted her interest. "According to local legend, there were three brothers who offended a powerful sorceress. She turned them into stone. The highest peak is the 'older brother,' the two lower ones his younger twin brothers. They are said to shake off the spell every hundred years and come to life. According to Domingo the hundred years was up a decade ago, but the brothers' didn't even do so much as yawn."

"Knowing Domingo, I imagine he's quite disappointed."

"Not at all. At his birth, the *curanderia* predicted that he would live to see the brothers awaken again. That's why he thinks he's more or less immortal. And, truth to tell, he's taken some injuries that would have killed many a younger and stronger man."

They turned along the river road, and the great peaks were lost to view. As they rode on, Rafferty grilled Thomasina on the several things they might expect to find when they examined their patient, and on what the proper treatment would be for each. He was a good teacher, she discovered, urging her to use her book knowledge and sense of reasoning instead of spoon-feeding her the answers. Before she knew it they were on the approach to the Zavala place.

Slowing his horse to a walk, Rafferty leaned toward Thomasina. "Remember, say nothing if at all possible. Geraldo knows a good deal of English." His eyes held hers sternly. "And if anyone asks, you are Mrs. Brendan Rafferty." Thomasina nodded but didn't reply.

They found their patient was doing as well as could be expected. Young Geraldo lay awake, but in great pain. While Señora Zavala hovered anxiously, Rafferty and Thomasina changed the dressing. They were greatly relieved to note there was no sign of infection.

"You were born under a lucky star. It will heal well," Rafferty assured the young man and his mother. Geraldo closed his eyes and murmured a prayer. He clutched at the doctor's wrist, murmuring *"Gracias!"* over and over when he realized he was in no danger of losing his leg.

"You are a fortunate young man," Rafferty told him in Spanish. "Don Carlos's bull is the most ferocious beast in all creation."

Geraldo's face clouded. "I do not know how the bull got loose. It was safe in the enclosure when I went past. Then it was upon me. I had no chance at all."

Thomasina was frustrated by not understanding the language, but her powers of observation were keen. Rafferty had been trying to draw information from Geraldo. As the doctor listened to the young man's responses his face had taken on a grave and thoughtful expression.

Later, on the ride back, Thomasina questioned Rafferty about it without success. "Don't meddle with the locals until you know your way around their customs and language. Things are different here.''

''I'll expect you to be my guide until I learn more of the language.''

''You have a few other things to learn. Twice, while we were with the Zavalas, you addressed me as Dr. Rafferty. Dammit all, that's not the way a wife would address her husband.''

Thomasina affected a demure expression. ''They will merely think I was being respectful.''

''Hah! Wait until they know you better.'' He turned in the saddle. ''What the devil am I supposed to call you?''

She stared back stonily. ''You needn't try to distract me with questions and oaths. My given name, as you know quite well, is Thomasina. And I still want to know what your conversation with Geraldo Zavala was all about.''

He shrugged. ''My dear Miss...er...'' His face grew redder. ''*Thomasina*. Fix your attention on learning what I have to teach you and we'll all be the happier for it.''

She said no more about the matter, but there was a mystery, and she was determined to get to the bottom of it. Domingo would tell her. He claimed to know everything that happened in the village and the surrounding countryside, and he seemed eager to pass on whatever he learned.

Rafferty's thoughts were on the old man, too. It still rankled him that Domingo had led him to believe he neither spoke nor understood English. He wondered what indiscreet things he might have done or said over the years and whether Domingo had repeated any of it to others. It was highly likely. Domingo seemed to think of himself as a sort of town crier. Perhaps, the doctor mused, that was why he had attached himself to the surgery, where something dramatic was usually happening.

As they skirted a grove of trees, Thomasina suddenly reined in. Another green valley fell away to the left of her, hidden previously by the arching willows. Wide, cultivated fields filled the lower end. Squinting against the sun, she thought she was seeing a mirage—a Moorish castle made of glazed tile rose behind massive adobe walls. Pillared porticos, arched windows and towers added to the incredible sight.

"It seems you have a wealthy neighbor, Dr. Rafferty."

"Don Carlos Valverde." He spit the name out as if it were poison. "He owns the entire valley. If he had his way, he'd own everything, including the people's souls."

His vehemence surprised Thomasina. "You dislike him."

"I loathe and detest the man. He is everything I abhor. However, I'm in no position to judge another man's soul. You're quite free to form your own opinion."

Another mystery. "I am, Dr. Rafferty. And I shall."

She was glad to see that she'd nettled him. He nudged his horse forward. "I was christened Brendan. My family... my friends call me Bren."

Bren, indeed. Thomasina pretended she hadn't noticed that peculiar pause in his speech. Another mystery. There was more to occupy her in San Juan than learning diagnosis and treatment. The breeze fanned her pink cheeks, and a ripple of excitement ran through her. She did love a challenge!

Rafferty saw the way Thomasina's face lit with inner radiance. A proper young female of her station in life wouldn't show such enthusiasm for what was, after all, a demanding and rather primitive way of life. Evidently, Miss Wentworth hadn't learned the rules. He liked her all the better for it. In his experience, determination got more done than all the goodwill in the world. Determination was one of the qualities he'd been castigated for in the past—some people called it obstinate bullheadedness—but it was a trait that he admired, and Miss Wentworth had an abundance of it.

There was a lot to be admired in his new assistant, including her splendid figure. But that, he reminded himself hastily, was something he must do his best to forget. In his eyes, she would be just another doctor in training, like Henry Appleby or Jebediah Grundy. Rafferty's hands tightened on the reins. She would have to be, especially if they planned to carry out their little charade successfully.

In the few days since her arrival, he hadn't had time to weigh the changes in Thomasina since their first meeting or to guess at what had caused them. That air of confidence—was it as genuine as it seemed? The previous day, when the men had swept down from the hills, he had seen something cross her face that was more than normal surprise or panic. The incident had frozen her to stone. Then she had raised her riding crop and fought like a lioness.

Rafferty puzzled over it for a mile or two, but came up with no clear-cut picture of his new assistant. Miss Thomasina Wentworth...er, Thomasina *Rafferty*—Gad, that would take some getting used to!—was a very complex young woman.

They reached the outskirts of San Juan, each caught up in private thoughts.

The news that the villagers thought Thomasina was Rafferty's wife had disturbed her more than she had let him suspect. On the one hand, it would make her life much easier. A single woman making her way alone in the world was liable to meet with obstacles and insult. Women trying to become doctors, diagnosing and treating bodily ills, were looked upon as odd, unfeminine and, perhaps, of easy morals. As a married woman, she would be under her husband's protection, safe from gossip and any unwanted attentions. The villagers' misunderstanding had also paved the way for her initial acceptance by the people.

On the other hand, the prospect of posing as Rafferty's wife and carrying it off for the three years of their contract filled her with severe misgivings. She wasn't put off by his sharp tongue or gruff ways. In fact, she preferred his blunt-but-honest approach over mealymouthed platitudes. His shouting and arm waving didn't intimidate her, either. But although they would be working side by side, Rafferty would be her superior as well as her teacher. He would also be her principal, perhaps her only, companion. They were two people of the same culture and background, bound by common goals and interests, who would be thrown together day after day. It was an alarming situation, at best. The potential for disaster was great. Without warning, Thomasina felt a tiny tendril of anxiety curl around her heart.

Then she glanced at Rafferty. The square jaw spoke of stubbornness and his slashing eyebrows warned of a volatile disposition. His eyes were keen and fierce, and his mouth firm, yet sensual. With a different character, he could have been arrogant and cruel. But Thomasina saw neither quality in him. Despite his sound and fury, Rafferty was a good man. He was a dedicated physician and surgeon, not a bogey man. She couldn't imagine him ever being like...like...

The memories rolled over her like a black wave, and she struggled to vanquish them. Her pulse drummed in her ears, and her breath was trapped in her lungs until she saw dark spots dancing before her eyes. Thomasina suddenly gave her mare its head. She didn't hear Rafferty's shout of surprise. Crouching low over the mare's neck, feeling the stretch of the horse's sleek muscle and bone and the wind tearing at her hair, she raced over the ground toward the safety of the surgery. Raced from the memories...

Rafferty watched her go galloping across the open plain with the wind. The pins came out and her hair fell free, streaming behind her like a river of red gold light. She and the mare were a breathtaking sight. A matched pair. Courage, stamina and beauty.

He pushed the last thought away as if it stung. It had come out of nowhere, jolting him to the core. If they were to work together without complications, he must think of her in the same way as he had his other assistants. A gloom descended over the doctor. He had great faith in the power of mind over matter, but even his strong will couldn't transform a lovely, glowing young woman into the skinny, speckled Dr. Pease or the red-faced Dr. Muchingham with his thin moustache.

Lugh pranced with eagerness to join in the race, but Rafferty reined him to a walk. "Let her go, old fellow. Sometimes, a woman just needs to be alone. Afterward, she'll feel all the better for it."

Thomasina didn't look to see if the doctor was gaining on her. She cleared her mind of thought and immersed herself in sensation: the heat of the sun on her cool skin; the paint-box blue of the sky; the scents on the clean breeze; the strong spring and thrust of Scheherazade's legs and the mare's joy in the wild run. Thomasina made herself a part of them all, submerging her own identity in them until she'd outstripped the fear. The memories . . .

She went over the rise and saw the surgery below, with the village of San Juan basking just beyond. The thin line of the river wound away to the left, fringed by leafy trees. The panic went out of her, leaving her drained and empty. As she rode up to the surgery, Thomasina hoped for a quick wash, a change of clothes and a cup of fragrant tea. Instead, she found a visitor.

A spirited mare was tethered to the post, Arabian blood showing in every elegant line. Domingo, accompanied by a small boy, was seeing to the horse's needs.

The owner of the lovely Arabian had not strayed far. She had been watching Thomasina from the archway that led to the small courtyard enclosed by the surgery's walls. She appeared to be about Thomasina's age and she was lovely, with a small, pointed face and hair like spun gold drawn into an elaborate knot at her nape. From the top of her head to her tiny feet, she was polished to perfection. Her riding habit was wonderfully tailored from a soft raspberry twill, and no finer bonnet could have been found in all of Paris or New York.

Thomasina was torn between curiosity and embarrassment at the spectacle she'd made of herself, pelting across the open ground like a wild woman. She was very aware of the odd appearance she must make, coated with dust and sweat with her hair flying loose. If the young woman had come to the surgery, there was trouble afoot and the services of a physician required. There was no time to waste.

Thomasina swung down from her mount as Domingo reached for the mare's bridle. "*Gracias,* Domingo. Dr. Rafferty is behind me by a few minutes time. I will attend to the problem."

The blond girl appeared in the archway once more and answered curtly in accented English. "I do not want you. I have come to see Dr. Rafferty."

Her rudeness incensed Thomasina. "Then you may safely discuss the matter with me. I am a physician in training to him."

The results were hardly gratifying. The girl stopped dead. "A woman! No. He would not be such a fool!"

Rafferty rode up, doffing his hat. "Unfortunately, I am that and more. *Buenas Tardes,* Señorita Valverde. I didn't know you'd returned to us. I trust there is nothing wrong at the hacienda?"

The *señorita*'s face lit up at the doctor's arrival, and she ran forward to greet him. All traces of impatience were wiped off her angelic features. "We are all well, thank you. I have come to extend an invitation to you. My father has guests and wishes to give a dinner party and a great fandango in their honor. It is for Wednesday next. Do say you'll come."

She had turned her back on Thomasina, excluding her from the invitation.

While Rafferty and the girl spoke, Domingo approached Thomasina. A boy of eight or nine hovered nearby. "I have prepared for some refreshments, *señora,* in the *placita.*"

"Thank you. That was very kind." Thomasina pushed her hair back from her heated forehead. "I'm afraid I gave Scheherazade a workout on the ride back."

Domingo bobbed his head. "The mare, she was anxious for a good gallop. Lorenzo—" he indicated the boy "—will rub her down well." He eyed his new mistress. "Perhaps you would like to wash after the long ride."

Thomasina was pleased. She was hot and sticky. And determined to show the pretty *señorita* that she could look just as presentable. She marched into the surgery and beyond to the bedroom. She selected a day dress of pale blue silk trimmed with navy ribbon. It was stylishly cut and perhaps a bit too elegant for the surroundings, but Thomasina didn't care. She was about to be formally introduced as Rafferty's wife and medical assistant, and was determined to make an impression.

The water was marvellously cool. Shedding her serviceable skirt and shirtwaist, Thomasina scrubbed until her skin was rosy. From time to time, the murmur of conversation came to her, muffled by the heavy shutters, which were closed against the heat.

She peeked through a chink in the unpainted wood. Señorita Valverde was perched on the best chair at the table beneath the trees. She sat stiffly, as if afraid the chair would ruin her expensive riding habit. Thomasina summed the newcomer up quickly as she plied a brush through her tangled curls. The visitor's golden tresses were woven into an artfully artless arrangement. Señorita Valverde was, Thomasina decided, a very calculating young woman. Each curl had been placed with precision and the expensive habit was cut to accentuate every feminine curve. There appeared to be little about her that was easy and spontaneous— everything from the movement of her hands to the way she looked up through her thick lashes had been thoroughly rehearsed.

Thomasina's mouth tightened. Señorita Valverde looked too perfect—like a wax-work doll.

Stripped to her camisole and knickers, her damp hair hanging down her back, Thomasina felt like an old burlap sack beside a swatch of gold brocade. Her knuckle was scraped, and her hands red from washing them with carbolic. The roil of emotions within her was completely unfamiliar. It's the heat, she told herself. The heat and the lack of sleep last night. It couldn't be jealousy. And Thomasina's arrangement with Rafferty was purely platonic.

Thomasina put on the dress and checked the spotted shaving mirror. Her image looked back solemnly. *Serviceable* was the word that came to mind. She shrugged it away. After all, she was a physician in training, not a fashion plate like *some* people. Nevertheless, she took her cameo set from her jewelry box. She centered the brooch at her neckline, put the wire loops of the eardrops in her lobes and, at the last minute, took out her white kid boots and exchanged them for the black ones she'd worn all day.

A tinkle of laughter caught her ear. Knotting her hair high upon her head, Thomasina peeked through the crack again. Rafferty was looking down at Señorita Valverde with a fatuous grin. It set Thomasina's teeth on edge. On impulse she unlatched the shutters. They swung open noiselessly on gold leather hinges.

It was a cozy little scene. Domingo had set out cool drinks in the footed glasses that Thomasina had brought from San Francisco, and he had served a plate of the buttery shortbread.

"My brother is glad that I have come to practice my English upon you." Señorita Valverde took a piece of shortbread and nibbled it daintily.

Rafferty downed his glass of cold water at a gulp. "Practice all you like, Margarita. However, I fear I have no interesting conversation to offer you. I was away in the hills for the past weeks, so my only news is of the people there."

"That will do. I am starved for conversation. It is so isolated out on the hacienda without anyone worth talking to for miles and miles." Margarita smiled. "Do you know, I haven't seen a new face all year, except for that poor, sad creature who rode up just ahead of you, covered with dust. Who is she and what is she doing in San Juan?"

A strange look came over Rafferty's face. Thomasina guessed that he'd forgotten her existence until now.

Thomasina had always prided herself on being immune to the legendary temperament that was said to go with red hair. In that single heartbeat, she learned that she'd been wrong. Her temper flamed. She stood on the bed and leaned out of the window.

"Good afternoon. To answer your second query, as I told you, I am here to work with the good doctor as his assistant." Thomasina leaned out a little farther. "As to who I am, my name is Thomasina Rafferty—and I am *Brendan*'s wife."

Thomasina was surprised at how easily the lie came to her lips. She was more surprised when the golden-haired woman stared at her in horror. Then, without warning, Señorita Valverde fainted dead away.

Rafferty gave Thomasina a look that would have stopped a train in its tracks before he jumped up and went to the *señorita*'s aide. "Margarita!"

He bent over the stricken woman and chaffed her pale hands between his. Thomasina had seen enough. She ducked back into the bedchamber and hurried through the surgery and out to the *placita*.

The girl was stretched out in the shade of the olive tree, her head propped by the doctor's jacket.

Thomasina stooped down beside them. "What on earth caused her to faint like this?"

Rafferty gritted his teeth. "We'll discuss it later. Get your smelling salts."

"I am not in the habit of swooning. I have never owned a bottle of smelling salts in my life."

"Then get the hartshorn from the cabinet."

"No need. I'm sure that lady carries one on her person at all times."

Thomasina tugged on a thin gold chain attached to the woman's waist, pulling out a bottle of frosted crystal topped with a cabachon emerald. "This should bring her around in no time."

As she twisted off the cap the sharp, nose-prickling odor of ammonia wafted on the breeze. Rafferty was still trying to restore Señorita Valverde to consciousness. Looking closely, Thomasina swore there was a faint flicker of eyelid and a gleam of dark eye beneath it. She knelt beside the woman. Yes, the *señorita* had roused from her faint and was taking advantage of being the center of the doctor's attentions. Well, there was a quick way to cure that.

Thomasina waited until Margarita's chest rose on an intake of breath and then waved the smelling salts beneath the woman's dainty nose. The results were immediate. Margarita Valverde sniffed, coughed and grimaced. Gasping in another breath, she sat upright like a marionette whose strings had been jerked, her nostrils red and eyes watering. The look she gave Thomasina was one of pure venom.

Margarita shoved the vial of salts away so quickly the movement was only a blur. Then the same pale hand, which had pushed so hard, drifted up to the woman's white throat. Margarita moaned again and closed her eyes. Rafferty was concerned. "She's overcome by the sun," he announced. "I'll carry her inside."

The woman might look fragile as a broken lily, but Thomasina was sure that there was hard steel beneath her velvet petals. She watched the little charade with her mouth firmly closed. To be fair, she had to admit that the *señorita*'s initial faint was probably genuine. No woman with the smallest degree of vanity would have plopped so gracelessly headfirst into the shortbread.

Thomasina followed them into the house. She was in time to see a masterful demonstration of female technique as the doctor set Margarita Valverde down upon the wooden settle—the eyelids fluttering just so, the tremble of tapering fingers as they clutched at Rafferty's sun-browned hands, the arch of swanlike neck and high bosom as the *señorita* pretended to try to sit up. The actions had only one aim. They were perfectly calculated to raise every protective and chivalrous instinct in the male of the species. Brendan Rafferty, Thomasina saw through narrowed eyes, was not exempt.

She was gravely disappointed in him. For some reason, she had expected a man of his intelligence to be able to see through such an obvious piece of playacting. He wouldn't have stood such nonsense from *her* for a moment, Thomasina thought, fuming. Why, if she had put on such an affecting performance at Geraldo Zavala's bedside during the surgery, Rafferty would have ordered her from the house without so much as a backward glance. She swallowed around the lump in her throat. Men could be such fools.

The doctor rose and stalked over to Thomasina. "Look what you've done now. What in God's name made you blurt out a thing like that!"

Thomasina squared her chin and glared back at Rafferty. His fingers were digging into her arm. "Why, don't you remember? You gave me precise instructions only a short time ago. And you had better lower your voice at once or she'll hear you."

Before Rafferty could reply, Domingo entered. As usual, he seemed to know everything that was going on and had anticipated the doctor's wishes. "I have harnessed the gray to the wagon and put up the canvas top for the *señorita*. Do you wish me to tie her mare behind the wagon or to take it to the hacienda Valverde?"

Rafferty thought the question over. Thomasina recalled the bitterness in his voice when he'd spoken of Don Carlos Valverde earlier. She wondered if the fair Margarita was the reason for it. Finally, the doctor nodded. "Yes, take the mare back, if you please, Domingo, and tell them I will bring the *señorita* back in the wagon after she rests awhile. Her constitution is too tender for the midday heat."

Thomasina bridled. Not once on the ride home had Rafferty bothered to ask her how she was faring. "Perhaps if the lady dressed more for the climate than for the sake of fashion, she would not have succumbed. If you will both vacate the room, I shall loosen her stays—which are laced far too tightly."

A strange expression flickered over the doctor's mobile face. It almost looked like suppressed laughter. Then he was his usual self again, and Thomasina wondered if she'd imagined it. She turned away and advanced on the young woman, who sat up quickly, apparently cured.

"I—I feel much better," Margarita announced hastily, her dark eyes snapping with energy. "As you said, Dr. Rafferty, it was only the midday heat. I shouldn't have ventured out until later, but I was so eager to extend my invitation that I didn't stop to think. I am perfectly able to make the return trip in the wagon with you."

With pretty thanks, she accepted the cold mug of water Rafferty poured for her. She ignored Thomasina completely. "Do say you'll come to the dinner and the fandango, Bren—Dr. Rafferty. I think...I hope that General Vasquez will be there. It might work to your advantage."

"Thank you. I'll let you know tomorrow."

With a warning look to Thomasina, Rafferty escorted Margarita Valverde from the surgery and out to the waiting wagon. *Not now,* his eyes warned, and Thomasina held her peace. If the doctor was to be her mentor, companion and mock husband, she had to learn to trust him. Since he was normally outspoken to a fault, there had to be a good reason for his silence now.

Satisfied for the moment, she watched them ride away in the cumbersome supply wagon, Rafferty

holding the reins and the beautiful *señorita* perched
beside him like an exotic butterfly.

After cleaning up the refreshments, Thomasina
took down the chicken carcass that Domingo had
plucked and brought it inside. Since she had never
cooked a chicken, she decided that now was not the
time to learn. It didn't seem safe to leave fresh meat
out to spoil, so she filled a heavy pot with icy well water and immersed the chicken in it.

The heat and lack of sleep made her tired. Thomasina felt she'd earned a rest. Stretching out on the bed
with her well-thumbed copy of Browning's *Diseases of
the Tropics* for company, she found her eyes too weary
for reading. A section on African Fever caught her
attention, and she managed to stumble through it. It
was good to know that Rafferty's fever was unlikely
to return for several months, and that when it did, the
attack would be much milder.

Thomasina yawned. At the moment, she needed a
cure for sleepiness. Terms like "scrofulous lesions"
and "membranous erythema" blurred together hope-
lessly. She sighed, closed the book and set it on the side
table. A nap seemed the best treatment for what ailed
her. She drew the shutters closed against the bright
sun. Within minutes, she was fast in dreams.

Sometime later, she awoke, still hazy with sleep, and
realized she wasn't alone in the room. Footsteps too
heavy to be Domingo's and too stealthy to be Rafferty's, came toward the bed where she lay. One of the
boards squeaked. More footsteps and then something
sharp poked her in the ribs. Thomasina became fully
alert.

"Wake up, old friend," a low voice growled. "I have need of your skills."

"Who are you?" she challenged groggily.

The voice muttered a curse and then the man reached across her to open the shutters an inch. *"¡Caramba!"*

A callused palm clamped over her mouth, and she found herself staring into the startled eyes of a swarthy stranger. "Who are you?" he demanded.

"I believe that I asked first." Her words were muffled against his hand.

"Where is Brendan Rafferty?"

"Who wishes to know?" She sat up, pushing the hand away. "And why should I tell you in any case?"

As she swung her legs over the side of the bed, the man made no effort to stop her. Although the interior of the room was cool with its thick adobe walls, she saw that the intruder was sweating heavily.

"Are you ill?"

"Sí, señora. Sick to death of Don Carlos and his villainous lot! But it is his bullet, lodged in my shoulder, that has brought me here."

She stood up and came around the man, gently removing the serape thrown over his shoulder. The back of his cotton shirt was soaked with blood despite the makeshift bandage. He'd lost quite a bit of it and was in grave danger of losing more.

"Come into the surgery and I'll—"

The sound of pounding hoofbeats interrupted her. The man rolled his eyes. "Don Carlos and his men...you must hide me, I beg of you. They mean to kill me."

His terror was real. Thomasina made a split-second decision. "Under the bed. Quickly. And don't come out for anything, unless I tell you to."

She smoothed the blanket back and piled some of the garments from the wardrobe on top of it, as if she'd been unpacking. Outside, horses snorted and a man spoke. "See. There is blood by the side of the house. He has come this way."

There was no time to be lost. Thomasina hurried into the surgery. A large splotch of blood marred the clean surface of the floor. Picking up the pot with the chicken, she sloshed some water over the stain and dribbled more from the table to the door.

Not ten seconds later, a man came in with a pistol in his hand. "*¡Hola!* El Doctore?"

Still clutching the pot, Thomasina faced the newcomer squarely. "I *beg* your pardon!" she said icily. "I am *not* used to people brandishing guns in *my* presence. Kindly leave at once."

The man understood the tone if not the words. As he gaped at her, another fellow entered the surgery. He was taller by a head, with dark hair and eyes as black as sloe berries. Despite the difference in coloring, Thomasina could tell he was related to the beautiful Margarita Valverde. He carried himself with authority and a magnetic sort of arrogance. But when he saw Thomasina, he was momentarily startled out of his composure.

His recovery was quick. With a graceful gesture, he swept off his hat and made an elegant bow. "*Buenas Tardes, señorita.* We have come to speak with Dr. Rafferty."

Thomasina kept her spine straight and her chin up. "Then you have missed him by an hour and more. He has escorted Señorita Valverde back to the hacienda of Don Carlos." Her arm tightened around the pot holding the chicken. "I expect him back in time for his supper."

The black eyes held hers, weighing and testing, then followed the splashes of water across the floor. "You will forgive my ignorance, *señorita*. I am Don Carlos Valverde." Another seeping bow. "How is it that I have never made your acquaintance?"

"My arrival in San Juan is very recent." She offered no other explanation.

Don Carlos glanced around the room. "I do not wish to alarm you, but a bandit was seen in the vicinity. One of my men shot him, but he managed to escape. It would be well for you to remain close to the surgery until he is apprehended."

"Thank you. I shall take your advice."

A final bow, and Don Carlos left, taking his man with him. Thomasina returned to the table and set the pot down. Her hands were trembling badly. Knowing she could be seen from the doorway, she took a knife and began slicing onions with apparent unconcern. Fortunately, she only knicked one finger in the process.

She was worried about the wounded man hidden beneath the bed. If she went to him too soon, she might bring the wolf pack down on him. If she waited too long, he might bleed to death. After several minutes passed, she went outside to pick a few of the pink blossoms growing on the trailing vine. The task gave her a good reason to reach around and obtain a clear view of the road. A haze of dust told her the horsemen had gone on to the village.

With a bouquet of the fragrant flowers in her hands, she stepped back inside. Once over the threshold, she dumped the blossoms unceremoniously and hastened to the bedchamber. "It's safe. They've gone."

There was no reply. Thomasina feared the worst. Kneeling beside the bed, she lifted the blanket and peered under it. Except for the sticky spot where he'd lain, there was no sign of the injured stranger. She found a bloody handprint on the windowsill showing how he'd made his silent departure. She scrubbed it clean.

When Rafferty returned some time later, Thomasina was seated on the bench outside, calmly shelling peas. "Where is Domingo?" he asked, getting down from the wagon. His keen eyes had noted the hoofprints of many horses in the dust.

"I don't know. He hasn't returned." Thomasina carefully stripped a pod and tossed the shell onto the discard heap. "However, there were several visitors in your absence."

She'd only meant to tease Rafferty a bit by drawing out her announcement, but the tension in his body made her think again. It all came out in a rush. "Don Carlos came with several of his men, searching for a man who'd been shot. A bandit, they said."

Rafferty paled beneath his permanent tan. "Did they find him?"

"No. I hid him under the bed."

"Did you, by Gad! Well done! Where is he now? How serious is the injury?"

"It's likely to prove mortal without treatment, but the man left while I was diverting Don Carlos."

"Describe him to me."

Thomasina did, as succinctly as possible. Rafferty didn't wait to hear more. He strode to the stables and made a rapid search without results. "Dammit all," he said beneath his breath, "Pablo should have waited for me."

He ducked inside the surgery, then came out again with his coat, special saddlebags and a rifle. While Thomasina watched in astonishment, Domingo's young companion, Lorenzo, appeared from behind the building with the suddenness of a genie from a bottle. In the flick of an eyelash, he had Lugh saddled and awaiting his master. Rafferty thanked him and was on horseback immediately, wheeling the great golden beast around to the north.

"Where are you going?" Thomasina asked.

"I won't be back before morning," Rafferty told her. "The boy will remain with you until Domingo returns. Meanwhile, stay inside and keep the door barred. You'll come to no harm."

She watched Rafferty disappear over the ridge. "A fine way to begin a honeymoon," she muttered.

The boy shrugged. *"No comprende, señora."*

Thomasina held the door open and waved the boy through. "I don't suppose you know how to cook a chicken, do you?"

The boy's culinary skills turned out to be as sketchy as her own. Conversation proved difficult, due to the language barrier, but Thomasina made some progress with her halting attempts at speaking Spanish. The evening hours stretched out unbroken, except for the occasional crumble of wood in the fireplace and the sound of pages turning as she tried—in vain—to study a text. She kept seeing the blood on Pablo's shirt and the grim look on Rafferty's face.

Long after the meal of burnt peas and undercooked chicken was finished and the boy curled up before the hearth, Thomasina paced the floor, praying and waiting for Rafferty's return.

Chapter Eight

Domingo came back the next morning. Thomasina hurried to the door when she heard him whistling in the yard. "I was concerned when you didn't return from the hacienda, Domingo."

He looked surprised. "I had things to do, *señora*."

"I didn't know you'd be gone the entire night. Dr. Rafferty was called away."

"Lorenzo was here to see to you. He is a good boy." Domingo offered no other explanation for his disappearance, and Thomasina quickly learned there was no point in pressing him.

The passing hours weighed heavily on her hands. No one came to the surgery, which seemed odd to her since Rafferty had claimed there was so much work, he required an assistant to share the load. Frustrated, Thomasina tried to apply her mind to studying her tomes on tropical diseases and on child care, but she couldn't concentrate.

Needing something to do, she rode out to the Zavala place, accompanied by Lorenzo on his mule, to check on the progress of young Geraldo.

Thomasina felt strange conducting the examination without Rafferty present. Señora Zavala hovered in the background, clucking and fussing. She spoke sharply to her son in rapid Spanish whenever he protested. If the rest of San Juan was avoiding her, Thomasina thought, at least she was welcome in this household. As she peeled off the bandages, Geraldo winced suddenly. "I'm sorry," Thomasina said quickly. "I didn't mean to hurt you."

Geraldo replied in halting English. "The pain is less, *señora*. Do what you must."

"I'll try to be gentler."

She wrapped a fresh bandage the way she'd seen Rafferty do it, and she was pleased with the result. "I'll see you again tomorrow," she told her patient when she'd finished. Geraldo smiled weakly.

Thomasina was embarrassed she could not offer anything in Spanish except "good day" and "thank you." If she intended to stay in San Juan, it was as necessary for her to learn to speak the language fluently as it was for her to study the practice of medicine.

She hoped to talk about Spanish lessons with Rafferty, but there was no sign of him when she returned to the surgery. It was strange, but the rooms seemed much larger and rather empty without the doctor's booming voice and vital presence.

That evening, Domingo went to the cantina in the village. Thomasina sat at the desk, pouring over one of her medical texts, with only Lorenzo for company again. The illustrated chapter on breech birth couldn't hold her interest. She turned a page and sighed.

Lorenzo lifted his head and gave her a reassuring smile. Apparently the boy had appointed himself as Thomasina's protector and aide. He seemed to sense when she needed a companion and when she wished to be alone.

As the days passed, Thomasina would occasionally ask Domingo if he had heard any news of the doctor. His reply was always the same. "El Doctore will return when he returns."

Rafferty didn't return until the end of the week. Thomasina had been reading a page on milk leg for the third time, without comprehending a word of it, when she heard hoofbeats coming slowly up the road. The hoofbeats quickened as the horse came nearer the surgery.

Thomasina went out to greet the arrival and saw Lugh and his rider. The golden creature looked well cared for, as always, but weary. Rafferty looked worse. Thomasina was shocked by his three-day growth of beard and the shadows beneath his eyes. The crinkles at their corners fanned out more deeply, and fresh lines were etched in his forehead.

"I was afraid something untoward had happened to you," she said, trying to hide her anxiety.

Rafferty didn't respond. His hand gripped the reins so tightly, his knuckles were white. She thought perhaps his fever had returned, until she saw the emptiness in his eyes.

"What news of Pablo?" she whispered as the doctor swung down from Lugh's broad back.

"Pablo is dead."

Rafferty unstrapped his saddlebags and went into the surgery, leaving her to stare after him. Domingo took Lugh to the stables. Thomasina sighed and went into the house, where she found Rafferty in the bed-chamber, splashing water on his dust-streaked face. His eyes were as red as pimentos.

"I'm sorry about Pablo," she said quietly. "I had hoped that the wound wasn't as serious as it looked."

Rafferty blotted his face on the towel. "It wasn't."

"Then what killed him?"

The doctor examined his red-eyed reflection in the small mirror. "One might say that it was a passion for justice and love of his country. However, I believe it was the bullet to his head that actually did the trick. Don Carlos conducted the execution himself. He is an excellent shot."

Thomasina sank down on the bed abruptly. *Don Carlos!* In her mind's eye, she saw Pablo's face again, filled with terror and a desperate resignation. A rush of dizziness passed over her. "Is it true that Pablo was a dangerous brigand?"

Rafferty turned to her. "No more so than I, my dear. But the less you know, the better. At least for now."

For once, she was inclined to agree with him. He sat beside her and began pulling off his boots, yawning. "I'm going to catch forty winks in here, if you've no objection. Tonight, we're to attend a dinner party at the hacienda of Don Carlos."

"I thought the invitation was for you alone."

She got to her feet, and he swung his legs up on the mattress without bothering to undress. "The situation has been altered. Tonight, you'll meet the local gentry as Mrs. Brendan Rafferty.'' The ghost of a smile flickered over his features. ''Wear your best finery. I want my wife to do me proud.''

Thomasina blushed to the roots of her hair. She recovered her composure and started to ask him about the dinner party, but it was too late. He'd already fallen asleep. Rafferty was like a cat, she thought, able to curl up and sleep anywhere and awaken refreshed. It was an excellent habit for a doctor to have and one that she hoped to cultivate.

For a few minutes, she stood beside the bed, watching Rafferty sleep. His chest rose and fell in a regular rhythm. He looked younger and much more vulnerable with the lines of care smoothed from his face. How luxuriant his lashes were. And she'd never noticed before the particular way his hair grew back from his forehead, because it always seemed to flop forward. Lovely hair for a man, really. Dark with just a hint of auburn fire in it.

The day was cloudy and the room was cool. Thomasina drew the sheet up to Rafferty's shoulders to prevent a chill. She brushed away the lock of hair at his temple, shocked by the unexpected wave of tenderness that swept over her. She smiled to herself as she went out, closing the door behind her. It seemed that she was always tucking Rafferty in.

But after all, wasn't that one of the things that a wife was supposed to do?

Don Carlos had sent his carriage to pick them up at the appointed time. It was shiny black with red wheels, well sprung, and lined with red velvet upholstery. There was real glass in the sidelights and pleated shades that rolled down for privacy. The groom and footman wore splendid red-and-black livery trimmed with gold lace. Thomasina gave a sigh of pleasure. After Domingo's bouncy wagon and the hours in Sheherezade's saddle, this was luxury indeed.

"Pining for the finer things in life?" Rafferty asked.

"No. But only a fool would find anything to quibble about. I didn't expect to find such lavishness in San Juan."

"My dear, you have seen nothing yet." Rafferty looked out the window as they rolled away and kept further thoughts to himself.

Thomasina smoothed her gloved hand over the mulled silk of her skirts. The rich garnet-colored gown had been a gift from her mother and was most becoming. "Don't be afraid to wear red because of your hair," Patrice had said at the time. "It's all a matter of choosing the proper shade."

Thomasina glanced at her tiny reflection in the brass trimmings of the door. The gown brought out the deeper tones in her hair and flushed her cheeks with delicate color. To complement the ensemble, she'd selected the triple strand of pearls with the diamond clasp that had been part of Cousin Agatha's legacy to her. Certainly not as splendid as the choker with the Valnoy sapphire—but holding far happier memories.

Suddenly Thomasina's stomach twisted and knotted. The last formal event she'd attended had been on that terrible evening when Rafferty had rescued her on the docks. Since that time, Thomasina had been unable to abide the smell of the sea. It had also been the last time she'd been able to face a party of her peers.

She didn't like the memories that were crowding back upon her. She clasped her hands together tightly. Although she'd said none of this to Rafferty, tonight would be a true test of her mettle. Her breathing came more quickly, and she felt as if all the air had been removed from the carriage. If I can meet their prying eyes with my head high and ignore Margarita's arrogant snubs, I'll be able to face anything.

Suddenly, Rafferty's big hand covered hers in a gesture of reassurance. All her panic fled. She gave him a tremulous smile in the light of the sunset. It was clear that he'd guessed her thoughts. "I'll be all right," she whispered.

"Of course, you will."

He removed his hand, and she felt alone again, but less so than before.

With the fine horses pulling the carriage they made the journey to the hacienda quickly. The sun was lowering, turning the treetops from emerald to gold, and the river ran like a stream of molten metal beneath the wooden bridge. As they came onto Valverde land, Thomasina had her first real view of the great house itself.

Earlier, she'd glimpsed adobe walls and tile roofs, and had anticipated something in vaguely Moorish style. Now she realized that what she'd seen were merely the outbuildings and the roof of a chapel. She hadn't envisioned such grandeur. The sprawling house, set like a jewel in the prongs of the valley's high walls, exceeded her expectations. It was an enormous mansion with fancy tilework and arches and towers and domes. A turret surmounted the main gate with a crennelated parapet along the protective walls. Don Carlos lived like a prince.

Evidently, she'd spoken aloud. Rafferty stared out the window. "More than a prince. In this valley and for miles beyond his actual domain, he is prince, god, judge and jury."

And executioner. The unspoken words echoed in Thomasina's head. She shivered and drew her heavy silk shawl around her shoulders. What could Pablo, a simple man in a homespun shirt, have done to earn the wrath of Don Carlos? And why had Don Carlos said the man was a brigand?

Thomasina felt overwhelmed. Why was everything so complicated? Life, she decided, was really much easier when lived between the pages of a medical book.

The huge gates swung open to admit them, and the carriage rolled through into the paved courtyard. Two more footmen came out to open the carriage door and let down the steps. The scene seemed unreal. From up close, the house was even more intimidating, a bastion of feudal pomp and pageantry set down in the remote countryside. Rafferty offered Thomasina an arm, and she placed her hand upon it as they mounted the wide stairs leading to a wide portico.

Thomasina looked around in awe. "It's like a picture-book drawing of a castle in Grenada."

"The first Valverde landed in Vera Cruz with Cortez in 1519." The bitterness was back in Rafferty's voice. "After helping to plunder the Aztec wealth and subjugate the people who'd welcomed them in friendship, Guillermo Valverde was given a royal grant of land here. In Mexico now, the few live in ease and splendor while the majority eke out their existence from day to day.''

Thomasina wondered again at the doctor's relationship with the Valverde family. He seemed on good terms with Margarita, but the slightest mention of Don Carlos had him snarling like a lion. Under the circumstances, she was curious as to why Rafferty had accepted the invitation. She tried to draw him out without him knowing it.

"Don Carlos must be incredibly wealthy. I didn't know such magnificence existed outside of Mexico City."

Her attempt backfired. Rafferty stopped short. "And when have you been to Mexico City? I was under the distinct impression that this was your first visit to this country."

"It is. I'll explain later."

She hurried up the steps, the hem of her silk gown whispering over the stone. Rafferty had no choice but to follow. They reached the top of the stairs and were greeted by a major domo, who led them through a vaulted reception hall. A fountain covered in colorful tiles splashed in the center of the room. Ceiling-high doors studded with great nailheads led to a candlelit room beyond.

Thomasina's impression was of enormous paintings and tapestries swirling with color and of massive chandeliers blazing with light. She half-expected to find ladies in ancient court dress and men in velvet doublets. Instead, men in sober European evening dress gathered in groups here and there. There wasn't another woman in sight.

One of the men detached himself from a group and crossed the huge floor toward them. He was thin and not in his youth. He wore a diagonal sash of red silk decorated with a foreign order. He held out both hands to Rafferty, smiling with genuine warmth.

"Ah, Brendan! Welcome, welcome, my old friend. I was not sure if we would see you this evening." He turned his brilliant smile to Thomasina. "I will make the apologies for my niece and nephew. Carlos and Margarita have taken the other ladies into the rose garden to watch the fireflies."

Rafferty made quick work of the introductions. "Julianno, may I present to you my wife, Señora Rafferty."

The man executed a graceful bow. Only the slight quirk of his eyebrow betrayed surprise. Rafferty put his hand on Thomasina's arm. "My dear, this is Julianno de Palmar, fifth Baron of Altemira and ambassador to Mexico from the nation of Costa Brava. He is one of the worst rogues—and one of the finest scientists—it has ever been my pleasure to meet."

The ambassador laughed as he took Thomasina's hand and bowed low over it. His black eyes twinkled with amusement. "I am charmed, Señora Rafferty. But you must not listen to your husband's stories. I am a staid and sober man of affairs now, with my adventuring days far behind me."

Thomasina inquired about his interest in science, and learned that de Palmar had been a chemist before called by his king to serve his country in the diplomatic corps. He still devoted what little spare time he had to his experiments. She was drawn to the man with his sparkling eyes and ready smile.

"I am pleased to know that Dr.... that my husband counts you as one of his oldest friends, Baron de Palmar."

For just a moment, Thomasina feared the words were going to stick in her throat. She would have to be very careful. Getting used to her new, if counterfeit, relationship with Rafferty was going to be a bit tricky.

No one else approached them, although Thomasina was aware of many glances cast their way. Some were curious, others seemed almost hostile. She was very glad to keep her arm tucked through Rafferty's. They engaged in pleasant conversation with Baron de Palmar for several minutes.

After a while, Thomasina sensed that the doctor was eager to speak with de Palmar alone. She wasn't at all anxious to leave his side. "Wouldn't you care to join the other ladies?" Rafferty finally said in exasperation.

She glanced up at him through her lashes. "Why, this place is so large, I'm afraid I would become lost."

"Then I'll come looking for you."

Thomasina was not about to be dumped unceremoniously among total strangers. She tucked her arm through his more firmly. "I wouldn't think of putting you to the trouble."

Three women in expensive toilettes came in from the garden together, arms linked. Thomasina's stomach tightened. Two more followed, one of them Margarita Valverde. She wondered what the gorgeous *señorita* would say when they met. Thomasina was sure she'd never be forgiven for her bald announcement. She should never have let Rafferty talk her into this!

"It's a command performance," he'd told her. "No *ifs, ands* or *buts*. They are very influential, and if you wish to work in San Juan, you will need their patronage."

His aboutface had surprised her. "If you dislike Don Carlos, why do you court his approval?"

"I don't give a damn about it personally, but let us just say that I have my reasons. For the moment."

She'd had to be satisfied with that. When Rafferty vented his spleen, the entire neighborhood knew about it—and when he decided to hold his tongue, he was as silent as an oyster. The sound of a soft voice at her elbow brought Thomasina out of her reverie with a start.

"Ah, Señora Rafferty. How happy I am that you have graced my poor house with your beauty."

"Speak of the devil," Rafferty murmured, a little too loudly for politeness's sake.

Thomasina was torn between consternation and laughter. She hoped it didn't show on her face. "Good evening, Don Carlos. Thank you for your kind invitation."

Their host took Thomasina's hand and raised it to his lips. He was resplendent in black silk velvet trimmed with silver lace and matching buttons of intricate filigree. His eyes were warm with admiration.

"It is I who should be grateful that you have accepted my humble invitation. I am a selfish man, *se-*

ñora. I prefer to surround myself with beautiful things, whenever possible.''

Unused to such a blatant attempt at flattery—one which fell flat to Thomasina's ears—she merely smiled and inclined her head. Don Carlos surveyed the room.

''There is an American lady visiting with us for a few weeks, but I do not see her in the room. You will, of course, meet her this evening. She is eager to encounter a fellow countrywoman so far from her home. I shall make a point of it to introduce you myself.''

''Thank you. I shall be delighted to make her acquaintance.''

Don Carlos smiled benignly, then moved away. The man had immense charm and, for the moment, it was turned on her full force. It was difficult to imagine him as an executioner, but Thomasina knew that Rafferty would not have lied to her. The doctor was impulsive, impatient and hotheaded—but he was just. Thomasina admired that in a man.

She looked around for him, but he'd gone off with de Palmar. Thomasina found herself alone in a group of people who were all well-known to one another. The old familiar panic came flooding back and she felt exposed and vulnerable. There must be someone she could talk to, someone to anchor her to the present before the unreasoning panic burst forth.

As Thomasina pivoted, looking in vain for Rafferty again, her hostess spotted her. Señorita Valverde was well trained in the social arts. It was not right for a guest to be left unattended, especially one who was a stranger. Margarita came forward graciously, a glittering smile on her beautiful face. She didn't recognize the fashionably garbed young woman as the dust-covered scarecrow of the previous week.

Then Rafferty returned with de Palmar and sent Thomasina a wink across the width of the room. Señora Valverde came to an abrupt halt. She looked from one to the other, her face alternately flushed red and then white.

With a haughty look at Thomasina, she spun about on the sole of her dainty blue slippers and went in the other direction.

Thomasina ducked behind a carved pillar inlaid with intricate glazed tiles. It was going to be a long and uncomfortable evening.

Her respite wasn't long. More people were filtering back from the garden, Don Carlos among them. He spied Thomasina at once and sought her out. "How is it that you are all alone, Señora Rafferty? Come. If you will permit, I shall personally escort you around to make you known to my guests."

Rafferty came up out of nowhere. From the stubborn set of his jaw, Thomasina thought he meant to carry her off somewhere. Don Carlos moved between them with the quick grace of a bullfighter.

"Although much indulgence is given a doting husband during the early weeks of marriage, I cannot allow you to monopolize your lovely bride this evening, Doctor." He looped his arm through Thomasina's. "You will forgive me, Dr. Rafferty, but I have promised the Countess of Castellena that I would bring your wife over to her for a little chat. I believe that Margarita has been looking for you. My sister wishes to speak with you about the plans for the hospital near Santa Cruz.''

So deftly that she didn't know quite how it was done, Thomasina found herself escorted away from Rafferty. As she passed one of the many mirrors, she had a glimpse of the doctor and Margarita Valverde slipping through a door.

Don Carlos tucked Thomasina's hand in his arm and swept her along beside him. His eyes smiled as he looked down at her. ''My sister and your husband are old friends. Margarita's nose will surely be out of joint now that you have come here. I hope you are finding San Juan a pleasant place. It is primitive compared to what you are used to and—perhaps—more primitive than you had expected?''

''But far more beautiful, Don Carlos. I am delighted with the valleys and mountains, and quite enchanted with the village of San Juan.''

He sketched her a mocking bow. ''As the wife of a doctor, you are truly charming, *señora*. As the wife of a diplomat, you might have truly found your calling. A woman of such wit and beauty would wield formidable power.''

Thomasina had wearied of his courtly games. ''The only power I would wish for is the power to heal the sick and mend the broken. But that power resides in a Higher Source than myself.''

She had expected him to be nettled, but was surprised by his reaction. Don Carlos's smile grew wider, and his glowing eyes mirrored his appreciation. Thomasina met him glance for glance. ''You find me amusing, no doubt for my naïveté.''

"No, *señora,* for your honesty. It is refreshing."

They had reached a knot of people, and there was no time for further banter. Thomasina was relieved. When Don Carlos was so clever and complimentary, it was hard to remember that he had "executed" Pablo. For the first time, she began to doubt Rafferty. His view of the matter was evidently quite different from that of Don Carlos, and probably just as prejudiced. Perhaps one man's seeker of justice was another man's brigand. Men could do strange things with words, twisting their meanings until white was black and down was up. But she trusted Rafferty.

She gathered her thoughts hastily. Introductions were being made. Trying to sort and label everyone occupied her for the next half hour as they moved from group to group. Thomasina smiled and curtsied to a sweet-faced older lady, who turned out to be the Countess of Castillena and cousin to the King of Spain. The proud man with the aristocratic face was not the diplomat she'd imagined, but a cattle buyer, and the plump, grandmotherly woman in green satin, who was his wife, had the disposition of a spider.

Among all the people she met, Thomasina was most drawn to Roberto Vega and his sister. Roberto was a serious young man with thoughtful eyes and a slight limp. He was distant cousin of Don Carlos and served as the hacendado's private secretary. Thomasina wondered if he was any relationship to Alonzo de Vega, the man who was called a rebel bandit by the landowners and a hero by the villagers. Roberto bowed low over her hand.

"I have heard much praise of you spoken in the Zavala household, Señora Rafferty. I am most pleased to make your acquaintance."

He introduced Thomasina to his sister. "Marisa has been eager to meet you."

Thomasina smiled at the girl. She was dark-eyed and quiet, with a pleasing roundness of figure that had caught more than one gentleman's eye. But Marisa seemed oblivious to them all. "I hope we may call upon you at the surgery, *Señora.*"

"Please do. I would be delighted."

Then Don Carlos finished his aside with the countess and whisked Thomasina away. There were thirty-odd people gathered in all. Some had come from rancheros on the far side of the mountain, and others all the way from Mexico City. So many names and titles and faces. Her head began to ache with the effort. The heat of hundreds of candles exacerbated the lingering warmth of the evening. Names and faces blurred together. When she was finally able to slip away, Thomasina chose the nearest door and escaped.

She found herself in a parlor that was much smaller and less grandiose than the formal reception room. It had been decorated with a feminine hand, and the light fragrance in the air reminded her of Margarita Valverde. Thomasina looked around the chamber. It was simple yet elegant, with the small personal touches that give a room character.

The wall sconces hadn't been lit, but a lamp with a crystal shade puddled amber light around the graceful secretaire. As she stepped nearer, Thomasina noticed the gold ink stand, trimmed in white onyx and malachite. Around the base was inscribed, in Spanish, "To Margarita from her loving brother, Carlos."

Thomasina found it strange that the room was at such odds with the woman to whom it belonged. It was graceful and serene, with none of the overblown fashion or florid style she expected of a woman like Margarita Valverde. Very strange, indeed.

Thomasina crossed the room and passed through the other door. Instead of entering another room as she'd expected, Thomasina found herself in a small courtyard. The *placita* was pleasant and dim, with only the light from the room behind her to hint at its daytime loveliness. A stone seat beckoned her, promising a quiet rest and time to think things over among the profusion of roses in the garden.

As she started toward the bench, Thomasina felt something catch at her skirts. She stopped to see what had happened and found she had brushed too close to a climbing rose. She was annoyed to think she might have torn her best gown, and she bent down, hoping to extricate the fabric without damaging it severely. It was then that she realized she was not alone.

Two people were talking at the far side of the *placita*. One of them was Rafferty.

"Dammit, Margarita, I was too tired and feverish to think clearly. Before I knew it, the woman was ensconced in my surgery and Domingo had spread the word through the village that Señora Rafferty had come to San Juan to join me."

Thomasina pricked her finger on a thorn in her haste to get free. She didn't want to hear any more.

"But you didn't act then."

"It was too late. I couldn't take the chance of a scandal ruining all my plans."

"Your plans? What of *our* plans? Did you think of them for one minute before acting so rashly?"

"Listen to me," Rafferty said impatiently, "I tell you I couldn't do otherwise. I had no choice."

"Oh!" Margarita's gasp was horrified. "You mean...that you have gotten her...that she is expecting your child? Oh, Brendan, how could you!"

She pushed past him and ran from the *placita*. Rafferty tried to follow, but his way was blocked. Margarita had slammed and bolted the door. He spun toward the other door—and found Thomasina frozen on the threshold. "Eavesdropping, my dear? It's a nasty habit, and one you would be well rid of."

Without apologies or explanations, Thomasina ripped her skirts loose from the thorns and raced back to the reception room before the doctor could catch up with her. In a quiet fury, she wove her way in and out of the crowd with more speed than elegance, aware that more than one person turned to stare. The evening was turning into a nightmare, and the dreaded dinner was still a half hour away. Thomasina wished she could transport herself magically back to the surgery. Failing that, she wanted nothing more than to slip into the anonymity of the garden and indulge in a quiet cry.

She almost succeeded. Two more people came in from the garden and stood just inside the door. Thomasina realized that one of them was Don Carlos. The other was a woman dressed in the palest of blue satin. The black velvet and thick silver braid of his Spanish-style garment and the icy gleam of her gown made them a striking pair, almost as if moonlight and shadows had shaped themselves into human forms.

Don Carlos looked up and saw Thomasina. "Ah," he exclaimed genially, "here is the little compatriot of yours whom I promised to introduce to you."

The woman turned slowly to face Thomasina. Clear gray eyes very like Thomasina's green ones swept a glance over her from head to toe. In that split second, her heart turned over in her chest.

Maman! Thomasina only mouthed the word. Her throat was too dry and constricted to say it aloud. Don Carlos was making the introductions, but she seemed to have become deaf as well as mute.

"How do you do?" Patrice Wentworth said as Thomasina's ears cleared. She extended her kid-gloved hand to clasp her daughter's, for all the world as if they'd never met. "I'm delighted to make your acquaintance, Mrs. Rafferty. I hope you find Mexico to your liking."

Thomasina fumbled for words. "It—it is everything I expected—and more."

Patrice inclined her head. "I might say the very same thing. We must try to find a few minutes alone to discuss our travels and our mutual acquaintanceship in San Francisco."

"Of—of course. I should—should like that very much."

"Excellent. After dinner, perhaps?" Patrice smiled coolly and turned back to Don Carlos.

While Thomasina stood rooted in place, heart thumping like a boiler, she realized Rafferty had come up beside her. She put her arm through his for support because her knees felt shaky.

"What the he— Ow!" Rafferty's question was silenced by Thomasina's fingers digging into his arm. The doctor sent her a sharp look. "Let us take a little stroll upon the terrace...*my dear.*"

Their opportunity to speak privately was lost as dinner was announced. Thomasina didn't know whether to be glad or sorry. Julianno de Palmar came to claim her as his dinner partner. To her left sat a dour German who spoke no English. Since they could not communicate, except through nods and smiles, she spent most of her time being entertained by the ambassador. It was a breach of etiquette, but no one seemed to mind. Since the lady seated on the other side of de Palmar was deaf as a tombstone, it worked out well for everyone.

Thomasina couldn't see either Rafferty or her mother, who were seated on the same side of the board as herself. The only thing spoiling Thomasina's enjoyment of the meal was the knowledge that her mother was twenty feet away and that the hour of judgment was fast approaching.

The serving of the fourteen courses flew by with the swiftness of a lightning strike. The cheese and fruit were cleared away and Thomasina knew the hour was at hand. Unlike English and American parties, there was no hard-and-fast separation of the sexes after dinner. Some of the men congregated in the gold salon to smoke cigars and talk of world affairs. A sprinkling of women were among them. Other ladies retired to freshen their faces with a touch of rouge or to have their hair attended to by their maids. A few less-hardy souls went upstairs to rest before the dancing began.

At first, Thomasina was glad to take a corner of the settee in the salon and listen, until she realized all the conversation was in Spanish. Finally, she decided that this was a good time to slip out and find her mother. She was a grown woman, Thomasina told herself, and she refused to cower from the consequences of her actions.

The main reception room was deserted, although candles still burned brightly. A glimpse of Patrice Wentworth through the open doors of an anteroom sent Thomasina in her direction.

A big, bronzed hand caught her arm, and she found herself propelled toward the garden instead.

"I believe a little private chat is in order," Rafferty growled.

The garden was deserted. A fountain splashed softly, drowning out the night sounds. The heady scent of roses filled the air, and the stars made a canopy of diamonds overhead. Thomasina looked up at them. "How beautiful."

"Very romantic, I'm sure," Rafferty said. "But this is neither the time nor the place." He led her deeper into the garden, along a graveled path. "All right. What the devil was that little charade earlier all about? If that woman is not your mother, then I'm not the sixth son of Seamus and Aileen Rafferty! And I know damned well that I am."

"I don't know—"

"Don't play games with me. If there's something going on here, I'd like to know about it—especially since you're here masquerading as my wife!"

"Shh. You don't have to shout." Thomasina glanced over her shoulder. The terrace was deserted. "Both our reputations are at stake—my mother's too, perhaps. No," she whispered. "Be quiet, and I'll try and explain . . . at least what I know of it."

Rafferty folded his arms. He looked quite formidable, looming over her in the velvet shadows of the garden. "Well . . . ?"

"And don't say a word until I've finished." Thomasina knitted her fingers together and plunged in. "I suppose you've guessed some of it already. My mother and I made a pact that morning in San Francisco when you took me back to Cousin Agatha's. If I was still of the same mind in two years, she would give her blessing to my great desire to become a trained physician. In fact, she would help me in any way she could."

Voices raised in laughter were wafted on the breeze, but Thomasina was too intent on her story to notice. "But first we would travel. During that I would play the social debutante to the best of my ability. I kept my word. My mother didn't."

"I see. And so when you made your . . . er . . . arrangements with me by letter, you didn't tell your mother about them. Instead, you waited until the two of you were touring through Mexico—and then you packed your trunks and vanished."

Thomasina lifted her head in the darkness and the starlight caught her eyes. "Not quite. There is a deep bond of affection between my mother and myself, although we were sometimes separated for long periods of time. I would never do anything to hurt her.''

Thomasina's voice was filled with sudden passion. ''I told her all along what I intended to do, but she thought it was just a pipedream. When I departed the hotel, I left a letter informing her of where I had gone and why. You see, I had to do something drastic. It was the only way to make her believe that I really mean to dedicate my life to medicine.''

It was impossible to make out the expression on Rafferty's face. He gazed down at her silently while the seconds spun out into minutes. Thomasina shivered. She wouldn't go back. She couldn't. ''I suppose you will do your best to get rid of me now. I can just imagine how your mind is working.''

To her surprise, he uttered a low, rich chuckle. ''Wrong again. I was thinking that it took a great deal of enterprise for you to order supplies and equipment and pack them away without alerting your mother to the fact. It must have been quite a feat stuffing things like Schumhoffer-Braus chloroform masks in among your, uh, your unmentionables.''

Relief made her giddy. ''I believe the word you're looking for is *lingerie.* Or perhaps *chemises* and *petticoats* and...and *corsets!* If we're to keep up our pretense of being man and wife, you might as well stop tiptoeing around words a husband would know.''

He laughed again. ''Believe me, my dear, I'm quite familiar with women's cors—lingerie. Now, let us put our heads together and decide what is to be done. Evidently, your mother is willing to go along with our ruse, at least for now. Why is something that you can probably tell more easily than I.''

Thomasina thought a moment. Suddenly everything became perfectly clear.

''I would guess that it is because my mother has no wish to discredit me. Your friend, Baron de Palmar...does he have a stepson?''

''Yes. A handsome young wastrel, with neither his stepfather's brains nor his integrity. He fills his days with fine horses, aged wines and young and pretty girls. Why did you ask?''

''Because,'' she replied slowly, ''for the past six months, letters have been flying back and forth between my mother and her old friend, Count de Palmar. You see, my mother has been trying to make up to me for everything that happened in the only way she thinks possible. No matter what you may think of her, she loves me very much.''

Thomasina blinked away the bright sting of tears. ''When my father died, my mother was thrust out in the world, alone and friendless and expecting a child. Knowing what it is like to be cast adrift, since I was born, she has wanted more than anything to protect and shelter me from the mistakes of her past. Now, without discussing the matter, she has tried to arrange a secure future for me as the wife of a powerful man in a foreign country.''

Thomasina was too busy twisting her hands together to notice the expression on Rafferty's face. The famous roar of the Red Raffertys was stuck in his throat like a bone splinter. His fingers curled as if they were pressing into Patrice Wentworth's swanlike throat. Two years ago, the woman had thrown her daughter to the society wolves of Nob Hill, and now, to make amends, she intended to sell her—complete with dowry—to the highest bidder. Was there no end to the woman's ridiculous ambitions?

"Your mother has certainly been busy since our last meeting," he said, barely containing his rage. "And I assume—correct me if I am in error—that she went about this without so much as a by-your-leave."

"She had been hinting at it quite strongly long before we left California. I was horrified."

"I'm sure you were!"

Thomasina cupped a rose blossom. The petals were black as velvet in the moonlight. They trembled and fell, scattering like ashes at her feet. Her voice was so low that Rafferty could hardly hear it. "In fact, the day I left our hotel in Mexico City, she finally admitted everything. All along, she had discounted my plans of becoming a physician as unrealistic—and she was sure that once everything was settled, I would be dazzled by the opportunity to be a countess. You see, she had brought me to Mexico with one end in mind—to finalize the contracts promising me in marriage to Baron de Palmar's stepson."

Chapter Nine

The hour was late when the Valverde carriage wound up from the valley floor, carrying its occupants back toward San Juan. Thomasina smothered a yawn that owed more to an evening of boredom than to tiredness. Despite the advanced hour, she felt wide awake.

"What a long-winded company that was. I thought the party would never break up," she said.

"You mean that you thought your mother would never give up and retire without having a little talk with you. By Gad, you clung to me like a leech."

"I had every intention of speaking with her. You know that I was seeking her out when you hustled me off to the garden so rudely. I was only following your express instructions."

"So you were."

Rafferty fell silent. The vehicle swayed beneath a canopy of trees, plunging them briefly into darkness so intense that the carriage lights hardly pierced it. Rafferty had been staggered by Thomasina's revelations about the proposed marriage of convenience between her and de Palmar's stepson. Was there no end to Patrice Wentworth's gall? It was all very well for the girl to defend her mother's reasons, but the boy was a wastrel—and a muslin chaser to boot. How she could think she was protecting her daughter or securing her future by marrying her off to Fernando de Palmar was more than Rafferty could see.

By Gad! he thought fiercely, it was a good thing that Thomasina was *his* wife—or rather, masquerading as his wife—and couldn't be forced into marrying Fernando. That pretty-faced, lily-livered jack-o'-napes. Rafferty scowled into the darkness. Baron de Palmar, not knowing Thomasina's true identity, had admitted he'd encouraged Patrice Wentworth's schemes.

"If the daughter is as ambitious as the mother, it would not be a bad thing for her," he'd explained. "She would be a countess with a fine hacienda and many servants. As for Fernando, the boy is running through his inheritance at a scandalous pace. If a rich American's dowry can save his worthless neck and both are willing, then who am I to come between them?"

Rafferty's blood boiled just thinking of it. At least he'd saved her from *that* fate.

But now, what was he going to do with her? A year was a long time, three years, an eternity. And she was too innocent to see the complications that would inevitably arise. Either that, or she saw him as too old and tired to have a grain of lust in his body or a spark of blood in his veins. He crossed his arms and settled himself stiffly beside her.

Thomasina didn't notice. She was staring out the window, engrossed. It seemed strange to be abroad in open country at such a desolate hour, and she almost wished they'd stayed on at the hacienda. Don Carlos had offered the hospitality of his house and had urged Thomasina and the doctor to spend the night. Rafferty had politely, but firmly, declined.

"The invitation is appreciated, but I must check on Geraldo Zavala first thing tomorrow morning and see how he is coming along."

"That young fool!" Don Carlos had replied. "He is luckier than he deserves, trespassing through that field when my black bull was out."

Rafferty's eyes had narrowed. "He told me the field was empty when he started across."

"The boy is a liar and a troublemaker, like his father and grandfather before him." Don Carlos had shrugged. "My carriage will be ready at whatever time you say."

Such high-handed tactics hadn't worked with Rafferty. "I prefer not to be away from the surgery for long periods at such a time."

Don Carlos had given the doctor a hard glance, and Thomasina had wondered if he knew that Rafferty had been away for several days. It was highly likely. Don Carlos seemed to know everything that happened for two hundred miles around.

Thomasina leaned her head back against the velvet squabs. "At least I've gained a few hour's grace. Maman is going to come to the surgery tomorrow afternoon so we may speak privately without fear of being overheard."

"The sooner you get your stories straight, the better for all concerned. I don't imagine your mother wants any hint of scandal attached to either of your names. It would ruin her plans. But how you expect to be private in the midst of all the surgery visitors is beyond me.''

Thomasina sank deeper into the upholstery. ''If the visitors are anything like the ones who came in your absence, we shall have the place quite to ourselves. Not one person came by with so much as a finger prick.''

''Not one?''

''If you're going to keep on repeating everything I say, I will... will...''

Words failed her. Thomasina looked out the window at the black-and-white landscape. She was tired and edgy. Between Margarita Valverde and her own mother, she had not drawn an easy breath the entire evening. There were too many things that just didn't add up. And this business with de Palmar's stepson was the final straw.

Evidently, Rafferty's mind ran on the same tack. His eyes glittered. ''I suppose she will want to set a date for your marriage to Fernando de Palmar—that miserable, prancing, popinjay!''

''Don't be ridiculous. How can she arrange a marriage to another man when as far as she knows, I am already married to you?''

There was a period of silence as the doctor paused for reflection. He cleared his throat. ''So, then. You mean to carry out the masquerade?''

''To the bitter end. You and I, my dear Dr. Rafferty, have a written agreement—and if, in order to keep that agreement, I have to pose as your wife, I will do so. Any breach of our contract will have to come from you.''

Without warning, the carriage hit a deep rut. Rafferty grabbed at the hanging strap and remained upright, but Thomasina was bounced across his lap. Beneath her arm, his chest was hard as steel, and as she seized his collar, her fingers grazed a warm and whiskery jaw. He'd shaved earlier that evening, but already, his dark beard was asserting itself. She rather liked the way it felt.

The lurching and swaying of the vehicle continued a bit, and they were unable to separate. Supported by his strong arm, Thomasina had no course but to hold on to him to keep from being jounced to the floor. As the carriage rounded a bend, moonlight fell full upon their faces. Rafferty was looking at her with a most peculiar expression. His features seemed sterner, somehow, yet softened by the heat in his eyes.

Thomasina was caught by that dark, burning look and held. It sparked—no, more than that—it lit a tiny flame inside her that warmed her blood. She was drawn to him, overwhelmed by the urge to touch his face and to trace her fingertips around the firm outlines of his mouth. His arms tightened, although the carriage was now on smoother ground. She lifted her head, unconsciously inviting the kiss that seemed inevitable. His lips seemed only a whisper away.

Then she was suffocating, trapped once again in the smothering panic, assaulted by broken fragments of memory. Her body went rigid as she fought off the demons of her past.

Rafferty released Thomasina immediately and settled her back on the seat beside him. Good Lord, that had been a close call. For the split second when she'd filled his arms, the light scent of her hair had clouded his thinking.

One year was a very, very long time. Three years, an eternity. And they would be thrown together day and night under the most intimate circumstances. Rafferty almost groaned. At the moment, the situation was more than he could bear.

Thomasina sat as if she'd been carved from granite, her hands clenched tightly in her lap. He cast about for something—anything—to ease the tension that ran between them like a tightly coiled spring. The carriage wheels hit another tortured patch of road.

"This road is a cursed abomination," he rumbled. "It still amazes me that you would wish to immure yourself in a tiny place like San Juan when you could be leading a life of ease and luxury in much more civilized surroundings."

His plan succeeded. Thomasina laughed. "I have often thought the same of you. It seems, Dr. Rafferty, that you and I are two of a kind."

She hastily grabbed the strap as the carriage bumped along over another particularly nasty stretch, and the discussion ended.

Rafferty was left to wonder what might have occurred if she hadn't frozen like an icicle—and to warn himself that he must maintain a certain reserve in their relationship. This was one more cursed complication, at a time when he needed to watch his every step. He turned his head and stared abstractedly at the moonlit countryside. The river shone like polished jet, and the valley of San Juan was gobbled up by velvet blackness.

Thomasina leaned toward her window, engrossed. The landscape was stark and majestic, a pen-and-ink drawing from a master hand. If she didn't know better, she could imagine that the occupants of the swaying carriage were the only people for a thousand miles in any direction.

As the carriage made a wide turn, a wonderful panorama unfolded. Los Tres Hermanos ruled the night, the snow-covered triple peaks of the massive volcanic cone gleaming like silver. The mountain dominated earth and sky, a brooding presence with its own, very real personality, born in fire and cataclysm but sleeping now. Cool and remote. She closed her eyes. The mountain was still there. She could feel it, almost as if it were alive. Watching.

With a start she realized she'd dozed off. Her cheek was pressed against Rafferty's shoulder—and had been for some time. Thomasina was glad the darkness covered her embarrassment. She sat up as the horses slowed down before the surgery.

The mellow glow of a lamp showed around the edges of the closed shutters. She pictured Domingo inside, dozing in the rocker as he waited to hear all about the grand dinner party. A warm, contented feeling rose inside her. It took a few seconds before she recognized what it meant: homecoming.

She grinned. This tiny part of the world would be her home for the next few years—and she was glad of it. Tonight, she'd had a little reminder of the greater world upon which she'd turned her back. Her grin widened. It was good to be home.

The footman got down from his perch and opened the door. Rafferty descended first, handed Thomasina from the carriage, then turned to slip a coin to the driver. The footman had already shut the door and was clambering into his seat. The driver apparently didn't hear Rafferty call out to him. He snapped the reins and gave the horses the office to start. The carriage clattered out of the yard in a veil of dust and moonlight.

"Well, they are certainly anxious for their bed—"

Thomasina wasn't allowed to finish. Her words were cut short as Rafferty grabbed her and pushed her forward. She stumbled and fell.

"What are you—"

Her angry cry was cut off sharply as the doctor launched himself through the air. Something whizzed overhead and hit the side of the house. There was a puff of white adobe dust and an abrupt boom of thunder. Thomasina felt the wind knocked out of her, and she heard the rattle of hooves and the sound of coach wheels going away at a mad pace.

"Stay down," Rafferty ordered.

He crawled toward the shadow of the building, half dragging Thomasina with him. Another shot clipped the brass bell that hung from the end of the protruding viga, sending out a shrill peal of alarm.

Domingo called out, and the door opened. The lamp had been extinguished, but a few coals glowed redly in the fireplace. Rafferty pushed at Thomasina. "Hurry."

She scrambled across the threshold as quickly as she could. The doctor was right behind her. He slammed the door and thrust the bolt home. Before her eyes had fully adjusted to the deeper darkness, Rafferty had his shotgun ready.

Domingo edged toward the window with a rifle. Rafferty signaled for the older man to stay inside while he went out the back way into the *placita*. Moments later, the roar of a shotgun blast made Thomasina back into the medicine cupboard. She waited, scarcely daring to breathe, for what seemed like an hour. There were no further incidents.

Rafferty returned, his face darkened with dirt and his jacket buttoned up to hide his white shirt. "They got away, damn their eyes. Slunk away to their dens like the cowardly curs they are."

"If only the driver and footman had stayed," Thomasina said as Domingo relit the lantern, "they might have helped us."

Rafferty poured water into a basin and began to wash his hands and face. "Your powers of observation are not very sharp tonight, my dear, or you would have noticed one critical fact. The footman was up and the driver sprung his horses a split second before that first shot was fired."

Thomasina went to him. "You are saying that they knew an attack was going to be made...?"

The doctor splashed water over his face. "Perhaps I'm jumping to conclusions. Shall we give them the benefit of a doubt? I saw moonlight gleam along rifle barrels. The servants of Don Carlos might have seen the same."

"But you don't believe that." She looked down at her best ballgown, torn and stained beyond repair. "I don't understand. Why were they shooting at us?"

Having completed his ablutions, the doctor set the shotgun down where it would be ready at a moment's notice. "It could be many things." He took her face between his hands. "Are you sure you haven't changed your mind about staying, my dear?"

Her heart speeded up at his touch. "Not one whit."

"Good girl." Rafferty put his arm around her and gave her a quick squeeze. "Tomorrow is likely to be a busy day. Get some sleep."

"I'll wait up with you."

"No. There are things I need to discuss with Domingo."

The gentleness in Rafferty's voice unnerved Thomasina. She was used to his booming giant's roar. His habitual bellow stiffened her spine, but his softer tones had turned her bones to jelly.

"Look at your arm!" he exclaimed in her ear a second later.

Thomasina realized her left arm was beginning to sting abominably. She felt suddenly faint. Turning her head, she saw a dozen tiny rivulets of blood streaming down from her shoulder.

Rafferty examined it and cursed. "Here, let's get that gown off."

"Domingo..." she said in protest.

"Very well. Into the bedchamber with you." He spoke to Domingo in Spanish, then helped her to the bed.

The dizziness was worse. Thomasina put her head down, knowing it would help relieve the horrible feeling. Rafferty struck a light. "Lie down before you fall down."

For once, she was glad to give in without protest. It was one thing to be brave and stoic, quite another to try to stay upright when the whole room was tilting. Suddenly Rafferty's arm was there to lower her easily to the pillow. His hands were warm and incredibly gentle, his fingers deft and sure as he explored her injury.

"I'll have to do some digging, I'm afraid."

Thomasina winced. She remembered being slammed to the ground, hard, and thinking that the doctor had been responsible. "Am I . . . was I *shot?*"

"Grazed. Perhaps there's a good reason, after all, for some of these ridiculous feminine fashions. I believe you were hit by a ricochet." He cut away the ruffled and beribboned straps of her camisole. "These folderols at the shoulder saved you from a nastier injury."

Rafferty left the room for a moment. He returned with a basin of water and a soft cloth. He began to sponge the blood away. There was pain as he prodded lightly at her arm, and a sick feeling in the pit of her stomach. More than a simple graze, she was sure.

"Is it very bad?"

Rafferty paused just long enough to worry her. "Nothing serious, I hope. However, there are several embedded fragments, one or two of them deep. Bits of shattered stone, most likely."

Thomasina sighed. "Better the stone than my arm. I thought something was terribly wrong when you didn't answer at once."

He didn't reply. It was the satin feel of her skin beneath his fingertips, its rounded contour and smooth perfection that had made him hesitate—and the knowledge of what he must do to set it to rights again. In his years as a physician, Rafferty had performed hundreds of surgeries, some requiring more skill and technical knowledge. His hands were always steady, his nerves nonexistent.

Until now.

Rafferty felt like a rank apprentice. His hands had sprouted at least a dozen thumbs apiece—and everyone of them was thick and clumsy as a piece of wood.

Thomasina had her face turned away from him. "Do whatever you have to do," she said quietly.

"But, you see, my dear, I'm not sure that I can..."

There was a pungent, remembered smell and the sensation of metal touching her face. Then Thomasina slipped down a dark blue funnel, whirling down and down and down until she knew no more.

She woke to pain and to the sound of her name being called. It was too much effort to answer. Thomasina wanted to go back down that whirling blue funnel, away from the throbbing. Gentle hands turned her and arranged her pillows. A few drops of fluid were spooned into her mouth, bitter and astringent. Later, the same hands did something to her shoulder, but her head was still fuzzy. She wanted to say something or ask something, but she forgot just what it was. It didn't really seem very important. She stopped fighting it and drifted ... drifted....

Her next impression was of hot sunlight shining through her closed eyelids and a sharp, concerned voice. "Thomasina? Thomasina! Oh, what have you done to her!"

Her mother's voice was strained and more than a little angry. The cool accents had melted away beneath the fire of Patrice's emotions. "I hold you totally responsible for this bandit attack, Dr. Rafferty! How could you take a gently raised young female and thrust her into the dangers of your harsh way of life? It isn't right!"

There was a familiar rumble of outrage as Rafferty's voice rose to its usual roar. "Madame, you are in no position to talk! The injury is a mere scratch—and your daughter's current status is less dangerous now than in the situation from which I rescued her on the San Francisco docks!"

Thomasina heard angry pacing in the wake of their heated exchange. She wished they would go away.

Patrice spoke again. "I can understand why you despise me, Dr. Rafferty, and I am grateful that you didn't expose me before Don Carlos and his guests. I am fully aware that I owe you some sort of explanation. After my late husband's death ... the circumstances were such that—"

Rafferty broke in hastily. "You need say nothing more. I am not here to judge you, and I have no intention of exposing your charade. It is none of my concern. At the moment, my most pressing duty is to see that Thomasina is restored to health."

"You are very good." Patrice leaned down and Thomasina felt her mother's hand cover her own. "My darling . . . I know that you can hear me. Wake up. Oh, what is wrong with her, Doctor? Why won't she wake up?"

"Well," Rafferty answered from just beside her, "let's close the shutters now that you've reassured yourself that she's alive. I imagine she's got one hell of a headache. I had to give her a whopping good dose of Wojcik's elixer just to keep her from climbing out of bed."

"My daughter is a very determined young woman."

"If you mean she has the tenacity of a bulldog, I heartily agree."

Thomasina blinked an eye open and fixed Rafferty with a baleful glare. He was grinning down at her. He looked younger and rather boyish. She shifted her head an inch. The result was a major increase in the throbbing at her temples and an unobstructed view of her mother. She groaned. There was a lot to discuss, but she didn't have the energy to do it now.

Patrice was not to be put off. She gave a tiny nod of dismissal to Rafferty. He didn't budge. "No doubt you have things to talk over. However, I'd like to have a look at the dressing first," he said. "If you'll wait in the *placita*, Mrs. Wentworth. Domingo is preparing some fresh tea and he'll bring you out a cup."

He held the door open, and Patrice had no choice but to go out. Rafferty closed the door behind her.

Thomasina tried to sit up. "I suppose you're going to do something horrid to my wound again. Tell me about it."

"The site is clean and without any sign of infection. The scars, if there are any, will be slight."

The throbbing in her head made Thomasina cranky. "Not that. What I meant was, what did you dig out of me and how did you repair the damage."

The expression on his face hovered between amusement and admiration. He filled in the details in a concise, professional manner, as if they were discussing a third party. "I hope that meets with your approval," he added drily.

She missed the irony in his tone. "I can't think of anything I would have done differently. Well, get on with whatever else you have to do. My mother won't be happy kicking her heels for long."

"I only said I had to check your dressing to get rid of your mother for a few minutes. I changed it earlier when I put you into my nightshirt."

Thomasina looked down. Sure enough, it was a man's full nightshirt that covered the bulky bandage. She lifted the sheet. As far as she could tell, she was wearing nothing else. Anger warred with embarrassment. "*You* undressed me?"

"I was only returning the favor, my dear. If you'll recall, you did the same thing for me on your first night in San Juan."

A deep flush spread upward from her chest to her throat, sweeping up to her brow. "I was saying that to tease you. It was really Domingo who stripped off your clothes and put you to bed."

Rafferty turned away to hide his smile. He'd guessed that himself. "That's neither here nor there. Now that you're back among the living, we had better get our facts straight. What do you intend to tell your mother?''

Thomasina pushed the tumble of curls up off her forehead. "First of all, I suppose I'll say how sorry I am if I've caused her any distress. Then I'll let her know—in the strongest terms—that I have no intention of going back with her."

"No," Rafferty said impatiently. "I mean about *us.*"

It took several seconds for his words to sink in. "About us . . . do you mean that you haven't told her . . . that she thinks . . . ?"

The doctor sat on the edge of the narrow bed. "Exactly. As far as your mother knows, you and I are legally man and wife."

"I see . . ." That made everything simpler. If her mother thought she was actually wed to Rafferty, Patrice would have to give in and hold her peace. Thomasina weighed the pros and cons.

"It would go very much against the grain to deceive my mother more than I already have—yet I think that it would be for the best. Earlier, I heard you say that I was as stubborn as a bulldog." She sent him a look of appeal. "But you see, I am my mother's daughter and have inherited the trait from her."

Rafferty got up and stood with his back to her, unaware that Thomasina could see his reflection in the mirror. "Then we will not admit her into our confidence."

"No. When my apprenticeship is done, I will have to tell her that . . . that we didn't suit . . . Perhaps I will say we've had the marriage annulled."

"Say whatever you like. It makes no matter to me. I'll send her in to you."

He left the room, shutting the door so hard, the mirror shook. Thomasina was puzzled. Rafferty's voice hadn't changed, but his face had looked like a thundercloud. No doubt he was regretting their arrangement already. Well, that was just too bad, she thought angrily.

Her head pounded, her shoulder ached, and she was about to perpetrate a hoax on the mother whom she dearly loved. It was necessary to do so because otherwise Patrice might expose their ruse and create a scandal. It was all very difficult. It was no wonder Thomasina felt like crying.

When Patrice Wentworth came back, Thomasina was propped up against the pillows, her face wan and her eyelids reddened. Patrice went at once to her daughter's side.

"Oh, my dear! I hope you are not in a great deal of pain." Pulling up the straight-backed chair from the desk, she sat next to the bed. "It was a great shock to see you laid so low, however Dr. Rafferty assured me that you would be quite recovered in a few days."

"I feel much better already, now that you are here. I know I have been a great disappointment to you, Maman, and I am very sorry for it...."

"No, child." The regret on Patrice's elegant features was genuine. "Don't apologize. It is I who have been gravely at fault. Please, hear me out."

She folded her hands precisely. "I wanted—desperately—for you to have all the things you deserved ... all the things that I had missed in my own youth.

I didn't...*couldn't* believe that the very things that mattered so greatly to me meant nothing at all to you. Now—'' Patrice sighed ''—now that you have proven that you are a grown woman with a mind of your own, I will step back and let you get on with your own life.''

Leaning down, she kissed Thomasina on the forehead. ''I will be back again tomorrow.'' With a swish of expensive clothing, she stood and proceeded to the door. Patrice paused with one hand on the doorjamb and sent her daughter a sweet and sad smile. ''Goodbye until then—Mrs. Rafferty.'' Patrice shut the door quietly, like an actress making her exit after a dramatic renunciation scene.

And that, Thomasina thought shrewdly, is exactly what it was. Her mother had some subtle trick up her sleeve, which only time—and the properly staged moment—would reveal. Thomasina wracked her brain for possibilities. The most likely one was that her mother was sure that the drudgery of life in a poor village would soon pall.

The snort of horses and the clopping of hooves said Patrice was on the journey back to the Valverde hacienda.

Thomasina slept away most of the day, but by suppertime, she felt much refreshed. She attempted to sit up and to swing her legs over the side of the bed. The effort was too much too soon, and she fell back against the pillow with a groan.

Rafferty came in shortly after with a bowl of gruel. His trained eye took in the mauve shadows beneath her eyes at a glance. Digging after those rock fragments had technically been an easy task—but it had been one of the hardest surgeries he'd ever had to perform. For the first time in his professional life, Dr. Brendan Rafferty had been unable to dissociate himself from his patient. He had felt the bite of the scalpel and the sting of the probe as if it had been his own flesh. Although he didn't know why it had transpired that way, the experience had been acutely uncomfortable. He didn't ever want it to happen again.

Thomasina was glad to see Rafferty at first. But by the looks of him, he was in a foul temper. He plunked himself down in the chair Patrice had vacated. The sturdy wood groaned beneath his solid weight. The gruel he spooned up looked thick and unappetizing.

"I am not an infant," Thomasina said mildly. "I can feed myself... and I would much prefer to get up and fix something myself."

"Hah!" the doctor snorted. "I've heard of your cooking."

Thomasina sank back against the pillow. "Go away if you mean to be in such a hateful mood. My shoulder is aching abominably."

Instantly, he was contrite. "Is it, my dear? I'll mix you up some more of Wojcik's elixir." He set the gruel down.

Domingo poked his head inside the room. "The carriage of Don Carlos is returning with Señora Wentworth."

Rafferty cursed beneath his breath and was rewarded with a scold from his patient. "I'll try to mend my wicked ways," he said through gritted teeth. "It's just that that damned woman is up to something and

I'd like to know exactly what, before she brings a hornet's nest down around our ears."

"May I remind you that that 'damned woman' is my mother." There was no real rancor in Thomasina's response. She had already admitted as much to herself. What could her mother be up to? The light suddenly dawned with blinding clarity. Patrice Wentworth was no fool. The hard years in New Orleans had taught her many things—and one of them was the ability to sum up another woman.

"I believe I have the answer. She either knows or senses that there is nothing of the husband and wife about us. While she may not know the truth, I think she at least suspects it. It is only a matter of time until she begins trying to find out just when and where our wedding took place."

Patrice's voice floated in to them. "And how is my darling daughter this afternoon, Domingo?"

Thomasina signaled to Rafferty. "Be on your guard. We must think of some way to erase her doubts."

"I already have," the doctor said softly.

Before Thomasina knew what he meant to do, Rafferty leaned over the bed and slipped one of his hands behind her head. She felt his breath at her temple. Then his long fingers tangled in her auburn curls and he lowered his mouth until it met hers. His arm was strong, his lips warm and firm. She expected a quick peck to simulate affection—and was taken completely by surprise.

Rafferty's nearness confused her, and the warmth of his kiss sent her senses spiraling dizzily. Almost like the effect of the ether, she thought in the brief space before she became totally overwhelmed. His mouth moved on hers in a way that sent ripples of pleasure through her entire body. All the intensity of his nature was concentrated in the touch of his lips upon hers. He drew her against his hard chest and she felt the heat radiating from him. It found its twin in her.

There seemed to be a glowing heap of embers somewhere in the region of her solar plexus. It grew until it filled her, sending flames of desire licking out along her nerve endings. The kiss—Rafferty's kiss—consumed her. Thomasina caught his shirt collar and clutched it for all she was worth. She didn't want the kiss to stop. Ever. It had taken her, in the span of a few heartbeats, from the innocence of girlhood through an awakening and into the ripening knowledge of womanhood.

Rafferty felt as if he were falling through time and space. What had begun as a sham became suddenly, startlingly real. The need that had been growing, unwelcomed and barely acknowledged, burst forth with such power, it shook him to the core. There was a woman—soft, warm, responsive—in his arms and in his bed. And that was exactly where he wanted her.

Not just any woman, but this particular, this prickly and vulnerable one. Dear God, but it had been a long time since he'd lost his head so totally! One meeting of their lips and she had broken through the prickly barriers to intimacy that he'd erected long ago. He had tried so hard to lock away his passions toward anything but his work, as if they were unruly beasts, whose very existence he denied.

Rafferty groaned and took the kiss deeper. Her mouth opened to him, warm and sweet as honey. A madness came over him. He kissed her until they were both breathless and yearning. One hand remained in the soft curls at her nape while the other sought the womanly contours of her breast. It molded to the palm of his hand as if it had been made to fit it. Impatient with the intervening cloth of the nightshirt, he pushed the wide neck open and slipped his hand inside.

Thomasina sighed as Rafferty's fingers brushed along the side of her breast. She gasped when he cupped her breast in his hand. Her nipple hardened in response, filling her with a hot, dark pleasure. Years of careful control vanished like smoke. She was greedy for more. She forgot everything—the Spartan room, the throbbing in her shoulder—even her mother's arrival, which had precipitated Rafferty's action.

''Oh!'' Patrice's small exclamation was as loud as a thunderclap.

Rafferty released Thomasina and twisted around, his face flushed and eyes half-dazed with the heat of his desire. Cursing beneath his breath, he pulled his hand away and slipped it out of the nightshirt.

With Rafferty's warmth withdrawn from her skin, Thomasina felt cold. Her mouth was swollen with kisses, and her breast still tingled. She pulled the sheet up to her chin, feeling waves of crimson flow over her face.

Her mother was the first to recover her composure. Patrice set down the armful of flowers she was carrying at the foot of the bed. There was an odd, speculative look in her eyes.

"Well, Thomasina! I'm so glad to see that you're much improved since this morning. Don Carlos and his sister have sent you these lovely roses from their garden to cheer you, and the promise of a visit as soon as you are able to tolerate it."

Rafferty muttered a curt greeting and pushed past Patrice, leaving the two women alone.

Thomasina's face was still flooded with red. It wasn't because her mother had caught them in mid-kiss that she was so mortified, but because of the way she felt. She wanted her mother to go away. She wanted Rafferty to touch her again. She wanted to drop through the floor.

The panic returned, overwhelming her senses. It robbed her of breath and set her heart racing until she was light-headed and trembling. She drew up her knees beneath the sheet, covered her face with her hands and gasped for air. Her skin was clammy and her teeth chattered like castanets.

Patrice flew to her side. "My dear, what is wrong? Are you in pain?"

Thomasina was too upset to speak. She rolled on her side, away from her mother. "Please ... I want to be alone for a while."

"Come, Mrs. Wentworth. Your daughter needs her rest." As if by magic, Rafferty had returned and was drawing Patrice away from the bed and out of the room.

Thomasina wept into her pillow. There was no way to explain that Rafferty's kiss had sent her tumbling from bliss into terror from one breath to the next. She struggled with her inner demons for control. She had to conquer and vanquish them if she meant to stay on at the surgery.

Rafferty was a virile man with a man's needs, and she—God help her—was a woman. Thomasina castigated herself for the naive thinking that had brought her to San Juan without considering all the implications. She prayed for guidance and the strength to keep Rafferty at arm's length—because if he ever touched her again, the results would be disastrous.

Chapter Ten

Thomasina's shoulder healed quickly. Her relationship with Rafferty did not. That one smoldering kiss, that urgent, hungry touch that had sent their passions blazing almost out of control, had come between them like a wedge of stark, cold steel. The easy camaraderie that had just been forming was rent asunder by the fact that they were man and woman.

Over the long days of her convalescence, their eyes did not meet except accidentally, and the moments of shared laughter were gone as if they had never been. The mere touch of his sleeve against her arm or the brush of her skirts too near his trousered leg sent them hopping away like scalded cats.

Thomasina set about improving her Spanish to pass the time and Lorenzo was a willing teacher. Rafferty refused to let her get on horseback, and he insisted that the wagon was too ill sprung for her to venture out in. There were no rides across the valley through the early-morning dew to visit Geraldo Zavala.

The birth of twin girls to one of the village women had taken place while Thomasina was laid up. It was a terrible disappointment to her. Rafferty hadn't told her about the confinement until after the dramatic event.

"I already had one difficult patient on my hands," he had snapped by way of explanation. "I did not need another."

It had been a bone of contention between them ever since. There were others. A week passed with Thomasina chafing under Rafferty's watchful eye. The usual parade of injuries and illnesses that occupied him still left him plenty of time to see that she followed his instructions. One afternoon, she braved his wrath to walk out to the stable where he and Domingo were removing a wheel from the wagon. They were so engrossed that she sat down on the wooden bench and watched them for some time before Rafferty noticed.

"What the devil do you think you're doing?" he roared.

"Getting my strength up. For the past week, you've restricted my activity as if I were an invalid and, in general, acted like a hen with one chick. I am not made of butter, you know. The sun won't melt me," she retorted. "And I refuse to lie about any longer with nothing to occupy my mind."

The doctor's jaw set in stubborn, familiar lines. "Your system suffered a severe shock. Inflammation might set in—and then I'd have an even bigger problem on my hands."

Despite his blunt words, Thomasina was not offended. Rafferty had a point...and she saw that he was motivated by true concern for her welfare. It touched her, but it did not dissuade her. "You are much too conservative, *Doctor* Rafferty. Bed rest and hearty food are well and good, but I prescribe daily walks and some mental exercise for myself."

He conceded reluctantly. "But not alone, mind you. I don't want you straying too far."

"Then you're afraid the bandits might return." It was a statement rather than a question.

Lorenzo had been running about the yard, using a long stick as a hobbyhorse. He came to a halt. "Bandits!" he said disdainfully. "Bandits would not attack anyone under the protection of El Doctore. He is their friend."

Domingo came to the stable door and called to the child sharply. Lorenzo looked from one to the other, then neighed loudly and trotted down the road to the village, dragging his steed with him.

"The boy is young and foolish," Domingo said carelessly. Thomasina was not convinced. Lorenzo was exceedingly bright. And if the men who attacked them were not bandits...?

That night, she was awakened by a thumping from the front door. She drew her robe on and hurried into the main room of the surgery, where Rafferty slept. He was already at the door, a revolver in his hand. She froze in place, fearing that whoever had shot at them the week before had returned to finish the business. Then Rafferty lowered the revolver and ripped a bundle of cloth from where it had been nailed to the outside of the door. Domingo appeared, the shotgun slung through his arm.

Thomasina hurried forward. "I heard the noise and... is it the bandits?"

"Go back to bed," Rafferty barked. "There will be no more bandits in San Juan."

There was such stern command in his voice that she obeyed instinctively—but there was one other thing that sent her fleeing to the bedchamber. As Rafferty had wheeled around, something had slipped from the bundle, small and pale and wrinkled.

"What is that . . . ?"

"A gift," he said with a strange smile, "from an admirer. Sleep soundly."

Thomasina went back to the bedchamber and shut the door. She leaned against it trying to convince herself that the object which had fallen was not what she thought it was. No, it couldn't be . . . could it?

She had only gotten a quick glimpse and she wasn't quite certain—but it had looked very much like a severed ear.

Her dreams were restless, and Thomasina awakened not long after dawn feeling tired and dispirited. She threw back the sheets. There was no sense staring at the ceiling. She intended to question Rafferty more about the shooting incident and the strange happening in the night. Up till now, he had managed to dodge her queries on one pretext or another, but she was determined to get answers.

She heard him talking in low tones and hurried into her clothes. She found the doctor in the surgery, attending to a farmer with a badly sprained ankle. The room reeked of spirits of camphor and green liniment. The man was in a good deal of pain, but his mental agony was greater. It was the busy season, and a man who could not tend his crops and animals was useless.

Rafferty probed the bruised foot gingerly, gently flexing and rotating it. "No broken bones," he told the farmer, who smiled and crossed himself, offering thanks to God and to El Doctore in equal measure. "You must keep off it for three days and put it up on a bench or stool to keep the swelling down."

"*Sí*, El Doctore. *Gracias. ¡Muchas gracias!*"

Suddenly, Thomasina realized the entire conversation had taken place in Spanish—and that she had understood. She was pleased and encouraged by her progress.

Rafferty finished winding a bandage around the farmer's foot for support. The man thanked him and, with the aid of a stout stick, hobbled out to the donkey cart where his brother waited.

As he splashed water into the basin, Rafferty examined Thomasina shrewdly. "You should still be abed. You look like something the dog dug up after two days—and then reburied."

She laughed. There was no sense in being angry. If there was one thing she'd learned, it was that Rafferty always spoke the truth—no matter how bald it might be. And she *had* seen herself in the speckled mirror, a white and hollow-eyed spectre floating in the dim, morning light. But she couldn't resist a jab in his direction.

"How original, Dr. Rafferty. But you shouldn't spoil me with such pretty compliments. They might turn my head."

He had the grace to grin. "Unlike my old friend de Palmar, I would have made a poor diplomat." He came closer, drying his hands on a linen towel, and studied her face. "You do look done in this morning."

As she was about to protest, Thomasina felt suddenly overcome by wave upon wave of dizziness. It came out of nowhere and distorted her vision oddly. The plastered adobe walls seemed to ripple and she had the sensation of being *here* one instant and *there* the next.

Then she became aware of a distant bell tolling and the instruments and bottles rattling in the cupboard. The cup Rafferty had left on the table skittered to the edge and fell to the floor in an explosion of splintered pottery. The doctor was rooted in surprise.

Thomasina ran past him and tried to pick Lorenzo up in her arms. Pain zigzagged down her arm like lightning and she almost dropped him.

Rafferty scooped the boy up and hustled Thomasina out of the surgery.

Domingo was sprawled in the dirt a few feet outside the stable. He scrambled up, staring at the peaks of Los Tres Hermanos, mirror bright in the dazzling sun. The snowy summit shimmered and danced with sequined light.

Rafferty thought he heard Domingo cry out in a low, agonized voice, but almost instantly, he realized his mistake. It was the earth groaning beneath gigantic forces loosed by an earthquake. The doctor had never experienced one. The power of it amazed him. The trees shook their leafy heads, and spurts of dust announced the collapse of a section of the rough logging road leading up the mountain's flank. The quake ended as suddenly as it had begun, leaving his ears ringing and his sense of balance disturbed.

Three tiny aftershocks reminded Rafferty of a giant beast trying to flick flies from its ear. Only in this case, the flies were human beings. To his astonishment, the surgery and stable remained intact.

Domingo hastily crossed himself. "It is like the legend says, El Doctore. One hundred years have passed and the three brothers are awakening. In the days of my father's father, the mountain rained fire upon the people of Old San Juan. The three brothers wakened, and the mountain melted, drowning the village."

"Nonsense. It was probably a landslide on the upper slopes. Mountains don't melt, Domingo. And look at those trees. They have been there for decades without disturbance. We are in no danger."

"No," Thomasina said with conviction. "It was an earthquake. Of that, I'm sure. I've known them in San Francisco. I hope there was no damage in the village."

Everyone looked toward the valley. Then Rafferty and Domingo conferred in Spanish so rapid, Thomasina didn't understand a single word.

The doctor turned back to her. "I'll have a look at that shoulder of yours and then go down to the village. There might be some injuries there."

"My shoulder is fine. I'll go along. You might need my assistance."

He lifted her chin in his hand and examined her face. "I saw your pain when you tried to pick up the boy. You're white as chalk."

Thomasina bit her lip. It was true, and she hated it. All the strength had run out of her, like water pouring down a drainpipe. She had come to San Juan in order to become a physician, and she had become a patient instead. "Very well. But if I am needed—"

"Then I swear I'll send for you." Rafferty's voice gentled. "I have no doubt of your courage, my dear, but at the moment, you'd only hinder me."

She blinked back tears, then she stepped back and Rafferty let his hand fall. The tension crackled between them, stronger than ever. Thomasina resorted to crispness.

"It's best to stay out in the open in case there's another quake. Make sure you tell the villagers that— and to stay away from the adobe walls. They might crumble and collapse. Not that they'd listen to any advice from me," she added bitterly.

Rafferty sent her a curious look. "You are more highly thought of in the village than you know."

When he left with Domingo, Thomasina sat down on the wooden bench next to Lorenzo. He had not spoken since the first rumble of the earthquake. Suddenly, he pointed toward Los Tres Hermanos. *"¡Señora!"*

Thomasina shaded her eyes against the glare and inspected the mountain. Nothing appeared to have changed. Then, as she watched, a small cloud formed on the lowest peak and grew, an ominous gray flag against the flawless blue sky.

Lorenzo began to talk worriedly. Thomasina didn't understand his words, but she realized that, as young as he was, he, too, had heard the legend of the three brothers. She tried to comfort him as best she could, and as her reassurances took hold, she looked back at the triple peaks.

The little cloud was thinning away to gauze. Soon, there was nothing left of it.

There had been no serious damage in the village, and after a few more aftershocks, the three giants slumbered once more and life in San Juan resumed its normal rhythms.

Thomasina tried hard to buck Rafferty's decisions regarding her own case, but she then thought better of it, settled down and began to follow his advice. She was determined to be fit and ready to ride out with the doctor when needed. Soon, she was able to sustain a leisurely stroll to the village and back, although Rafferty still ruled out riding.

The nights stayed cool, but the days grew hotter. Thomasina avoided the worst heat of the day by taking the requisite siesta or by sitting beneath the shady tree enclosed by the three walls of the *placita*. There were always tasks to be done. While shelling beans with Domingo or examining the treasures Lorenzo collected about the countryside—rocks and horse nails and bird's nests—Thomasina worked on learning Spanish.

Domingo was diplomatic enough that he rarely smiled at her mistakes. Lorenzo hooted and capered about like a monkey. More than once, she made an utter fool of herself by confusing two similar-sounding words.

"You are very . . . very droll, *señora,*" Lorenzo said in Spanish one morning, between guffaws.

"*Gracias,*" she replied gravely, as if he'd given her an extravagant compliment.

That, of course, sent the boy laughing again, and Thomasina joined in.

Rafferty had been inside all morning, dealing with correspondence. He was in a dark mood and came roaring out, demanding a little decorum. "They can probably hear you cackling all the way up to the logging camp."

Domingo looked up from the harness he was mending. "Better laughter than tears, El Doctore."

"Three against one," Rafferty exclaimed, throwing up his hands. "It's a fine thing when a man is outvoted in his own house."

Thomasina was curious. "What is that you're working on that takes such concentration?"

The doctor blushed to the roots of his hair. She didn't think he intended to answer. He loosened his collar. "A book," he said shortly. "I am completing a companion volume to a book I had published several years ago. And I require a little less noise in order to do so."

Then he glowered and retreated to the surgery. The little scene stuck in Thomasina's mind afterward. She knew so little about Rafferty and had no idea that he'd published a medical tome. It was something to pursue later, as was that strange reaction of his to Domingo's reply. Although the doctor had laughed, there had been shadows in his eyes. Thomasina would not have been a woman born if she hadn't wondered what had put them there.

The more she saw of Rafferty, the more she realized how little she knew of him personally. He had a past, and not a happy one, if she was any judge. But he never spoke of anything except medicine or his work in San Juan. Thomasina wondered about that.

Patrice, on one of her frequent visits, raised the same question. She was perched on the wooden bench of the *placita,* twirling the furled parasol that matched her blue silk dress.

"But really, Thomasina, surely you must know something about your *husband's* background! He must have spoken of the family who raised him and how he ended up in San Juan. What on earth do the two of you talk about when you're alone?"

Thomasina blushed. "There's so much to learn...so much to read...that we haven't had time. I've often wondered myself why he never married." She realized her error. "Until now, that is."

Patrice pounced. "If you know so little about him, what drew you together so quickly?"

The pit yawned before Thomasina. She had never been able to lie well, especially to her own mother. If she said that she and Rafferty had married for reasons of convenience and to avoid scandal, Patrice would leave no stone unturned to separate them. Thomasina knew her mother was not happy that her only child had tied herself to a provincial doctor. Fortunately, they were interrupted by the arrival of Margarita Valverde.

Thomasina and Patrice were still keeping up the pretense that they were not related, and it was proving to be quite a strain. In accepting the Valverde invitation, Patrice had told her hosts that her daughter had stayed behind in Monterrey. If they found out the truth, Patrice would be discredited, and so would Thomasina. Fearing to cause trouble for Rafferty, Thomasina had agreed to maintain the deception. At the same time, it had seemed like a minor concession to smooth over potential awkwardness—but she had regretted her decision ever since.

Domingo ushered Margarita into the *placita*. She paused when she saw Patrice. "Had I known you intended to visit Señora Rafferty, I would have accompanied you."

Patrice gave her an ingenious smile, but her voice held an edge. "Ah, but you were walking in the garden with Ambassador de Palmar, and I did not want to disturb you."

Margarita waved away the chair Thomasina offered. "Thank you, but I have come to speak to Dr. Rafferty. He can usually be found in the surgery at this time of day."

Thomasina felt the blood rush to her face. "He has gone to the village. There was an emergency."

"That is unfortunate, for I need to speak to him. In that case, I shall be on my way," Margarita said. She paused at the door, then to Thomasina, she said, "When you are quite recovered, you must visit the *curandaria*. Her name is Ophelia. It would be well for you to court her friendship. You might learn a good deal."

Thomasina was surprised. "I thought the healing women were primarily midwives."

Margarita didn't try to hide her annoyance. "She is much more. You think that you know so much with your books and patent medicines, Señora Rafferty. But you will find that my people are wiser still, in many ways."

Her vehemence surprised Thomasina even more. Don Carlos referred to the local people as if they were serfs and he the great lord, but Margarita had said "my people."

There is more to her than I imagined, Thomasina thought. I shall have to cultivate her friendship, as well as that of the healing woman.

Patrice sipped at her glass of lemonade and eyed her daughter. "Before either of you venture out, you should be aware of a vile rumor flying around..." She paused for effect.

Thomasina distrusted her mother in such a mood. There was something up her sleeve. Thomasina had to discover what it was. "What rumor is that?"

"Someone has started a whispering campaign. I hope you'll not be offended, my *dear* Mrs. Rafferty, but I think it is time you knew about it. There are those who say that you and the good doctor are *not* man and wife."

Thomasina's heart jumped against her ribs so hard, she was sure her mother could see it. Patrice went on. "Most ridiculous, of course, and so I have told everyone. Why, Dr. Rafferty told me all about it. You were married at the mission of San Pedro near Huacatapetl—isn't that right?"

"Why, yes." Thomasina was relieved that Rafferty had had the sense to palm the story off on her mother—until she looked up and caught the blaze of victory in Patrice's eyes. She'd seen the trap too late. After walking straight into it.

With a sinking feeling in the pit of her stomach, Thomasina realized that the doctor had probably given some other name for the place of their alleged wedding. She grasped at a straw. "San Pedro. Or was it San Pablo? I always get Saint Peter and Saint Paul mixed up in their Spanish versions. You would think I would know the name of the place where I was married."

"Yes," Patrice replied smoothly, "one would think so. But I imagine that you have been so busy in the past weeks that you haven't had time to be bothered with . . . details."

Thomasina could have cheerfully throttled Patrice. Why was her mother playing these cat-and-mouse games? It didn't make sense. At this point, after pretending to have just met Señora Rafferty at the Valverde hacienda, revealing the truth would rebound on her with just as disastrous an effect as it would upon her daughter.

As the hostess, Thomasina skillfully turned the conversation into other channels, but inwardly, she was seething. As soon as Rafferty got back, they would have to get their stories straight and make sure the "facts" matched. Thomasina's head began to ache. It had always distressed her to tell even a small untruth—and now she was living a lie of major proportions.

Patrice finished her glass of lemonade. "That was delightful, Mrs. Rafferty. And now, since Señorita Valverde is here, I will accompany her on her ride. I understand it is quite a long way out to the Zavala ranchero. In such troubled times, it isn't wise for a young lady to travel so far unescorted."

Margarita was jolted out of her pensive mood. She flushed to the roots of her hair. "That is kind of you, Señora Wentworth, but unnecessary. I assure you, I am quite used to ranging far and wide over the countryside. The Zavala property runs along the southern boundary of my brother's lands. I will be perfectly safe."

"Doubly so for my company," Patrice murmured dulcetly. "And I shall be charmed to meet some of the local people."

There was no polite way that Margarita could refuse. "Of course, Señora Wentworth." The smile didn't quite reach her eyes. "It is very kind of you," she repeated hollowly. "I will ride a little bit ahead of the carriage. The road is narrow and I would not wish to cover you with dust."

Outside, Margarita's magnificent Arabian mare waited near the carriage. As Domingo helped Margarita mount, Patrice sent her daughter a particularly charming smile. "Oh, how forgetful of me. I don't think I mentioned that this will be my last visit for a while. I am returning to Mexico City for a few weeks. I will be leaving in the morning. When I return I hope to call upon you again."

"I am sure you will," Thomasina replied with a veiled look. "I wish you a safe journey—and God-speed."

"Thank you, my dear." Patrice raised her ruffled blue parasol. She leaned closer and lowered her voice. "What lovely manners you have. I am sure your mother is very proud of you." With a mischievous wink, she turned and stepped up into the carriage.

The visit gave Thomasina food for thought. Her mother had known that Margarita intended to visit the Zavala household, although the girl hadn't mentioned her plans. That was mystery number one.

The second, and more puzzling was the mystery of why Margarita would ride out to the Zavala place alone at the risk of her brother's displeasure. Yes, there was much more to the lovely *señorita* than Thomasina had imagined. It was a valuable lesson for her in not judging by first appearances.

Her lessons did not end there. Each evening, Rafferty had taken to quizzing her about her day's studies. They had slipped into the roles of pupil and mentor, awkwardly at first, and then with increasing ease, and Thomasina had discovered that Rafferty was an excellent teacher with a keen mind and a marvelous way of explaining things.

For his part, Rafferty was pleased by Thomasina's ready grasp and the logical way she strung together cause and effect, and action and reaction, into a lucid whole. At times, their minds seemed linked and the excitement of their discussion carried them away. Then a meeting of glances or an inadvertent touch as they pored over a volume of medical works would leave them tense and self-conscious.

The weeks passed. One morning when Rafferty had gone to the Zavala place, Thomasina decided to walk to the village to make rounds. It was a fine day, warm and sunny, with the scent of summer on the breeze. Usually Lorenzo accompanied her, but he had gone off chasing the blue-and-yellow butterflies that swarmed across the flower-covered meadows. It wasn't often that he went off to do nothing but be a boy on a hot summer day, and she was happy for him.

She stopped in the *mercado* to look over the baskets of fruits and vegetables. Fresh from the countryside, they were as gorgeous as jewels—tomatos and peppers glowing like rubies and emeralds, silvery squash and copper beans and corn as rich as gold. They looked so ripe and colorful, she was tempted to try her hand at one of Domingo's recipes, though Rafferty had declared her talents with knives and needles were not in the least domestic. "Do your sewing and slicing on consenting human beings," he had counseled when presented with yet another inedible concoction, "and not on hapless vegetables and rice."

Thomasina decided not to put herself to the test and set the peppers down with a tiny sigh. Cooking seemed to be a mysterious art to her, one she would never master.

As she made her way past the individual stalls, she realized the townspeople were watching her, yet avoiding any contact. The same people who had danced and cheered and carried her upon their shoulders were vanishing into their homes as if she carried bubonic plague.

The rumors about her relationship with Rafferty had gained great foothold in the past weeks and Thomasina wondered how long it would be before there was an ugly confrontation. If anyone bothered to check the records at the San Pedro mission, all the good the doctor had accomplished, all his plans to establish a hospital and train doctors and nurses from among the people of the area, would be undone.

Perhaps she might disarm the rumors with friendliness and a few well-chosen words. Her Spanish was not fluent, but she'd made great strides in learning the language. She pretended not to notice any hostility and smiled and greeted everyone she saw.

A fragrant melon caught her eye and she searched for the proper Spanish words. "I will have two of these, if you please. My husband is very fond of them."

The vendor didn't say much, but her attitude became slightly warmer. The gesture worked so well that Thomasina made the rounds of all the stalls. "What a lovely shirt," she told another woman. "Don't you think it would look very well on my husband?"

"Ah, *sí.*" The seller pointed out a woman's blouse decorated in the same colorful embroidery. Thomasina took the hint. By the time she'd finished, she had purchased enough items that she had to buy a handled basket to contain them. That accomplished, she carried out her original intentions.

Her first visit was to the little house of old Señora Estevez, where she learned that the dropsy medica-tion was working well. "The swelling is almost gone, *señora*," the woman said, crinkling up her wrinkled face in a pleased smile. "And my breathing much easier."

Thomasina beamed. She had convinced Rafferty to let her try one of the infusions she'd found in her medical books, adding Peruvian Bark to the regime that included the foxglove extract he'd prescribed for Señora Estevez. Thomasina had instructed the woman to take a teaspoon of the liquid morning and night without fail.

"I'm delighted to know it has helped you," she responded in her brand-new Spanish.

"Oh, yes. I do exactly as you told me to do. I rub it on myself twice a day—and it works wonderfully."

Thomasina was flabbergasted. Her instructions had not been as clear as she'd thought. Her one consolation was that Rafferty had not been present to learn of the mixup. He would have never let her live it down.

She racked her brain for a diplomatic way to straighten things out—one that would spare her blushes and not embarrass her patient. Before leaving the surgery she had brought another bottle of the Peruvian Bark infusion with her and that gave her an idea. "Excellent. I am glad to hear that—and I have brought you another one that will be even more effective. The only difference is that you must take it by mouth instead of rubbing it on your skin."

She explained the dosage slowly and had the woman repeat the instructions. "*Sí*, I will do that. A spoonful to be swallowed in the morning and again at night."

Disaster had been averted. With a sigh of relief, Thomasina continued on to her next destination, a stop to see the new *niñas* and to check on their mother. She was welcome in the home, but there was a good deal of reserve there and she left feeling very uncomfortable. On the walk back to the surgery, the humor of the situation with Señora Estevez struck her. Perhaps she would tell Rafferty after all. It would be worth it to see him smile and hear his hearty, booming laughter once more. She had missed it sorely.

Thomasina returned to the surgery to discover the doctor's horse saddled and waiting by the front door. Domingo was just securing a heavy blanket roll in place. The special saddlebags were already in place.

"What is it?" she asked Domingo. "Another accident in the logging camp?"

The forested slopes of Los Tres Hermanos were a prime source of timber for the surrounding area, and the close-knit families who lived on the high eastern slopes took great risks with their primitive equipment. A few days earlier, they had sent for Rafferty after a felled tree had broken away from its restraining ropes and crashed through their temporary camp. One man had been killed, a second permanently disabled in the tragedy.

Domingo buckled the straps and tested their strength. "*Sí, señora.*" He fiddled with the saddlebag flaps and didn't turn around.

Rafferty came out of the surgery, carrying his medical bag. He threw himself up into the saddle. "I didn't know I'd be leaving when you went into the village.

However, necessity dictates I must. I hope to return sometime late evening.''

Thomasina was dispirited. Was this not one of the reasons she'd come here—to learn medicine by observing and assisting? Again, she would be left behind. Irritated by his previous caution for her injuries, she was now perversely cruel. ''You needn't bother to hurry on my account. After being shot on my doorstep, nothing short of outright abduction would rattle me.''

''You weren't shot,'' Rafferty reminded her brusquely, and then he rode off.

Thomasina flounced into the house, feeling very put out. The villagers had been cool toward her and there had been no time to discuss the problem with Rafferty. No time to share with him the story of how she'd made a fool of herself with Señora Estevez. No time to laugh.

The afternoon dragged by slowly, relieved by the appearance of a small boy carrying an injured dog. Thomasina recognized Juanito Mendoza. He didn't say a word, only held out his small pet to her imploringly. ''Oh, poor creature! Bring him into the surgery.''

After her work with Cordell McGillicudy's veterinary patients, stitching up the slashed ear was a simple procedure. Thomasina was puzzled by the looks of the wound. It was not the work of another animal. ''How did this happen?'' she asked in Spanish.

''My dog was excited to see Don Carlos as he walked through the village. He is a very friendly dog, *señora*. Don Carlos struck him with his whip.'' The explanation was accompanied by the appropriate gestures.

"How wicked!" The dog was little more than a puppy, and even though she was hurting him as she sewed up his ear, his tail still wagged like a metronome. Thomasina was incensed. The animal's wound was bad enough, but Juan's acceptance of such unwarranted cruelty made her blood boil.

Since her visit to the hacienda, she had learned many things about Carlos Valverde. There was not a family in San Juan that had not been touched by his shadow. It was no wonder that some of the young men had joined the growing ranks of rebels in the hills.

When the boy left with his dog an hour later, Thomasina felt a mild glow of satisfaction. At least there was one person in the village—make that two, counting Señora Estevez—who had faith in her surgical skills. Perhaps now there would be others.

She made a lunch of the melon she'd bought in the *mercado,* and sat at Rafferty's desk, poring over the chapter he'd advised her to absorb. Finally, she closed the book with a sigh. She seemed to be doing a lot of that lately. There was more to being a doctor than book learning. Rafferty had all the fun. She was tired of reading, tired of being left behind and even more tired of having nothing to do. She had come to San Juan prepared to work. Instead she had found herself with more time on her hands than she'd ever had in her life. It was intolerable.

Thomasina looked around for something breakable and replaceable. She wanted to throw it. Self-control won out.

The time after supper was worse. Domingo went off to the cantina, as usual. Lorenzo had gone to his cousin's house. Thomasina was left to kick her heels until Rafferty's return. Dusk had fallen in the valley and was creeping up the road toward the surgery. Swimming in light high above, the three peaks of the mountain shone like polished gold.

Thomasina went inside and took down her hair, running an ivory-backed brush through the shining strands. It was a part of her evening ritual that she usually found relaxing, but tonight, it seemed to have the opposite effect. She was filled with restlessness. She pulled her hair into a loose knot, low on her nape and tried to read a book on herbal cures.

THE UMBELLIFERAE: An important order of plants which have a marked effect on the nervous and spinal system. Ingestion and subsequent overdosage may lead to symptoms of profound hysteria . . .

Try as she might, she could not interest herself in the *umbelliferae*. Rafferty surely should have returned by now. What could be detaining him? She tried again.

AETHUSA CYNAPIUM is a frightful poison which causes deep narcosis and permanent paresis when taken in excessive amounts. Despite these terrible effects, AETHUSA has its place in the modern pharmacopaeia. . . .

After a few paragraphs, the words swam back and

forth across the page until her eyes grew heavy. Thomasina rubbed her temples. Perhaps she should just give up and go to bed. Then, when Rafferty returned, he wouldn't guess that she had missed him or that she had grown worried as the lonely hours stretched out.

Unfortunately, she was too sleepy to read and too worried to sleep. Perhaps a change of books might help. There was an especially interesting one in the bottom drawer of the doctor's desk. She'd seen it when he was putting away his writing materials. Trying not to feel guilty—after all, he'd said more than once that she might read any of his texts—Thomasina opened the drawer and took out *Man and Woman: The Anatomy of Love.*

It certainly woke her up some.

The book was not a treatise on the anatomy and physiology of the human reproductive systems, but discourse on the art of lovemaking. She turned the pages, feeling like a voyeur. The language was beautiful and poetic; the drawings were done in a lyrical style, but were rather explicit. Although she was alone, Thomasina felt herself blushing.

My word! I didn't know that was even possible, she thought in surprise, examining one of the illustrations at length. And look at these two on the opposite page! They certainly seem to be enjoying themselves!

She pored over the pages, reading quotations drawn from the literature of the world. The words of the women stirred her more than the erotic drawings. She had never known that a woman would find the same pleasure in the act of love that a man did, but she had clearly been misinformed. The glittering house of her childhood memories, she knew now, was Pretty Polly's, a brothel in which tragedy lay only an inch beneath its gilded surfaces.

By the time Thomasina was ten, her mother had made enough money to give up the place and had fled with her daughter to Europe. Thomasina didn't recall much of those days either, but somehow, somewhere, she had come to believe that romance was a female's pale compensation for putting up with the stronger, darker needs of the male of the species.

Now it seemed she had been wrong. In truth, she had already learned that when Rafferty had kissed her. Only a deep, abiding fear had prevented her from accepting that knowledge. Her mother had loved and lost everything. Thomasina had never wanted to lose herself that completely. She had felt safe with her books and studies.

And then Rafferty had kissed her.

She remembered the strength and warmth of his mouth on hers, the hardness of his wide chest against her breasts, the hunger and yearning that had awakened her to her own loneliness and desire.

She closed the book.

The realization was terrible, but there was no getting around it. Without intending, without wanting to, she had fallen head over heels in love with Rafferty. The implications rattled her. She closed her eyes, only to be haunted by the images of entwined lovers she'd seen in the book. Thomasina wanted Rafferty to take her in his arms again, to hold and touch and stroke her like that. She wanted to know his fingers on her skin, his mouth on her breasts, and she wanted to do the same to him. Wanted it terribly.

It was plain that Rafferty didn't share her feelings. A man who returned a woman's sentiments didn't hide the fact from her, he courted her. Since that one scorching kiss, Rafferty had been scrupulously avoiding occasions that might allow another.

Thomasina understood about men. Her mother had explained it to her time and again. At times, men's reason was overruled by their desire. It happened to the best of them. Rafferty must have been as taken aback by the passions that kiss had ignited as she had been herself. No, even more so. And that was why he'd been ducking and sidestepping ever since.

Tiny tears squeezed from beneath her eyelids. She opened her eyes and dabbed at them with her handkerchief. The title of the book shimmered and glinted in the lamplight, the words stamped out in gold letters. *Man and Woman: The Anatomy of Love. A Scholarly Examination of Love and Eroticism—*

By Brendan P. T. Rafferty, M.D.

Thomasina was horrified. How embarrassing if he had returned and found her reading his book. She jumped up and went to the desk. She heard the surgery door open as she fumbled with the drawer. *"Damn!"* she said under her breath, without realizing it. She tried again to open the drawer and broke a fingernail. The drawer was stuck.

Thomasina muttered another oath, only vaguely aware that she was picking up the one habit of Rafferty's that she most deplored.

She was still trying to yank the drawer open when she realized that the man who had just entered was not the doctor. The steps were too light and had the wrong rhythm. She smelled garlic and woodsmoke and the unmistakable scent of an unwashed body.

"Buenas noches, señora."

Before she could turn, a hand clamped down upon her head, and she felt an edge of sharp steel against her throat.

Chapter Eleven

The keen edge of the knife pressed more deeply into her flesh. Thomasina didn't move. Or breathe.

"Where is the man called Rafferty?"

"I don't know."

"Don't lie to me, woman!"

Thomasina was pulled around by her hair, and she had a first, long look at her assailant. He was dressed like one of the hill men, in an embroidered overshirt tied by a wide, blue sash at his waist. He had a thick mustachio that covered his upper lip. A scar drew his right eye down at one corner. He smelled like a wet goat. The last observation was the most irrelevant and, strangely, that was the one thing she fixed on. It infuriated her.

"Take your dirty, filthy, stinking hand from me at once. *At once!*"

The man was taken aback. He'd expected fearful tears or screams. He hesitated just long enough for her to jerk away.

Thomasina whirled to face him, then looked him up and down with disdain. "Very well, state your business."

Her assailant goggled. "My business? *Señora—*" he advanced upon her, waving his knife like a magician's baton "—this is my business. Now, where is El Doctore? He is needed immediately."

Her arms akimbo, Thomasina stared at him without reply. The man's demeanor changed. *"Por favor, señora.* A child is ill, perhaps dying. He had the choking sickness and must have a doctor."

The choking sickness. Diphtheria. Thomasina grabbed her cloak. "How far is it from here?"

"In the hills, beyond the Old Way."

She knew the place. An ancient road of the Aztec empire had once run from the hills below Los Tres Hermanos to Mexico City. Now only a few remnants remained. "I will leave a note for El Doctore and go with you myself. I am his assistant."

She pulled out pen and paper and scribbled a hasty note for Rafferty, then gathered what she thought might be needed and threw a change of clothing into her small satchel. Before leaving, she demanded one thing of the man: why had he tried to frighten her at first.

"The lady, she said to bring you if El Doctore was not here—but she did not expect that you would come with me willingly."

Thomasina looked him up and down again. "I should think not!"

The man flushed in the lamplight. "I was not always what you see before you now, *señora*. Once I had my own fields and a few head of cattle. I bathed and laughed and went to church each Sunday with my family. Now, I am a hunted creature burrowing into the hills with—''

''With Alonzo de Vega,'' she said, saying what the man refused to. His eyes widened with fear. ''Don't look at me as if I were a witch,'' she added. ''It was only an educated guess.''

She was about to extinguish the lamp as usual, thinking that there would be enough light from the banked coals to keep Rafferty from falling over the furniture when he came in. But then she realized he might not see her note. Although she hated to leave a lighted lamp in an empty house, it was the lesser of two evils. Placing her note on his desk, where he could not fail to find it, she put on her cloak and followed the man into the moonlit hills.

The ride was long and lonely, the way often difficult. All the fury and shock that had kept her from crumbling earlier attacked her nerves with full force. This was an idiotic thing to be doing, going off with her fierce companion to his rebel camp—if there even *was* such a place. Thomasina's teeth chattered with a chill that was caused by more than the cold night air.

The scene was incredibly eerie. The hills and the lower slopes of the mountain were shapeless black presences, more guessed at than seen. Floating high in the sky, the triple peaks of Los Tres Hermanos seemed to glow with a cold witch light of their own. Only the picture of a young child suffocating from diphtheria sent Thomasina onward.

As her mare picked its way up the track, there were furtive rustlings. Thomasina had the sensation of being watched by dozens of clandestine eyes. It seemed entirely possible that things of the netherworld roamed the countryside, myths taking on frightful reality. A wild creature howled to the silvery moon, but whether coyote or wolf—or werewolf—she didn't know. By the time she spied the light of a campfire through a gap in the trees, Thomasina was tired, half-frozen and sure she was hallucinating. For a brief, happy moment, she thought it might all be a bad dream, that she was really still in the surgery, dreaming and snoozing over the dry dissertation on medicinal uses of *aethusa cynapium* and the *umbelliferae.*

Then she was through the gap and into the rebel camp. Someone ran up to catch her mare's bridle and lead the gallant beast away, while other hands were there to get Thomasina down from the saddle and unbuckle her satchel. Her hands were so numb from the cold, she couldn't undo it herself. Someone rode in behind them. She couldn't be sure, but he looked like Geraldo Zavala. She was surprised that he would be up and about already. Then she was led away.

"Thanks be to God," a woman said as Thomasina was hustled into a rude shelter. "Dr. Rafferty—he is with you?"

Thomasina received the shock of her life. A wick floated in a dish of pale oil, illuminating the face of Margarita Valverde. Her beautiful hair was pulled straight back, and her lovely features were haggard with worry as she glanced back at the child on the bed.

"No. He is away. I left a note." Thomasina didn't waste time explaining any more as she hurried to the fever victim. The boy was in sore distress, trying desperately to get air past the membrane that had formed in his throat. It was a dreadful thing to see. "I will need your help in holding him down."

Margarita and another woman, who Thomasina guessed was the child's mother or aunt, complied. First Thomasina attempted to remove the membrane with a hollow metal straw she'd brought along for the purpose. The membrane was too low for her to reach. It was hopeless. The boy was dying before her eyes. There was only one way to save him and she didn't know if she could do it.

"He needs..." The words were merely a squeak. She cleared her voice and started again. "He needs to have a hole made in his throat from the outside, so that he can breathe."

"Mother of God! Is there no other way?" Margarita gasped out. But it was plain to all that the boy was near death.

Thomasina gave terse instructions, as they listened and acted, preparing everything as she directed. "We will do what we can, *señora,*" the boy's relative said. Thomasina nodded. And I, she thought, God willing, will have to do the rest.

Her hands trembled as she laid out her instruments. Her knees were shaking and her spirit rebelled. I can't! she thought, agonized. I can't do it!

She was a faker and a fraud. All her medical knowledge was gleaned from books and a few discussions with Rafferty. The patching up she'd done at the veterinary surgery, under Cordell McGillicudy's encouraging eye, was nothing to this. One slip of the hand and she could slice through an artery.

I can't do it!

The sound of the boy's choking sent a cold wind dancing up her spine. She reached for the scalpel and her shaking stopped. Calmness flooded her, damping out the fear that had paralyzed her. I am a doctor, she said in her mind. I know what to do and I can do it.

It took only minutes to open the boy's airway. She kept it open with a flanged piece of metal she'd found in Rafferty's instrument cupboard. Thomasina heard someone enter behind her. She prayed that whoever it was wouldn't faint at the sight of what she was doing. When it was over, the boy's face pinked up nicely, his relative was reduced to grateful tears and Thomasina was drenched with sweat.

Margarita looked at her levelly across the rude bed. "I owe you an apology."

"And I, you." Thomasina smiled. "When he is comfortably settled, we shall have to have a long talk. I think that from this night on, you and I will be friends."

A shadow fell over the bed and a hand rested on her shoulder. "Well done, Thomasina. Well done."

She turned to find Rafferty standing behind her, his weary face creased with lines of strain.

Without thinking she threw herself into his arms. They closed around her tightly. Suddenly the doctor's mouth was on hers. The kiss that followed was a culmination of all the passion and emotion of the night. She clung to him for dear life until he pried her away gently.

Thomasina was embarrassed by her outburst. Margarita was stricken. She gave Thomasina a slow, sad smile. "We will still be friends, I think." Then she slipped out of the shelter into the night.

Rafferty and Thomasina turned to the bed and examined the boy together. The patient had fallen into an exhausted sleep. A young woman entered and took the stool beside the bed as Rafferty brushed the back of his hand over the boy's cheek. "He'll be all right. We can safely leave him with Elena. She is a very competent nurse."

"I'll stay with him," Thomasina persisted.

"Elena will call if there is any problem. Meanwhile, you must have a chance to rest."

"But I don't want to rest. I'm perfectly all right."

"Are you, my dear? Then why are you trembling like an aspen leaf in a windstorm?"

It was true. Thomasina suddenly realized her entire body was shaking. Her teeth clattered so violently that she bit her tongue. Rafferty put his arm around her. She was glad for the support since her limbs seemed as limp as noodles.

"Don't worry," he told her. "The reaction is often like this at first. Come, I'll get you some blankets and some warm broth. You'll be all right in no time."

He led her outside and to another shelter formed of adobe brick, half-disintegrated from decades of exposure, and a layer of sticks and thatch. Thomasina was amazed to see that the sky was already lightening to a pearly glow. Between the eerie ride and the boy's terrifying illness, she'd been so engrossed that the hours had passed as quickly as minutes. It was no wonder that she felt shaky.

Rafferty guided her inside the shelter. It was humble in the extreme, yet was as welcoming to her as a palace. A wick burned in a dish of oil, as in the other place. Its small glow was enough to show her a straw pallet covered with Rafferty's riding cloak, and his saddle and bridle placed neatly on the dirt floor beside his satchel and emergency kit. The floor was swept clean of all debris and there was an efficiency about the way things were arranged that told her Rafferty was no stranger here.

Thomasina stumbled. He caught her about the waist, saving her from a nasty fall. She warmed to his touch. Weariness and the sharp exhilaration of saving the boy's life blurred and blended into something stronger. Thomasina had run from her emotions far too long. There was no use in running now. She knew, with blinding clarity, that she loved Rafferty. Loved him beyond thought or reason.

That revelation on top of everything else overset all her careful restraints. She had faced a knife-wielding rebel, a ride through the dark night and the spectre of death. But it was realizing that she had fallen in love— for the first and last time—that brought the sting of tears to her eyes.

Rafferty heard her sniffle and saw the tears. They smote him to the heart. "My dear girl! Lie down, you're exhausted." He lowered her to the pallet and covered her with his cloak.

It smelled just like him—of leather and bay rum and tincture of green soap. It was very comforting.

He hunkered beside her and took her hand between his. "You're a brave woman."

"No, I'm not. I was frightened to death."

His grave eyes regarded her steadily. "But you did what had to be done." His grip tightened. "Don't you think I've ever been afraid? At times, the knowledge that a human life lies in my hands, that one error on my part can condemn a person to hell on earth—or death—is almost more than I can bear. But that is the choice I made in choosing medicine as my vocation. And every day of my life, I reap the reward or assume the burden of it. I can't let you give up your own life to medicine unless you understand the cost."

She pushed away the cloak and sat up. "I understand. I do! Especially after tonight. I thought I would be exhilarated. Instead, I was humbled by it."

She thought he wasn't going to respond. He was staring at the shadows on the walls as if his whole life were revealed there. "The call to the healing arts is a difficult one. A blessing and a curse, some say. In my time, I've thought it both."

There was such sadness in his voice that it tore at her heart. "Yes," she said huskily. "I've seen the joy on your face when you help someone—and I've seen the pain that shadows your face when you think that no one is looking."

He looked at her sharply. "You see too much."

There was a change in his eyes. For just an instant, he was caught off guard and she saw deep into his soul. Thomasina couldn't bear to see the anguish that haunted them. His vulnerability was unexpected. His loneliness shattered her. Rafferty had always seemed so self-sufficient, so sure of himself and his decisions, that he had fooled everyone—herself included.

Thomasina ached for him. Rafferty filled up others with his generosity of spirit, but his own cup was almost empty. She reached out to him, tracing the strong bones of his cheek with her fingertips. He closed his eyes and made a low, strangled sound. "Don't," he whispered hoarsely.

Her palm cupped his cheek and he raised his hand to push it away. Instead, his fingers closed around her wrist possessively. He was storm-tossed on a sea of chaotic emotions. She was his only lifeline. He pressed his mouth against the delicate underside of her wrist, inhaling the sweet perfume of her skin. Soft. Warm. Giving.

Rafferty opened his eyes. Thomasina's face was mere inches from his, her lips parted. He leaned down and with a groan, drew her into his arms, crushing her to his chest.

His hands roved over her body. During the long days of her convalescence, his hands had been gentle and impersonal when they touched her. There was no gentleness in them now, only blind, driving need. He breathed her name as if it were a prayer. "Thomasina..."

Then his mouth came down on hers with a strength and hunger that set her blood afire. Her lips clung to his, her body molded to him. His kisses burned against her mouth, her cheek, her throat. She wanted to get close to him...closer...

His wide palms swept over her back and sides, learning and memorizing. Thomasina's fingers dug into Rafferty's broad shoulders and she reveled in the feel of his hard muscles. When his fingers brushed over her breast, she gasped with a rush of desire. When he cupped their womanly roundness, she knew a hot, fierce joy.

He freed the buttons at her bodice and his mouth skimmed down the curve of her throat, seeking the sweetness of her breasts. She was overwhelmed with sensation and need. He pressed her down upon the pallet and slid lower, until his lips touched the pebbly softness at the peak. When he took the tip of her breast into his mouth, she was washed by alternating waves of heat and cold. The feathering of his breath across her skin was the most exquisite torture. There was a dizzying, pulling sensation deep inside her that filled her with wild, singing glory. Time was suspended. She reached out to him, enfolding him in her arms.

Rafferty groaned again and buried his face between Thomasina's breasts. He shifted his weight until he covered her, tangling his hands in her hair. This was the moment he had dreaded and longed for. The moment for which they had been destined long before their first passionate kiss. Rafferty fought to hold on to the tattered scraps of his reason. He had to know that she wanted this as much as he did. Once they crossed the final threshold, there would be no turning back.

He held her face between his hands. "Thomasina... I want you...."

She felt the heat rise in the pit of her stomach and curl outward until she gasped for breath. Then the terrible, familiar panic swept over her, sucking the air from her lungs. Smothering her.

Thomasina clawed at Rafferty, struggling and choking. She was suffocating. She was fighting for breath, for life...running, running down the long, empty corridor, running until her chest felt ready to burst and—

Rafferty caught Thomasina by the shoulders and shook her out of her panic. The fire of his desire had been extinguished. In place of the smoldering, would-be lover there was a hard-eyed physician trying to control a hysterical patient. One moment she had been a woman, pliant and responsive in his arms, the next, she was a frenzied, feral creature fighting for all she was worth.

"Let me go!" Thomasina's eyes were glazed, and Rafferty understood that she was reliving some horrifying memory. Her voice rose in pitch.

"Let *her* go. Don't hurt her. Oh, no! God..."

There was no bringing her out of it. Thomasina was sobbing incoherently, caught in the talons of a terrible hysteria. He had to break its grip. Rafferty drew back his hand and delivered a swift slap to her cheek.

Thomasina's whole body went rigid. She stared at him, wide-eyed, then buried her face in her hands. If Rafferty could have made himself sink through the ground, he would have willingly done so. He touched her arm lightly and she pulled back away from him. "Thomasina...!"

"Go away...please. Just go...."

He did. She watched his retreating back, then collapsed upon the pallet and wept up a storm.

Rafferty cursed, long and fluently as he strode through the camp. For a few precious minutes, he'd been lost in a delirium. He'd known, almost from the first, that she was a danger to him and the careful life he'd built. And that he was an even greater danger to her. He'd known and had still rushed in like a mad fool. He was every kind of a blackhearted knave that he'd ever been called, and worse.

He went to where Lugh stood tossing his golden mane in the early light. The horse neighed and shifted restlessly. A dog growled, low in its throat, from across the way. Rafferty scarcely noticed. His eyes were still filled with the image of Thomasina cowering in terror against the wall. It had burned into his mind like a brand and he was forever marked.

He turned and strode through the rocks and trees, to the high meadow. He wanted to lose himself on the mountain. He had never been so angry in his life. He was consumed with rage at his loss of control. It built in him like a giant red tide. It rose like boiling lava from deep, volcanic depths. It shook his entire body—

No, it was another earthquake. Clouds of dust puffed up against the pink dawn sky where an old wall had collapsed into the dirt. The dogs bayed, and a child screamed in terror. The tremor lasted for several very long seconds as the ground heaved beneath his feet like a living thing.

The sun shot up above the horizon unexpectedly, bathing the scene in lurid light. Then came the roar, loud and hot as a giant's breath on his back. Rafferty spun on his heel just in time to witness disaster. A great gout of smoke and flame belched forth from the side of Los Tres Hermanos.

The wind was blowing in the opposite direction, across the face of the mountain. When it cleared, with much smoke and rumbling, a steaming crack had opened on the mountain's surface, like a rift into hell. The air smelled of sulfur. The glow of lava was clearly visible in the jagged fracture, lighting the dawn like a second sun. Slowly, the rock and snow of the upper reaches shifted into a heavy veil of fog as the lava began to roll down the slope, a cauldron of boiling mud that snapped trees as it engulfed them and turned the mountain into a thick gray-brown sea. A towering cloud of ashy smoke grew upward into the sky as the flow raced downward, hissing and sputtering. The very air hummed.

The area where Rafferty stood was in no immediate danger from the lava flow, but the valley of San Juan was in its path. Hundreds of tons of lava bore down upon it, gathering speed, and there was no warning he could give in time. He said a swift prayer and, as if in answer, the bells of the church began to toll. The villagers were warned.

He ran to find Thomasina, but she was gone from the shelter. With a smothered oath he ran through the camp. He found her in the shelter with Elena and the boy whose life she'd saved. The walls listed but still held together. Another jolt might send them crashing down. Thomasina was gently picking up the boy. Her eyes, although red rimmed, were dry, and there was a sense of purpose about her that reassured Rafferty.

Her vocation would see her through the next hours. The need to help and soothe and ease would keep her from thinking. For now. But later, when she had time to dwell on what had passed between them ... He rushed them both outside.

Back on the high meadow, Rafferty watched the destruction below. The lava flow poured through a gap in the hills like thick syrup through a funnel, diverted from San Juan by a long ridge. Another ridge hid the flow from view, but its destructive path could be followed by the patterns of mingled smoke and steam. The Valverde lands were dead ahead of it.

Rafferty saddled Lugh and threw his bags over the horse's back. The horse was skittish, rolling his eyes and sidling until Rafferty stroked the animal's great golden neck. "Easy, old fellow. Easy."

There was incredible trust between man and beast. The horse shivered and went still. He snorted softly. Rafferty leapt into the saddle. Two riders had already taken off down the road, but the others were standing about, carefully not meeting his eyes. "What are you waiting for?" he roared. "The lava flow has reached the hacienda lands. They'll be needing every able hand we have."

One of the men spat in the dust. "Don Carlos!"

Another man, tall and commanding, pushed his way through the throng. "What do we care what has happened to that devil and his henchmen. He taxes his tenants unmercifully and rents out his lands at exorbitant fees. He takes what he wants, and the people pay the cost."

Rafferty was furious. "Dammit, have you no compassion, de Vega? Whatever your fight is with Don Carlos, there are others on the hacienda, as well—

servants and tenants and their families. We can't abandon them.''

The rebel leader faced the doctor squarely. ''Don Carlos is my sworn enemy, and I his. There is a price on my head—and he is the one who put it there. I would not lift one finger to save his filthy hide or to aide those who have thrown their lot in with him.''

''Then be damned, Alonzo de Vega, for you are not the man I thought you were.''

At Rafferty's words, there was an ominous stillness, broken only by the distant crackle and hiss of the flowing lava.

Thomasina had heard everything. She had settled her patient on the safety of the open ground as the drama unfolded. The faces of the men were suddenly ugly. They crowded around Lugh, closing their circle around horse and rider.

Thomasina rose slowly. Her mouth was dry. The slightest cause might turn them from a group of angry men into a mob. Suddenly, a young man broke through their ranks, the one she'd thought was Geraldo Zavala. In daylight, she saw her mistake. This man was leaner, older, fiercer. He fisted his hands at his sides.

''Listen to Dr. Rafferty,'' he urged. ''Don Carlos is your adversary, as he is mine—but there are innocent men, women and children down there, workers and servants and their families. And what of Margarita Valverde and all she has done for us... all she has risked to bring us food and supplies? Who knows what may have happened to her... ?''

Margarita came forward, her golden hair shining. "I am here, Luiz."

The man's face lit up. He stepped up to her and clasped her hands in his. "Margarita! Thank God you are safe. I didn't know you were in the camp." He closed his eyes tightly. "I thought...I thought you had gone back to the hacienda."

Margarita gazed at him in surprise. It was almost as if she'd never really seen him before. "I have been with Concepcion and her son. But I must go to the hacienda now. Come with me, if you will."

Margarita held out her hand to Luiz. He took it. "I will," he said.

Thomasina joined them. "And I."

Rafferty looked down at her from Lugh's great back. His features were set in stern lines and his eyes were bright and hard. Thomasina lifted her chin and met him, glance for glance. There was challenge in her expression and a deep, unspoken plea.

"I shall be glad of your assistance," he said quietly. "God knows, we will need it."

She flew to where one of the men was already saddling Scheherazade. Grabbing her gear, Thomasina let the man throw her up into the saddle. Her fear was gone, held in check by the need for swift action.

Rafferty wheeled Lugh around to meet her. They rode out of the camp together, followed by Margarita and Luiz.

They were halfway to the hacienda when Thomasina glanced over her shoulder. The rebels had also followed, led by Alonzo de Vega. Rafferty and Luiz *had* rallied the men. She cheered them on.

Rafferty was the first to reach the ridge above the valley. He reined in, and the others followed suit. "The bridge is gone," he said. "We'll have to ford the river."

The riverbed was half-exposed. Rafferty urged a quick crossing. "The lava has dammed the river higher up. When it breaks through, there will be hell to pay."

Alonzo de Vega shaded his eyes. "A flood would wash away half the valley, inundating what little is left. Perhaps we can break up the dam. I'll scout along the edge of the lava flow."

The doctor nodded. "We'll go on."

When the party reached the main buildings, Thomasina was stunned. The destruction was terrible. The mud and fiery flows had poured down the funnel of the upper valley until they covered the road, the cattle barn and the stables. The buildings had vanished completely beneath the thick ooze. The lava, glowing red and gold beneath its thick black crust, had reached the main buildings of the hacienda, as well, knocking down the outer wall of the courtyard before losing its impetus. The air was filled with popping, crackling sounds. The formal gardens and half of the dining hall lay buried. Margarita was devastated. The others were shocked into silence.

Most of the house servants were accounted for. The shock had immobilized them, and they milled about in dazed states. Rafferty took charge and began giving out orders for the care of the injured. Luiz set about organizing the able-bodied to help where needed. Meanwhile, de Vega and his men cleared the riverbed of debris. The danger of flood was averted.

Soon, Domingo and Lorenzo arrived with others from the village. Thomasina was relieved to know the older man and the boy were all right. She had grown to love them both dearly. There was no time to stop and speak with them.

Thomasina began evaluating the seriousness of each person's injuries, determining what must be done first. A serving woman stared at her with the wide, blank eyes of shock. She appealed to Thomasina. "*Señora,* what shall we do?"

"Are you hurt...? No...? Good, for I need someone to assist me. Get some of the others and fetch us water and linen for bandages."

The woman nodded and went off, relieved that someone had come to take charge.

Thomasina found herself busier than she'd ever thought possible. While de Vega's men and the servants dug survivors out of the rubble and searched for victims, Thomasina and Rafferty bandaged wounds and treated burns, stitched cuts and set broken bones. Whenever Thomasina needed a hand, Margarita was there to lend it, always willing to tackle the worst tasks without a murmur of complaint.

Thomasina felt badly that she'd so misjudged the girl. She knew now that it had been envy of Margarita's friendship with Rafferty that had blinded her. There had been jealousy on the fair *señorita*'s part, as well. It was plain that Margarita worshipped Rafferty with all the pangs of a first love. It was even more evident that he thought of her only as a friend. Thomasina was certain, from the expression on the girl's face when she watched him, that Margarita was beginning to realize he would never return her sentiments in the same way.

The three of them worked in desperate harmony throughout the long day. The sun had reached its zenith and begun sliding down the western sky before they had time for a bite of food. "You must eat something," Rafferty told Thomasina. "You've been through a lot more than you bargained for since this time yesterday."

She sat on the ground, weary but strangely exalted. Steam and gray smoke still swirled up in thick, lamb's-wool clouds from the top of the mountain, wreathing Los Tres Hermanos in mystery, but there had been no further outbursts.

"It is over," Domingo announced as he dipped out water for the workers with a hollow gourd. "My father and his father and their fathers before them all lived in the shadows of Los Tres Hermanos. The giants awaken, they stretch and yawn. Then they go back to sleep again for a hundred years."

"I pray that you are right," Thomasina replied, keeping her reservations to herself.

She rose and dusted off her hands. There was still work to do. The hacienda had suffered great damage, but from what she could see, there was nothing that could not be replaced.

Thomasina knew she had faced and passed her greatest test as Rafferty's medical assistant. That was cold comfort.

How ironic, she thought, that her success as a physician had come within hours of her failure as a woman.

Chapter Twelve

Twilight came early as the ashy sky blocked out the light. With the approach of true dusk, a gloom fell on the company. Thomasina had been wrong: something had been lost that couldn't be replaced. Don Carlos Valverde was dead. He had tried to rescue one of the old servants trapped in the debris. As he freed the sobbing woman, the walls had collapsed on top of him.

Thomasina was there with Rafferty when the body was found. She had never seen death at firsthand. It was all the worse, when it wore the face of someone she had met.

Rafferty knelt beside Don Carlos and felt for a pulse. It was merely a matter of form. He closed the staring eyes, rose slowly and stared out across the courtyard to the hacienda. Tonight, there were no lanterns and liveried footmen, only the bandaged remnants of a natural calamity. Beneath the odor of smoke was a lingering perfume of summer roses.

"Don Carlos was not loved in the district." Rafferty's jaw squared. "I didn't like the man—we butted heads often. But he wasn't the incarnation of evil, as de Vega and some of the others thought. He was raised in the old way, like a feudal prince. His greatest sin was arrogance.''

Thomasina sighed. ''He has made full reparation for it.''

Another emergency claimed the doctor's immediate attention, and he turned to Thomasina. ''Go to Margarita. She will want another woman with her.''

''Of course. I am sorry....'' Thomasina hurried across the courtyard, praying for strength if she had to break the terrible news to the dead man's sister.

Margarita had already heard. She stood alone in the shadows, softly weeping. Thomasina tried to comfort her, but her sympathy was spurned. ''Do not waste your time or mine,'' Margarita said proudly, dashing away her tears. ''I am a Valverde. I have a duty to my people. They will look to me for guidance now. I must be strong.''

Alonzo de Vega watched her go. ''Like her brother, she thinks that we are children to be led by the hand.''

He was challenged immediately by Luiz. ''You are wrong. Margarita knows full well that every man must seek his own destiny. And she knows that her example will help to prevent the troubles that could follow her brother's death.'' The darkness etched shadows in his face. ''I fear there may be evil times ahead.'' A shiver ran through Thomasina. Rumors of revolt were everywhere. Someday...

As the news of Don Carlos's passing traveled the camp some of the survivors cheered. Others were silent. Most wept.

Thomasina wandered through the ranks of the injured, offering what solace she could. There was more bad news. One of the men clearing away wreckage was struck by a sudden rain of tiles from the hacienda's Moorish tower. His arm was cut to the bone. "I don't know if we can save it," Rafferty said to the man's wife.

The woman blessed him. "You and the *señora* will bring my man through, God willing."

It was then that Thomasina realized that she and Rafferty had become a team in the eyes of the villagers.

They set up a crude operating table with three lanterns for their only light and tried to stanch the flow of blood. They worked well together, each anticipating the other's intentions. Once, when Thomasina looked across at Rafferty, she was appalled at how tired and worn he was. There were smudges beneath his eyes and grim lines at the corners of his mouth. He needed a haircut and a shave but, to Thomasina, he looked heroically beautiful in the flickering light.

Their labors to save the man's arm were in vain. Rafferty did what had to be done. When the surgery was finally over, their patient had mercifully passed out and he and Thomasina were both drained.

The next three days were a waking hell. Margarita threw open the hacienda and its resources to the ill and injured. The grand reception room was transformed into a hospital ward. Blankets lined the parquet floor and the villagers slept beneath the heavy chandeliers. Thomasina got up at dawn tired, and fell back asleep at night, exhausted. Her conversations with Rafferty covered only the necessary topics of infection, diagnosis and treatment. She listened, watched and learned by doing. Her skills matched her courage.

By the fifth day after the eruption, the pace slackened. The feared outbreak of diphtheria had never come to pass and proper emergency care had prevented more than one disaster.

Nightfall found Thomasina restless. Instead of retiring to the couch in Margarita's study, where she slept to be near her patients, Thomasina went outside. How different everything was from the first night she'd come to the hacienda! Only the garden seemed unchanged.

Scintillating light came from the thousands of stars that pricked the blackness overhead. It was incredibly beautiful. She leaned her head against a carved column of the portico and looked up to where the peaks of Los Tres Hermanos blotted out the stars. The giants had shrugged their massive shoulders a few more times and then fallen back into their slumber, as Domingo had predicted. Thomasina wondered if they would really sleep a hundred years.

A gravel path invited her to walk along it. She made her way to a huge tree with wide, spreading branches. The crunch of her boots on the gravel disturbed the night insects and when she sat beneath the tree, there was no sound except the soft breeze in the leaves overhead.

For the first time in almost a week, Thomasina had time to examine things. Someone had thrown a rush mat down beneath the tree and she stretched out on it to watch the heavens. The earth was soft and still warm from the sun's heat. It was very soothing after the hectic days that had just passed. She had learned a great deal about medicine—and more about herself. Despite the endless round of tasks and the many claims upon her time and energy, there had been a fulfilling purpose and rhythm to her days. When the worst was over, she found that she'd developed enormous affection and respect for the people of San Juan. This was what God had intended her to do with her life. This was where she belonged.

A deep peace came over her. She closed her eyes and let it wash over her.

Suddenly she was running down the echoing long, empty corridor of the nightmare house. Footsteps behind made her heart speed up. She ran faster and faster past the cold faces of the marble statues, seeing their mocking reflections in the long mirrors spaced at intervals. Her pursuer was gaining on her. She felt his breath upon the back of her neck, felt his hands reach out to snag her hair.

"*No!*" Thomasina ran and ran until her chest felt like it would burst with effort. She rounded a corner—and came face-to-face with a blank wall. There was no escape. Cowering in the corner, she waited for the attack. Hands grabbed her cruelly by the shoulder, shaking her violently—

"*Thomasina!*"

She thrashed out wildly. She had finally remembered—a dull, rainy day in the isolated chateau...the Duke, drunk and violent, and the sobbing, hysterical servant girl. She remembered screaming and screaming. Then the footsteps running behind her and the blind corridor where she had found herself trapped. Hands touching, tearing... Then her mother, rushing at the Duke, waving a heavy poker in her hand as if it were the sword of an avenging angel... the blood and the Duke's vile curses ringing in her ears... and silence.

The rest was fragmented—fleeing on foot through the rain, sleeping in ditches and under the thatch of a cottage... the seedy house along the wharf and the women who painted their lips and cheeks and laughed too heartily... her mother, smiling by night and weeping by day....

"Thomasina! Wake up!"

Thomasina opened her eyes. The chateau, the rainy French countryside, the wharfside rooms that smelled of whiskey and cabbage faded away. Rafferty was staring down at her in stark concern. Thomasina moaned in relief. She was safe in the haven of his arms. No nightmare could touch her as long as his strong arms protected her. She was safe with Rafferty.

His strength and sureness vanquished her fears. The child in her remembered the Duke de Montparnon as godlike one moment, demonic the next. The child in her had feared, on some basic level, that the same might be true of Rafferty. The adult in Thomasina realized that was impossible. There was nothing in Brendan Rafferty that was not true and good.

The moment she tried to move, he released her immediately. His face was set and stern in the starlight, his mouth carved in a harsh, bitter line. "I didn't mean to frighten you again."

"No, I was dreaming," she explained breathlessly, pulling away. "A nightmare... a terrible dream."

"You're awake now." His voice was cold. "I've been looking for you. This might be our last chance for a private talk."

At his words, cold fear coiled itself around Thomasina's heart. She knew what he was going to say even before he began.

"I think we have both come to realize that this charade of ours has been a terrible mistake. We can't continue on, pretending to be man and wife and sharing the same roof."

"You are saying that you want me to leave."

"I was a fool not to have sent you packing the day you arrived, and I've lived to regret it. Tomorrow, Ambassador de Palmar will leave for Mexico City to get relief supplies. You will go with him."

The stars blurred through Thomasina's tears. "I've worked beside you day and night, sharing your griefs and triumphs. I'm willing to work as long and hard as need be to learn what you have to teach me. Why can't I stay? Haven't I proved myself?"

His voice gentled. "A thousand times over."

"Then *why?*"

"Do you want the bald truth?"

"Yes. Yes, dammit! You owe it to me, Rafferty!"

He turned to face her, his features silvered by the pale light. "Very well, then. You can't stay because I am neither a saint nor a plaster statue, but a man of flesh and blood. What do you think it's like knowing that you're just an arm's length away—and that if I reach out, you'll shrink away from me? That my very touch is repugnant to you?"

His words sunk in slowly. Thomasina's despair was transformed into a wild hope. "Wrong again, Dr. Rafferty," she said softly. "You see, that's not at all the way it is."

"Isn't it?" he said savagely. "Then how is it?"

"Like this." She stepped closer—so close, she could feel his breath stirring her hair. She held out her arms. "Hold me."

Rafferty groaned. "Why are you doing this to me?"

Thomasina laughed. "Why are you always asking me questions at the most inappropriate times?" She moved closer still, until her breasts brushed against his chest. "It wasn't you I shrank away from, it was a painful memory...something I saw as a child. It has haunted me all my life, but now, I think—I *know* it is gone for good."

Her hands slid up his wide chest. Rafferty stepped back until he came up against the tree. "I am hallucinating," he murmured. "Domingo has fed me some of those damned mushrooms again, and I'm dreaming this."

"Then I am sharing your dream." Her arms twined around his neck. "Hold me, Rafferty. Touch me." Thomasina's eyes grew heavy with desire. "Make love to me...."

He caught her to him, crushing the breath from her with his fierceness. His mouth was hot, his kisses hotter. They sank beneath the sheltering branches of the tree and made love, with only the stars for witnesses.

Rafferty showered Thomasina with all the passion he had held in check for so long. He opened her bodice, pressing kisses down her neck and into the shadowed valley between her breasts.

Thomasina didn't shrink away. Her breasts ached for his hands, his lips, his tongue. He was ardent and skilled, leading her along paths of pleasure that she had never dreamed existed. The feathering of his hands upon her skin set her blood singing. She was ready and eager, but he led her on, teaching her all the ancient secrets of love. When his hand brushed along the inside of her thighs, a shudder of anticipation ran through her body. When his fingers touched her intimately, she gasped and caught his hand in hers, but only to urge him on. The sudden surge of sensation caught her by surprise. She hadn't dreamed it could be like this. The next surge came, stronger than before, leaving her delighted and shaken.

The moon rose, frosting them with cool light, but they were warm in the heat of their passion. Thomasina felt his readiness and thrust upward to meet him, the melding of their bodies sweet and fierce, accelerating to a dizzying rush that left them gasping and wanting more. The final surrender was mutual and complete.

Later, when the moon was winking behind the mountains, Rafferty and Thomasina walked hand in hand along the graveled path, whispering and laughing.

Domingo was curled up on a piece of blanket outside the door to the study, making sure no one came out of the house to surprise the lovers. El Doctore and the *señora* had worked hard and deserved their time alone. They probably hadn't stopped to wonder who it was that had left that rush mat beneath the tree.

Now, if he could only do something more to bring together Doña Margarita and Luiz Zavala, he would be a very happy man indeed.

As it turned out, the Ambassador did not arrive in San Juan until the following week. Life had almost returned to normal with Thomasina and Rafferty back at the surgery, reviewing the signs and symptoms of mushroom poisoning, when they received unexpected visitors. Thomasina glanced out the window at the sound of carriage wheels, then jumped up from her chair so fast she almost knocked it over. Rafferty steadied the chair and followed her to the door. A striking, dark-haired beauty and a handsome blond gentleman descended from the modish carriage, dressed in the height of fashion. They were accompanied by a plump nursemaid and a sturdy set of twin boys.

"Vivienne! And Deverill!" Thomasina embraced them and then knelt down and hugged the boys. Thomasina chattered happily in French with her visitors, lapsing back and forth into English.

Rafferty watched them from the doorway, not without a tinge of apprehension. The enchanting Madame Deverill and her famous husband were a part of Thomasina's past. The part that was best forgotten. Outside of Patrice Wentworth, these two were the only ones who could definitely link Thomasina to her mother's shadowed past. He stepped outside and approached them, scenting for danger and finding none. Vivienne clapped her hands together.

"Ah, so this is the handsome Dr. Rafferty I have heard so much about." She eyed him a moment, considering. Then she smiled. "You have a stubborn chin, wise eyes and a good mouth. I believe that you will make a good husband for my friend, Thomasina. You must take good care of her."

Rafferty flushed under her steady regard. "I shall." Then he took the little gloved hand extended to him and kissed it. Vivienne laughed, a charming ripple of bells. "Ah, handsome, intelligent and polished of manner. Yes, I see now why Thomasina has fallen in love with you."

Deverill shook Rafferty's hand. Once more Rafferty found himself under severe scrutiny. Then Captain Deverill smiled, also. "My wife is right. She always is. Congratulations, Dr. Rafferty. I hope you'll both be very happy. And if there is ever anything we can do to help you, you have only to ask."

Thomasina blushed deeply and the doctor's face was still red. He looked into Thomasina's eyes and she nodded. Rafferty relaxed. "There is something that you might do, at that. Won't you come inside while we discuss it?"

The men went into the house but Thomasina lingered a minute with Vivienne and her two boys, Phillipe and Gerard. "Are you happy, Thomasina, *ma petite?*"

"Oh, yes! Everything would be perfect if only I could get things straightened out here—and with my mother..."

Vivienne linked her arm through Thomasina's and they went into the surgery, talking a mile a minute.

The Deverills had brought a surprise with them. Vivienne handed Thomasina a wrapped package. Inside the Valnoy Sapphire and the double strand of pearls blazed against the blue velvet wrappings. "Regine Valnoy sent this. She said it is rightfully yours." Vivienne covered Thomasina's hand with hers. "On condition that you never see her again."

"I never want to!" Thomasina's anger blazed. "And I don't want the damned necklace." She was, she realized with a shock, most definitely picking up Rafferty's speech patterns.

"Then," Deverill interjected, "I'll find a buyer for the jewels, if you like. The profits on the sale could be put to good use here."

Rafferty did nothing to encourage Thomasina either way, but a slow smile came to her lips. "The hospital... the new surgery... a bigger house... perhaps a school..." Poetic justice.

Beaming, she handed the necklace to Deverill. "I would be very grateful to you if you'll handle the sale for me. And perhaps you could have a new microscope sent out as well."

Rafferty came forward and took Thomasina in his arms. "Spoken like a true doctor." They were still kissing when the others tiptoed out.

Vivienne, Deverill and their little family stayed on in San Juan for a week, with rather vague plans for the rest of their travels. Rafferty realized the sole reason for their trip to Mexico was to see if he was worthy of Miss Thomasina Wentworth. He was determined to be. Vivienne and Deverill rode away with their family when the time was up, well satisfied, with promises of more visits.

Rafferty was alone a few days later when Patrice came with the ambassador, bubbling with concern for the people of the area and stories of her travels. "I stopped in San Pedro and the Ambassador kindly offered to escort me here. It's very strange," she added casually, "but I was speaking of you to the priest of the mission—and he told me that a foreign doctor had been married there several years ago to a Mexican woman, but that there had been no marriages at the mission for two years."

Rafferty smiled genially. "Did I say San Pedro?" He crossed to his desk and pulled out the official record of the marriage of one Thomasina Yvette Valnoy to one Brendan Patrick Rafferty. He held it out, his thumb carefully concealing the recent date.

"Ah, how foolish of me. We were married at San Pablo mission." He put the marriage record away as Thomasina came in from the placita, and slipped his arm around her waist. "My wife is always chiding me about it."

Patrice bit her lip. "It is lovely to see two young people so happy together. Perhaps one day..."

She lowered her lashes but not before sending a winsome glance at de Palmar. The ambassador flushed with pride. "You two are not the only lovebirds," he announced. "Mrs. Wentworth has done me the honor of accepting my hand in marriage. We will exchange our vows as soon as it can be arranged."

Thomasina was startled but pleased. Rafferty grinned. "I hope your daughter will be at the ceremony."

Patrice swallowed, hard. "I hope so. But first I want to talk things over with Fernando."

"I can imagine so."

After Patrice and the ambassador left, Thomasina and Rafferty could only speculate. "I believe she'll tell him everything," Thomasina said. "There must be honesty between lovers." Rafferty glanced about guiltily and she raised her eyebrows.

"Do you mean to tell me you have a deep, dark secret you've kept from me?" Rafferty turned away so abruptly that her stomach sank. "What is it . . . ?"

When he turned back, his face was somber. "I don't know how to tell you. . . ."

Thomasina dug in her heels. "I won't move an inch until you do."

"Very well. Dr. Thomasina Rafferty, you are the world's most adorable woman—and its most dreadful cook." Rafferty's blue eyes took on an ardent glow. "And your other talents are remarkable."

"Well, I'm going to learn to cook in my spare time. Just wait and see. Now that I'm a respectably married woman, I should learn. Perhaps I'll try my hand at some paella tonight."

Rafferty's booming laugh was filled with joy. He picked Thomasina up off her feet and swung her around. "No more cooking—ever!"

"Put me down," she ordered. Her frown soon changed to a smile.

He held her close to him. "Domingo will be preparing supper. Lorenzo is occupied in the stable with the new kittens. I thought that you might want to take a walk—a long walk—down by the river."

Thomasina slipped her arm through his. "An excellent idea, Dr. Rafferty. That would be lovely—wouldn't it?"

"Is that a question or a challenge?"

The two Doctors Rafferty ran down the road and into the trees that fringed the river's edge. And it was very lovely, indeed.

* * * * *

HISTORICAL

Bring back heartwarming memories of Christmas past,
with Historical Christmas Stories 1991, a collection of
romantic stories by three popular authors:

Christmas Yet To Come
by Lynda Trent
A Season of Joy
by Caryn Cameron
Fortune's Gift
by DeLoras Scott

A perfect Christmas gift!

Don't miss these heartwarming stories, available in December at your favorite
retail outlet. Or order your copy now by sending your name, address, zip or
postal code, along with a check or money order for $4.99 (please do not send
cash), plus 75¢ postage and handling ($1.00 in Canada), payable to Harlequin
Books to:

In the U.S.

3010 Walden Ave.
P.O. Box 1396
Buffalo, NY 14269-1396

In Canada

P.O. Box 609
Fort Erie, Ontario
L2A 5X3

Please specify book title with your order.
Canadian residents add applicable federal and provincial taxes.

XM-91-2

presents
MARCH MADNESS!

Come March, we're lining up four wonderful stories by four dazzling newcomers—and we guarantee you won't be disappointed!
From the stark beauty of Medieval Wales to marauding *bandidos* in
Chihuahua, Mexico, return to the days of enchantment and high
adventure with characters who will touch your heart.

LOOK FOR
        STEAL THE STARS (HH #115) by *Miranda Jarrett*
        THE BANDIT'S BRIDE (HH #116) by *Ana Seymour*
        ARABESQUE (HH #117) by *Kit Gardner*
        A WARRIOR'S HEART (HH #118) by *Margaret Moore*

So rev up for spring with a bit of March Madness . . . only from
Harlequin Historicals!

Harlequin Intrigue®

Trust No One...

When you are outwitting a cunning killer, confronting dark secrets or unmasking a devious imposter, it's hard to know whom to trust. Strong arms reach out to embrace you—but are they a safe harbor...or a tiger's den?

When you're on the run, do you dare to fall in love?

For heart-stopping suspense and heart-stirring romance, read Harlequin Intrigue. Two new titles each month.

HARLEQUIN INTRIGUE—where you can expect the unexpected.

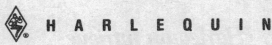

◆ H A R L E Q U I N

A Calendar of Romance

Be a part of American Romance's year-long celebration of love and the holidays of 1992. Experience all the passion of falling in love during the excitement of each month's holiday. Some of your favorite authors will help you celebrate those special times of the year, like the revelry of New Year's Eve, the romance of Valentine's Day, the magic of St. Patrick's Day.

Start counting down to the new year with

**#421 HAPPY NEW YEAR, DARLING
by Margaret St. George**

Read all the books in *A Calendar of Romance,* coming to you one each month, all year, from Harlequin American Romance.

American Romance®

COR1